Somewhere to Belong

White Dove | Book 1

by Maya William

SOMEWHERE TO BELONG: WHITE DOVE | BOOK 1

COVEY PUBLISHING, LLC

Published by Covey Publishing, LLC

PO Box 550219, Gastonia, NC 28055-0219

All rights reserved. No part of this publication may be reproduced, distributed, or transmitted in any form or by any means, including photocopying, recording, or other electronic or mechanical methods, without the prior written permission of the writer, except in the case of brief quotations embodied in critical reviews and certain other noncommercial uses permitted by copyright law.

This is a work of fiction. Names, characters, businesses, places, events and incidents are either the products of the author's imagination or used in a fictitious manner. Any resemblance to actual persons, living or dead, or actual events is purely coincidental.

Cover Design Copyright © 2017 Covey Publishing, LLC
Book Design by Covey Publishing, LLC
Production by CreateSpace

Copy Editing by Covey Publishing, LLC
Printed in the United States of America.

First Printing, 2017

www.coveypublishing.co

ALSO BY MAYA WILLIAMS

WHITE DOVE
Somewhere to Belong

To the Big Guy, who provided the inspiration for this story.
To my husband, who continuously encourages me during this journey.
To my mom, who patiently taught me English as a child.
To my father, who showed me to work to achieve my dreams.
To my kids, who go to sleep early and give mommy time to write.
To Monica, who can now flap her wings freely up in the sky.
To Annie, who is still putting up with me and my crazy ideas.
To the TAFF Facebook group, who believed in me and kept me going, even when Miss Inspiration is in tantrum mode.

CONTENTS

Chapter 1: The Test   1
Chapter 2: Welcome Home   12
Chapter 3: Rasputin   20
Chapter 4: Family Should Be Chosen   28
Chapter 5: Cooking Time   42
Chapter 6: Darcy   59
Chapter 7: The O'Flannagan's   72
Chapter 8: Change is Good   86
Chapter 9: The Market   104
Chapter 10: Second Chances   125
Chapter 11: Calvary   137
Chapter 12: Proper Introductions   153
Chapter 13: The Sound of Cooking   169
Chapter 14: Climb Every Moun…Wall   183
Chapter 15: The Lonely Goatherd   205
Chapter 16: The Beauty in Asymmetry   222
Chapter 17: Testing, Testing, One, Two, Three   235
Chapter 18: Making Bets   251
Chapter 19: I Am Sixteen Going On…Twelve   264
Chapter 20: Something Beautiful   283
Chapter 21: Night Closing In   301
Chapter 22: May Favorite Things   321

CHAPTER ONE
The Test

"Inhale, exhale." I quietly repeat my now hourly mantra as I try to steady my nerves, which are ramping with over-excitement at what lies ahead. My emotions control me.

Even though the dance course in Spain has me a little nervous, I couldn't be any happier, Big Guy.

I glance at the clock of the classroom, and my stomach does a small flip. Two more hours of class and then *Adios, hasta luego y nos vemos pronto*. Time for me to experience a new world in Barcelona.

Living at a boarding school means the campus provides for all my needs, and I don't get to leave school every day or even every year. Much like the chapel and the buildings at the boarding school, I became a constant fixture.

Might as well include me in the school inventory.

At the tender age of four, I lost my mother to a car accident and my home became Saint Magdalene's Catholic School for Girls, one of the VIP schools of the state, educating girls for the future. However, I shouldn't complain. After all, this high-quality school has an excellent dance program and strong values.

While I was sent away to receive a prestigious education, my grandmother took the responsibility for raising the twins by herself, which, according to her, was a challenge. My brother, Zacharias, rebelled against authority and my sister, Abigail, got in trouble at school more often than him.

I used to visit them for two weeks during the summer and for a week during Christmas break, but now two years have passed—

No, wait...*Has it actually been three years? Probably. But the constant emails sent and received keep me in touch with them.*

"Miss Melbourne, please stop mumbling to yourself and focus on your paper," Sister Agatha snaps my attention back to the test.

I didn't realize I spoke out loud while trying to calm my nerves with my breathing.

"Of course, Sister Agatha," I reply, immediately regretting it as I manage to dig myself deeper into the hole. I shut my mouth when Sister Agatha glances at me with a warning.

Oh shoot!

Over the years, the nuns became my friends, except Sister Agatha and Mother Superior, since I can never manage to get in their good graces. My voice could be louder, my chewing needs to be faster, I should arrive earlier for our daily prayer, and once they even complained about my breathing being too loud.

There's a private bench in the chapel reserved for me to kneel on and ask forgiveness to the Lord for all my *indiscretions*. All those times have allowed me to find a friend in Him.

I know Big Guy; some people might think I'm crazy. But, I know you are out there listening. And I shouldn't complain. There are a lot of people in the school whom I share a deep connection with.

Like Miss Johnson, who has been my ballet teacher since I entered Saint Magdalene. The long hours of training developed a strong relationship between us, at first while she taught me and now because we work together on new routines for the lower grades.

Or Sister Josie, the oldest nun at school, and also the one in charge of managing the kitchen. During the weekends and vacation seasons, she likes to enroll me as her minion to help her with the school cooking and the pastries she bakes to sell over the weekend to make some extra bucks for the school.

Thanks to her, I found another passion besides ballet. She gave me the chance to memorize all her *secret recipes*. Plus, taking advantage of her seniority and the fact that she cooks all of our meals, she bails me out of trouble or reduces my timeouts when I get in trouble with Mother Superior and Sister Agatha.

And nobody messes with the cook, right, Big Guy?

I should have friends my own age, but the new batch of girls who arrived for middle school enjoy different interests than me, making it hard to build a friendship. On the weekends, most of them return home, which is impossible for me because of the four-hour drive to Gram's. When they return, they discuss topics I don't understand, separating me further from any chance of making new friends.

I return my attention to the test and review my answers with all the stories, facts, and dates of Austen life I memorized, knowing my almost perfect GPA might suffer a big hit if I score low. While I love the idea of my two-month dancing camp at our sister school in Spain, I hate the idea that this grade will be the one I get for two months, especially if I do poorly because I'm excited.

"Psst," somebody whispers at my back.

I ignore the call, focusing on writing the last answer of the test. *Almost done!*

"Psst, Samantha," the whisper comes a little louder this time.

With an internal groan, I keep steady, not daring to turn my head an inch, hoping the girl shifts her attention to another victim.

"Melbourne, give me the answer to question number one." The raspy voice from behind allows me to identify the girl, Brittany Murphy.

Sweet Jesus! Have mercy on me. I roll my eyes and bite my lip.

I don't want to piss off the popular, beautiful, blond, rich girl and my own personal bully. Most of the time she gets her own way with a slight slap on the wrist if she gets in trouble.

The spoiled, little brat, she basically owns the school and the majority of the nuns are wrapped around her manicured, little finger. Including Sister Agatha.

For years, she tormented me. At least the punches ceased, but it came with a price. I agreed to do all her homework for the classes we share.

"I don't know," I whisper between clenched teeth, praying my voice doesn't reach Sister Agatha.

"Don't give me shit, Duckwalk. Clearly, the writing below the question is your answer. I'm not stupid," she hisses back, annoyed at my lack of *support*.

I beg to differ on the last statement, Big Guy.

The answer she wants makes my stomach quiver. Couldn't she ask for something simple instead of our opinion of Elizabeth Bennett rejecting Mr. Darcy's first proposition?

Better get it done before she gets me in trouble, or does something to me prior to my trip. I angle my body to one side and push my test to the other, leaving a clear view of it. If she wants the answer, let her do the work to get it.

Big Guy, does allowing her to copy qualify as cheating on my part? Unlike her, I studied for the test.

In my peripheral vision, I catch her craning her neck over my shoulder and quickly writing the answer on her paper. In my mind, I'm already forming a new answer, guessing she's not creative enough and will copy mine word-for-word. A total giveaway. Luckily, I always use a pencil to answer my tests in case of any last-minute changes, such as this one.

The time it takes her is complete agony. My gaze sticks to my test to avoid eye contact with Sister Agatha. I don't want my nervous state to be a giveaway, and if Brittany gets caught, I can claim I didn't know what was happening behind me.

Unlike Sister Agatha, who I'm certain has eyes on her back.

I give Brittany enough time, then return my body to block her view of my test. Quickly, I erase the answer and put in a new one.

"Not yet, I need answer number two."

Is she serious? How many answers does she plan on copying from me?

Nervously I glance at the clock, my stomach hitting the floor when I read the time. Nuts! Three minutes is a short time for Brittany to copy all twenty of my answers and a long one for Sister Agatha to discover us.

I keep my head straight to the test and again shift my body, accidentally hitting my backpack that rests at my feet, knocking it into the aisle dividing one line of desk from the other. The loud noise interrupts the silence of the classroom, scaring some of the girls. The one in front of me turns to the floor, alerting Sister Agatha to where the noise came from.

"Miss Melbourne, second warning," she grunts.

Afraid to get the third warning, I refrain from explaining the accident to my teacher. They say patience is a virtue, but they forgot to explain how nerve-racking the wait can be.

My nervous tic starts up, and I bite the tip of the pencil, all my hard work to stop this bad habit gone thanks to Brittany. But I need an outlet for my anxious energy. Re-directing it to the small school supply seems like the best idea.

"Move more, Bunhead. You're blocking the rest of the answers," Brittany orders.

Oh, Lord! If I scoot any closer to the edge of my seat it will be too suspicious, or I'll fall from the chair. Not willing to risk a third and final warning, I stay in place, eyes fixed on the clock.

Two minutes to finish this torture session and get out. I can practically taste the freedom.

"Oh, for Christ's sake!" Brittany exclaims, and before I can react, she whisks my test sheet from my desk, and a few seconds later a practically empty one lands in its place. Out of twenty, only the first two questions have answers.

I momentarily freeze. No, no, no!

The clock marks one minute left. I can practically see the big, red *F* scribbled in the top right corner. Unless time freezes, I'm doomed.

Years of being subjected to her bullying, hours spent

doing her homework, and for what? Not even a small thank you. Now she plans to affect my grades? Or my trip?

I don't think so.

I ignore all my internal warnings as the pit of my stomach burns. Anger toward Brittany's actions allows the sensation to creep up and take control of my body. I spin around, facing her fully. Glaring, my hand reaches for my test, grabbing one end of it. Brittany's fast reflex grabs ahold of the other end, initiating a tug of war between the two of us.

"Help, Sister Agatha," Brittany anxiously calls the teacher, using her most innocent and fearful voice. "Samantha is trying to steal my test."

What the…? How the…?

A scraping of the chair against the floor alerts me to the teacher rising from her seat.

"Miss Melbourne, drop Miss Murphy's test, immediately!" Sister Agatha orders, stomping her way to where we sit.

Technically, I'm obeying since Brittany's test still rests on the top of my desk. I stand to get a better hold, dropping my pencil to the floor. Brittany does the same, and the paper begins to rip.

"This is my test," I finally speak out, trying to explain my actions to our teacher and the rest of the class.

Pain radiates from my right ear, and I finally release the test. Brittany steps to the other side of the nun, using her as a shield.

When Sister Agatha lets go of my ear, she glares at me,

silently telling me to back up.

"Hand over both of your tests," she demands, stretching out her hand.

Brittany obeys immediately, a small smile on her lip and an innocent expression on her face. My mouth drops when I catch her name written on top of the sheet, mimicking perfectly my own handwriting. I turn around and grab the almost empty test, my stomach hitting rock-bottom when I notice my name written on it.

No! How could she?

"Miss Melbourne, your test," Sister Agatha asks severely.

Reluctantly, I obey, already anticipating the terrible end that awaits me. Our teacher analyzes our tests and purses her lips. Her eyes drift from the papers to me.

"She changed our names," I inform her, injecting a confident attitude into my voice, trying to convey I did nothing wrong.

"I didn't," Brittany retorts, acting all innocent as she bats her eyelashes and forms a small pout with her lips. "You tried stealing it from me."

Spoiled brat!

Sister Agatha's eyes go from Brittany to me, suspicion running thorough them.

"Miss Melbourne, go to Mother Superior's office," she orders and walks away.

Once my brain processes her words, my mouth falls open. Pointing my finger from my bully to me, I ask in disbelief, "She changed our names. Why do I need to go to the Principal's office and not her as well?"

Sister Agatha stops, turns around, and stares me. Her face flushes and the vein in her neck pops up, anger radiating from every pore.

Oops. Sister Angertha is showing her ugly face.

"Do as your told, Miss Melbourne," she orders.

The smart thing would be to back down, turn around, and obey. But I can't. I'd be accepting defeat. I need to fight this.

"Make a verbal test, Sister, or allow us to retake it. This way you will know who the cheater is," I plead in one last attempt to clear my name.

Ignoring my request, she gives me one last glare and turns around. In a more controlled voice, she directs, "Class is dismissed. Everybody leave your test on my desk."

The rest of the class, which remained quiet during the whole discussion, complies with the instructions.

I sigh in disappointment. I should probably stop by the kitchen and seek help from Sister Josie before pleading my case with Mother Superior. *You know, Big Guy, to improve my odds.*

I turn, preparing to store away my belongings and follow the orders, when I notice Brittany's victory face. I bite back any kind of retort I wish to say to her, not wanting to add another item to my list of offences. Hands balled, I let my nails dig into the inside of my hand to ease my anger while I consider a valid argument for Mother Superior.

"Seems you'll be staying with us the rest of the school year," Brittany whispers happily. Taking a step back, she waves goodbye with her hand. "Adios Barcelona."

This dance course was my goal for the past five years and now she ruined it so she can keep her personal minion here to continue doing her homework.

Straightening and pulling back my shoulders with resolve, I glare at her and step closer, prepared to inform her of my intention to fight the accusation. Instead, I find myself falling as I realize too late I tripped on my bag where it still lies in the aisle.

Reflexively, I fling my arms in front of myself to avoid hitting my face on the floor. My clenched hand connects with Brittany's nose, followed by a loud crack.

The odds are no longer in my favor, right, Big Guy?

CHAPTER TWO
Welcome Home

The four-hour drive from Saint Magdalene to Grand Forks, Colorado passed faster than expected, my mind constantly replaying the set of events that occurred after the moment my fist met Brittany's nose. Meanwhile, my heart breaks every time I consider what lies ahead: *Separation from the people I've called my family for the past twelve years.*

A sense of shame and disappointment flows through me when we enter the housing development where Gram's house is located. Every white, two-story tall house appears to be the same. I inch closer to the window, trying to identify the one with the missing tree at its entrance. My heart skips a beat when the car comes to a complete stop, dreading the moment when the beautiful, red door with number 249 on it will open.

"Are you sure you don't want to tell me what happened?" Miss Johnson asks once again when we reach my final destination.

If there were a chance to appeal my case, I would spill my guts right now. But I know Mother Superior's ruling is final, especially since Brittany's parents threatened to press charges.

I shake my head, dropping my eyes to the floor of the cab.

The driver gets out, hustles to the passenger door, and opens it. Miss Johnson steps out, takes his hand, and closes the door behind her.

"Hold the car. I need a ride back to the airport," my ballet teacher instructs the driver. "And, please, take out the smaller suitcase."

"Sure, ma'am," the driver replies calmly, walking to the back of the car to retrieve my belongings.

I chew my lower lip, regretting getting out of bed. We should both be on our way to the Spanish adventure instead of sitting in a cab at the beautiful entrance of 249 Solar Drive.

I get out and follow Miss Johnson through the stone path that leads to the door. Still wearing my school uniform, the blue-plaid, pleated skirt and the white, starched blouse with the navy-blue vest protects me from the cold October wind. I drag my feet on the pavement, stalling while keeping my head down in disgrace.

Gram's dove messed up big time.

Miss Johnson rings the bell and quietly waits for somebody to answer it. The driver sets down my suitcase. I nod, silently thanking him for his help; he gives me an encouraging smile before he turns around to return to his cab.

I step to one side, hiding behind Miss Johnson when the thud of footsteps approaches the door. She might be on the shorter side, but in case somebody peeks through the peephole, the step that leads to the house provides her the extra inches to hide me.

The door opens, sending my heart into a frantic beat. Time to face reality and finally meet Grandmother's angry side.

"Hello. How may I help you?" a tenor voice asks.

"Hi, my name is Miss Johnson. I come from Saint Magdalene Catholic School. May I speak with Mrs. Morris?" my guardian kindly asks.

A quick glimpse over my instructor's shoulder shows a guy stands in the doorway. It takes me a couple of seconds to recognize Zach, my older brother. His features appear older, sharper and masculine, leaving behind the adolescent boy I remember from three years ago. His hazel eyes focus on my dance instructor, recognition setting in when he identifies my school name.

Shoot!

I inch back to my place, cowardly hiding behind my ballet tutor.

"She's not currently home, but I'm her grandson. How may I help you?" he inquires, his voice serious.

"Oh!" Miss Johnson replies, surprised. "Well, is there a way we can contact her?"

"Unfortunately, she's out of town. How may I help you?" my older brother kindly offers again.

Could things get any worse, Big Guy? Honestly, she never mentioned in the weekend email any kind of travel plan. I would prefer to face her wrath than Zach's. At least I know she likes me, unlike my brother who avoids me like the plague when I visit them.

Miss Johnson sighs. "A situation came up today regarding Samantha, and we were unable to reach Mrs. Morris."

"Is everything all right with her?" His voice fills with concern, realizing there might be something wrong with me.

Miss Johnson steps aside and extends her arm, inviting me to come closer, which allows him to make his own personal assessment.

Nu-uh. This spot appears to be safer, especially since you're seconds away from dropping the explanation-bomb.

Zach's narrow eyes contemplate me, appearing confused for a second. "Samantha?"

I gaze down at my feet and put my arms behind my back, too intimidated to face him.

"This morning, an altercation erupted among two students during a test," Miss Johnson explains.

Three.

"A girl stole another student's test and afterward attacked her classmates."

Two.

"The girl in question is your sister, and as of today, she can no longer attend Saint Magdalene."

One.

"What!" he exclaims, full of surprise.

Kaboom! Whatever you do, avoid eye contact at all cost!

"We can't condone such an attitude from our students. I am here representing the school, to hand over—"

"Wait!" he interrupts Miss Johnson, bringing his hand up. "I find it hard to believe this about Samantha. The last email from Saint Magdalene placed her as one of the top students in her class, not to mention her straight A's report card from the last three years."

"Well..." Miss Johnson stammers.

Why would Zach know anything concerning my academic achievements? I wonder if Grams shares with him the news I tell her.

"It doesn't make sense, why would she need to cheat?" he continues.

"I don't know all the details. The investigation was cancelled due to the violence involved in the issue." Miss Johnson replies determinedly, straightening her spine while she faces my brother.

Ugh, Big Guy, I hate violence, and yet I got expelled because of it.

"Samantha wouldn't react in such a manner without a

provocation from another girl," my brother remains calm while arguing my case to Miss Johnson.

Big Guy, my brother presents a much better argument than Sister Josie's heated accusations. Why couldn't he be there during the confrontation with Brittany's parents?

"All the witnesses confirmed Samantha punched the other girl in the nose," Miss Johnson responds blankly.

Technically, I tripped on my backpack and hit Brittany's nose. Like it or not, there's a world of difference between purposely hitting her and the whole situation being an accident.

Zach's wide eyes stare at me, full of disbelief.

"Therefore, following school procedure, here is your sister, together with her school transcripts." Miss Johnson pulls a thick folder from her briefcase and hands it over to my brother.

Was it necessary to document every single one of my indiscretions? Apart from today's incident and the drunken one, all my misdeeds classify as minor slip ups.

"There has to be a mistake," Zach insists, returning his gaze to my dance teacher as he takes the folder and opens it to the last page. His eyes widen even more as he analyzes the dreadful picture, evidence of the power of my right hook.

The picture definitely did not capture Brittany's best look.

"Sorry to be the bearer of bad news, Mr. Melbourne, but Samantha can no longer attend Saint Magdalene," Miss Johnson states, cutting him off from any further discussion.

She turns, extends her arms, and reaches in for a hug. Not wanting to say goodbye, my eyes prickle while a knot in my throat chokes me.

She introduced ballet into my life and made sure I excelled at it. Not to mention all the times she went beyond her duty as a teacher, worrying about my health, keeping a close eye on my schoolwork.

"She can't stay here," my brother states flat-out, interrupting our farewell. "She needs to go back to school and to her dancing camp in Barcelona."

I stiffen at his harsh words and cold expression.

Years have passed since the last time I saw him, and even then, we were never close. Grams always acted as a buffer during our interaction. But the harshness of his words cuts deep inside my heart, especially coming from my alleged brother.

Miss Johnson turns around and Zach flinches, retreating a couple of steps.

I'll bet she just gave him the death glare.

"Mr. Melbourne," she snaps furiously. "I believe Samantha already over-extended her time in Saint Magdalene under our tutelage. It might be time for her to know something other than a nunnery—"

"You misinterpreted what I wanted to say." He brings his hands up, trying to calm her.

Too late, dear brother. Take it from me; you are way over your head.

"And it wouldn't hurt her to get in touch once again

with her real family," she continues, ignoring him.

"You don't understand. We have a lot on our plate right now…" he pleads again.

"Remember, family is a priority to the flock," she adds, her tone full of command, daring him to argue.

His retort dies at my instructor's words. His mouth closes, and he gives a brief nod, accepting her statement.

Miss Johnson turns and hugs me, again. "Take care, Samantha." Her voice breaks at the end. A tear escapes my eye, which she cleans with her thumb. "Be brave and smart. Time for the little dove to spread her wings and fly."

Without another word, she lets go. My eyes focus on the ground, not courageous enough to watch her leave. With each retreating footstep, my chest tightens with a pull at my heart, my world crumbling, leaving my boarding family behind to deal with my blood family. The door of the cab opens and closes, and the motor of the car slowly dissipates until I only hear the wind and the occasional chirp from a bird.

Trying to find some comfort, I remember the last encouraging words of Sister Josie, the school's cook. When a door closes, another one opens.

I bring my eyes up to find the door of the house open and no Zach there to welcome me in.

Well, Big Guy, this appears to be the start of a promising friendship, I sarcastically say to myself.

CHAPTER THREE
Rasputin

As I enter the house, a gasp escapes my lips when my eyes fall upon a completely different setting from the one I left behind three years ago. The walls, which divided the different living areas, are gone. Instead, a big, open space greets me together with new wood flooring to replace the old carpet.

In the living room, a large, flat-screen television hangs above the fireplace and modern pieces of furniture replace Gram's old ones. Next, in the dining room, a ten-seat rectangular, chocolate-brown table resides.

The previous wall that divided the kitchen from the dining area is now half the height with a countertop and five stools in front of it.

I inch closer to the kitchen, expecting to find Gram's floral wallpaper, the almond cabinets, and a cluttered counter. As with the rest of the house, the renovation crew also got ahold of this area, too, installing a modern kitchen in its place. The new white counter, stripped of all small appliances, only holds a fruit basket, which sits in one corner to disrupt its clean surface.

If I didn't catch the missing tree at the entrance and my brother didn't open the door, I would have guessed I entered the wrong house.

I wonder what the twins did this time for Grams to redecorate the house?

After dropping my suitcase at the entrance, I patiently wait for Zach to return. The house appears foreign to me with all the changes. However, his disappearance act leads me to believe I might be on my own for a while.

Zach, come out, come out wherever you are.

I tiptoe around the house, waiting for any sound to alert me to where he might be. When I return to the kitchen, my stomach growls. With the whole commotion at school, I skipped lunch. Closer to dinner now, it loudly complains at the lack of attention and the sight of fresh fruit.

Only the thought of adding another sin to my already growing list stops me from stealing one of the juicy apples.

I already did a lot of damage today to my current score with the Big Guy.

Luckily, my attention diverts as a noise comes from

the door leading to the garage.

Could Zach be in there?

I crack it open with the hopes of finding him. Something fast passes me, grazing my calf. Surprised, I jump at the touch, letting go of the door.

Near my feet, a little, brown Chihuahua stares up at me, its tiny head sizing me up. Its little black nose scrunches while it sniffs me.

"Oh, come here little fellow," I tell him softly, overpowered by its cuteness. I bend down and stretch out my hand, ready to pet its little head.

The little rat immediately growls at me, baring its minuscule teeth and yapping loudly. Its reaction takes me by surprise. I snap my hand back and jump up when it approaches me.

"Hey, wait a minute there..." I whisper softly, trying to calm it. I obtain the opposite reaction, the barking becoming louder, followed by growls. I back up, holding up my hands.

It corners me against one of the kitchen counters. In his eyes, I can tell he's prepared to do whatever it takes to remove me, the invader.

I jump on the counter, walloping my butt, but I don't let the pain slow me down. I pull my legs up, getting them away from his snapping little jaws.

Big Guy, can my bravery level get any lower? Retreating because of this small dog, shame on me.

The torture doesn't last long. The sound of the garage opening makes the dog stop yapping, giving me an opportunity to identify the sound of a vehicle parking inside the garage.

Please, Big Guy, distract him.

My prayers seem to work since the barking stops. The dog's head turns in the direction of the door that connects to the garage. I shift one millimeter to the side, inching toward the kitchen exit, but the dog's head snaps back to me, ready to attack if necessary.

I momentarily catch my reflection on the fridge door, making me realize how pathetic the whole display appears.

The door opens and in comes a guy, his face hidden behind some grocery bags.

"Zaaaachiiiieeee, I'm home!" a deep voice sing-songs the words to the tune of *honey, I'm home.* "And I come bearing food!!"

I freeze in place. After twelve years of practically being locked up in an all-girls school with limited contact with the opposite sex, my only real interaction with men came from the elderly priest and the old gardener. Even around Zach, I'm intimidated by his presence.

Could I be more pathetic? Cornered by the little rat with no way to hide.

As the tall figure steps inside, he closes the door with his shoulder. He wears tight jeans, showcasing his lean legs and small waist. A white shirt covers the top part of his body; the sleeves rolled up to show strong arms and big, masculine hands. His face hides behind the groceries bags, but I spot a few strands of honey-colored, short hair.

"Zach, did you let Rasputin in?" He questions while

he deposits the bags on top of the counter.

Distracted by my inspection of him, I miss when the little Chihuahua abandons his guarding post and stands on its hind legs, getting the attention of the newcomer.

"There you are, you annoying little thing!" The guy bends down and grabs the dog.

The *thing* licks his face, making the guy chuckle.

Ewww gross!

The guy's head snaps in my direction.

Shoot! I forgot to use my inner voice, again!

I find myself speechless, my tongue glued to the top of my mouth. The guy's tan face and strong, manly features complement his beautiful, sky-blue eyes, making my insides quiver.

Some of my classmates decorated their dorm rooms with pictures of their male friends or of some famous pop star. However, this guy reminds me more of the archangel's portrait, which hangs in the school library.

"Hey, Abigail," he casually greets me, rising and leaving Rasputin, the dog, down on the floor. "Is Zach home?"

Ugh, Big Guy, was the genetic pool not big enough? Zach is Abigail's twin, not me.

As expected, nodding seems to be the only response my body can provide.

Yay me! At least I managed to reply.

"Great, where..." he stops, his eye going up and down my face, analyzing me. "Hey, you finally allowed Barb to change your hair color."

He inches closer, spooking me by his approach. I retreat farther onto the counter until I reach the edge.

"She also put in extensions?" His hand comes closer, grabs a lock of my hair, and runs it through his fingers. "Wow! The expensive ones. Nice! Are you taking inspiration from Rapunzel, or do you want to appear younger?"

He lets go of my hair, and now his eyes travel to my outfit, his eyebrows rising while he contemplates me. He laughs after a few seconds.

"Hot, but you won't be able to pull off the Catholic girl act. Honestly, it's not your thing, Abigail. The closer you behave to your character, the easier it will be for us to investigate Calvary." He chuckles and retreats to unpack the grocery bags.

The little beast stays by his side, its evil eyes reguarding me from a distance. I test the waters and put one of my feet down, analyzing its reaction.

It stays puts.

I take advantage, put my other foot down, and tiptoe toward the exit, my eyes still on the dog. My peripheral vision catches the slightly open door that leads to the garden, giving me a chance to formulate my escape plan.

"You're never this quiet, Abigail. What's wrong?" The guy turns around and faces me. His intense gaze fixed on me, freezing me in place.

My cheeks burn as if he caught me red-handed.

"Are you wearing contacts?" His eyes zero in on mine and tilts his head to one side, analyzing me. After a few seconds, he walks closer.

For every step he advances, I take one backward, exiting the kitchen. Rasputin growls, catching my attention as its little steps quicken.

"Rasputin, what's wrong?" the guy asks the little Chihuahua as if it can answer him.

I increase my speed, putting more distance between the mutt and me. My back hits the dining room wall. I push through the door and reach the garden. A sharp, painful tug radiates from my calf as the little rat catches up to me.

Ouch!

"Rasputin, down boy!" The guy angrily commands.

Immediately, the strong pressure on my leg stops. The pain, though, continues.

Freaking, stupid mutt!

Between the guy and the dog bite, I don't pay attention to my surroundings. But I know something's clearly wrong when the ground disappears from beneath my feet. Reflexively, I throw my hands up to break my fall, however, the cold water takes me completely by surprise, and I panic when my body submerges in it.

Flashes of long forgotten memories return, followed by a loud crashing sound that rings in my ears, paralyzing my body. I sink like a rock, the water's surface inching away from me while my breath becomes nothing.

The small figure of the dog appears at the other side of the water followed by two tall ones.

I can't control myself. My feet touch the bottom of

the pool, and before I know it, I black out.

CHAPTER FOUR
Family Should Be a Choice

Air being pushed through my mouth brings me back to consciousness. Survival mode kicks in with a coughing fit. Somebody pushes my body to one side, allowing the water to escape freely from my mouth to the ground without choking me. The taste of chlorine remains after the coughing stops.

With each sharp breath, I thank the Big Guy for allowing air to flow through my system, oxygenating my body and keeping my heart pumping.

Not today, Big Guy.

When my eyes open, the pool rests a few feet from where I lie. I flip over to my back, removing its terrifying sight from my view and bringing back the memory of the boarding school's Olympic-sized pool.

As any average student, swimming classes were a mandatory requirement. But after the coach tried to throw me in the first time and found me clawed onto her leg, whimpering, the nuns opted to waive the requirement due to the traumatic experience I suffered and instead substituted it for an extra hour of Ballet. I never again set foot inside the school pool, but I knew the ballet studio as well as the back of my hand.

Truth be told, my fear for water runs deep, I avoid most bodies of water. I barely stand being near a shallow fountain, and I never allow the tub to fill.

Clearly getting inside the pool was not done by choice.

Opting to focus on something less terrifying, I enjoy the sight of the few stars that decorate the purple sky, wishing for the terrible day to finally come to an end.

Considering how things turned out, I believe my request is rather fair. *Don't You agree with me, Big Guy?*

Two faces appear, blocking my view of the sky. I recognize the guy I met in the kitchen and my brother, his hair dripping water and his clothes drenched.

"Are you all right?" Zach asks, full of concern as he runs a shaky hand through his soaked hair, his wide eyes analyzing me.

Overwhelmed by the whole drowning experience and the handsome, semi-archangel who stands next to my brother, words fail me, and so I simply nod.

Zach releases a breath and faces the other guy, a scowl

replacing his terrified expression. "Why did you push her?"

"Calm down, dude," the other guy puts his hands up in front of himself to calm Zach. "I didn't push her. She ran straight into it."

Zach's curious glance returns to me, his eyebrow shooting up as if to silently ask me what I was thinking?

But what can I say, the last time I visited, the garden was pool-free. Then again, if Grams went through a complete house overhaul, what would stop her from tackling this area of the house as well?

"When does Grams return?" I manage to ask, avoiding the embarrassment of explaining how a little Chihuahua chased me into it.

Zach clamps his lips shut as his frown returns. Instead of answering, he diverts his gaze to the other guy. "Archie, can I borrow your phone? Mine drowned."

When he extends his hand, the blue-eyed guy reaches into his back pocket and pulls out a phone.

"Wait, wait! Zach, who is she?" he questions, pulling his phone away from Zach's reach.

My brother glares at him, which makes Archie drop the phone into his hand and avoid further questioning.

"You should shower and change, use one of the bathrooms on the second floor. You can find towels inside the closets. I'll sort everything out," Zach orders, rising and turning his back to me, his soaked clothes clinging to his body.

Archie stands and offers his hand to help me up. Nervously, I take it, finding it strange how mine warms with his touch. Without any effort, he pulls me up. I try to let go as soon as I stabilize myself, but he hangs on.

"Hi, my name is Archibald," he shakes my hand. "Or Archie," he adds, his smile broadening.

He expectantly waits for an answer, but again, my tongue seems to glue inside my mouth. I drop my eyes to my feet, intimidated by his gaze. He releases my hand after a short while.

With my arms around my body to keep myself warm, I make sure my petite attacker has left before I follow Zach's instructions.

"Thank you, Archie." I mumble, not certain if he heard me and enter the house without a glimpse back at him or the pool.

~

I pull my suitcase up to the second floor, relieved to find the layout in this part of the house unchanged. The hall splits two ways. One side goes to our bedrooms while the other hall takes me to Gram's room and the attic door.

I head toward my room, eager to find something in the house still the same, together with the promise of a lovely, warm shower and dry clothes.

When I push open my bedroom door, I stop dead in my tracks and take in the abysmal changes inside. The girly pink room with the ballerina portraits and the white comforter on top of the bed has disappeared. In its place, there's an unmade bed with black sheets on top of it and a wall covered with manga posters.

Clearly, there's a new resident in the room. Not wanting to intrude, I take a step back into the hall and close the door. I skip the next room, the one that belongs to Abigail, as I remember all the warning she used to give me during my visits.

Guessing Zach changed rooms with me, I venture to the next one. Confusion sets in when I open the door and find a queen-size bed with a light-purple down comforter, the walls decorated with stripes in alternating colors of purple and pink. The furniture and woodwork resembles my old white ones with not a single item out of place, the room immaculate.

I inch back and close the door. Confused, I walk to the other end of the hall.

I guess Abigail and Zach decided to change the decoration of their rooms?

I face the two doors on the other side of the stairs. I know the door on my right leads to the attic where Grams stored the Christmas decorations during my last visit, which means the one to the left should be hers.

Once I enter, I freeze, gaze on a picture of a little girl fixing her gaze upward, smiling at a woman. I step closer, studying how the woman's black hair hangs loose, covering most of her face. However, the mirror that hangs on the wall facing her inside the picture reveals her beautiful smile, which she shares with the girl, her daughter, Abigail.

"You are the living image of your mother," Grams

once told me, the happy glint of her eyes disappearing and replaced by tears. "You and Abigail." A sigh escaped her lips as she remembered her daughter with great fondness.

My memories of Mom are practically zero, just a few flashes of her face and smile. I know Grams tries to fill the gap by telling me stories about her when my siblings aren't present. For so long, I wished I could remember her. But alas, she died before my brain could store her in my long-term memory.

With one last glance to the beautiful picture, I enter the bathroom and turn the water on, letting it warm up while I pull out a simple white t-shirt, my underwear, and some gray pants from my suitcase. I remove a towel from the closet and strip.

When I climb into the shower, the hot water feels like heaven after such a day. I lean my head back, letting the water wash away the chlorine from the pool and hope it can also remove what I assume is a spell of bad luck.

I take advantage of this small peaceful time to say a prayer.

Hey, Big Guy, Samantha again.

I want to ask for Your forgiveness. I allowed my emotions to overcome my serenity and self-control. I ended up harming Brittany. I ask if You could help her with a speedy recovery and a beautiful nose without any permanent damage. I will accept my punishment with grace and promise to learn my lesson.

I also want to ask You to keep my friends, the nuns, safe and happy doing Your glorious work.

Since You like to work in mysterious ways, I'll trust you know what is best for me. However, I do ask, please let me not become an inconvenience to my family. Please show me the path I should follow where we can all be happy.

Amen.

After turning the water off, I pull the curtain out of the way, wrapping the towel around my body. I grab another one and dry most of the water from my hair and brush it. I towel my body and notice the bite mark from Rasputin.

Shoot, the little bugger got me.

Once I put my clothes on, I open the drawer, searching for the medical kit Grams keeps here. I stop when I find a blow dryer and a curling iron instead.

Did Grams let her hair grow longer? Hmmm, funny, another thing she never mentioned.

After a closer inspection of the items on top of the counter, the quantity of make-up stands out.

Grams usually likes to keep it simple.

Inside the next drawer, I find a collection of different perfumes, none of which is the rose scented one she likes to wear.

When I re-enter the room, a gasp escapes my lips as reality hits me. After studying the decoration and items inside the bedroom, I realize none of them are Grams, but Abigail's.

Did I mess up and get the wrong room again?

Full of disbelief, I inspect the closet. To my great disappointment, I only find modern clothes, none of which suits Grams's style. I step into the hall, confused, wondering if Grams and Abigail switched rooms.

Bang!

My hand flies to my heart at the startling noise, stopping me from investigating any further. The loud sound comes from the front door slamming shut downstairs. I tiptoe to the top of the staircase, catching a quick glimpse of a group of four girls as they enter the living room.

"Zacharias! Get your ass out here, now!" an angry voice shouts at the top of her lungs.

Grams, where are you? *Big Guy, I need backup, ASAP.*

"No need to shout, Abigail. We can start once Oliver arrives," Zach answers.

Why would you need to wait for this Oliver guy? We only need Grams.

"No, we need to discuss this before he gets here!" Abigail replies furiously. "Are your guys here?"

"Samuel will arrive shortly," a deep, grave voice with a strong accent replies, the tone not matching Zach's or Archie's.

Nuts! More guys? How many guys are here?

"Where is she?" Abigail asks, calmer.

"Upstairs taking a shower." Zach shushes her. "Can you try keeping your voice down?"

"Abbie, darling, can you tell us why you called an emergency meeting?" a feminine voice questions, a thick southern accent in her voice.

"Abbie, darling," I recognize Archie's voice mimicking to perfection the southern accent. "Were you planning on telling us about your clone?" His chuckles quickly die, replaced by an *uff* sound.

"I don't have a clone, you asshole, only a twin which happens to be your fearless leader," she fires back.

Language! My cursing sensors rattle. We can add One Hail Mary to the count.

"Well, the little girl is your spitting image." He laughs at my sister.

In case You were wondering, Big Guy, no, I don't find Your lack of creativity regarding our features amusing. Millions of options for you to play with and yet we got stuck with practically the same combination.

"Shut up, Archie," Zach commands. The laughter immediately dies.

"Why the hell did you let her in?" Abigail asks, a little more controlled.

Two Hail M... wait, what?

Undoubtedly, my arrival took Zach by surprise. But comparing his reaction against Abigail, his now feels like the warm and fuzzy one.

"I wouldn't have opened the door if I knew what was on the other side," he defends himself.

Never mind about the warm and fuzzy welcome then. Grams, I really need you here, like right now.

"Do you guys care to share with the rest of us your problem?" This time, the question comes from a feminine voice with an Eastern accent.

"I blame you, Zacharias, therefore, you need to figure out what we do with her." Abigail continues ignoring the previous question.

"Nu-uh, she is both our responsibility. We need to deal with it as a family."

Wrong! Just grab a phone and get Grams on the line so she can decide what to do with me.

"Let's ship her back to the nunnery, then," Abigail proposes.

"She got expelled. They won't take her in anymore," he answers her firmly.

What gives them the right to treat me as trash? They can't dump me and forget about me. Grams won't allow it.

My chest tightens, and I hold my breath, waiting to hear their next hurtful words.

"Can you get expelled from a nunnery?" the male with a German accent asks.

"Then we will find a different boarding school! Joy, can you please find one? Preferably in Alaska," Abigail directs the question to one of the girls who entered the house with her.

Wait, what? Alaska? No! Joy, please don't!

"It's not going to be easy without pulling some strings," Zach answers.

"What the hell do you mean, Zacharias?" Abigail demands.

Time to re-live the bomb once again, because the first two times were hilarious. *Right, Big Guy?*

"She punched a girl and broke her nose after a nun caught her cheating on a test," Zach explains.

Silence.

I strain my ears, waiting for another stream of bad words to follow and increasing the quantity of Hail Marys to the count I'll be praying tonight.

Based on my previous experiences with Sister Angertha, a speechless reaction is a terrible omen. Quietly, I creep down and sit at the bottom of the stairs to get a peek at the group and their response.

"And, you said she wasn't your clone." Archie's joke breaks the uncomfortable silence.

"Shut up, Archibald!" Zach and Abigail command at the same time.

"And," Zach continues with the explanation, "she happened to punch Brittany Murphy, the daughter of Congressman Murphy."

I never knew her dad worked in Congress. No wonder she behaves as if she owns the place!

"Damn it! We will need to pull more than one string and call some of our contacts, Zach, and we can't burn all our opportunities. We might need additional aid in the investigation," Abigail rattles off. "I'm sick of this..."

How many Hail Marys do I already have?

"Now, now, darling." The southern girl intervenes with a calm tone of voice. "We can always find different options to accommodate the girl? Like public school? Or we can ask help from the Phoenix School headboard and check if they can work with her?"

"She can't stay here, Barb. We owe it to Oliver and his uncle to focus on the investigation. Not spend our precious time looking out for her." Abigail continues, "She behaves like a little girl, practically a child!"

When you were sixteen, you never thought of yourself as a child considering all the mischief you got yourself into. And I don't need a babysitter. Grams can take care of me.

Frustration, disappointment, and a room with boys inside stops me from arguing back. Instead, I remain quiet as a mouse while silent tears cloud my vision.

"Abigail, don't be harsh. Who are we talking about, sweetie?" somebody asks, trying to calm her.

"No, Grandma always over-protected her. The little brat lived her whole life in a bubble," Abigail continues. "And now, after Grams died, Zach and I inherited the problem she created."

For a moment, times stands still while all of my blood rushes to my feet, numbing all of my extremities along with my mind. My breathing stops as a hundred thoughts run through my mind.

Hold on! What do you mean with now, after Grams died? But… That can't be right. I got an email from her last weekend, wishing me good luck on the trip. She must have died within this week, but when? Why wasn't I notified, and why didn't Zach tell me anything when I got here? And he lied to Miss Johnson!

This painful information feels as if somebody plunged a knife straight into my heart, sliced a piece, and stole it, leaving a big hole behind.

Big Guy, why did you take Grams away from me a few hours after I lost the place I used to call home?

Not wanting to be discovered, I cover my mouth with

my hand, silencing the sobs daring to escape.

"Remember what Grandma always used to say, 'the family is a priority to the flock,'" Zach tells her, repeating the same phrase Miss Johnson used.

"Bullshit! Everybody should be entitled to choose the members of their flock!" she replies. "Blood doesn't mean a thing,"

Big Guy, please make it stop!

"Abbie, keep quiet!" Zachary warns her.

"No, Zach. Don't Abbie me. Fucking Samantha! She always manages to ruin everything!" she screams at the top of her lungs.

"Abigail Caroline Melbourne! Enough!" somebody orders her. "Stop talking about your sister that way!"

With all the commotion, I didn't hear the front door open. My head snaps in the direction the voice came from. Three newcomers stand at the entrance.

The two younger guys appear to be older than Zach and Abigail, one probably closer to his mid-twenties, while the other is harder to pinpoint because of the beard that covers his face. The last person of the group, I met him a couple of times when I got sick during my visits with Grams, and he was kind enough to check me. If I recall correctly, he is…was Grams's brother-in-law, Doctor Morris. His kind eyes fix upon me, his features softening.

With the back of my hand, I wipe away my tears without achieving anything. For every tear I clean, another one rolls down. Meanwhile, my sobs escape freely from my lips without the barrier of my hands to stop them.

"Samantha, honey, no! Get over here." Dr. Morris steps closer. He leans over, caressing my cheek with the back of his hand. The contact feels foreign, and I jerk away from his touch.

If I hurt my uncle with my action, he doesn't show it. Instead, he nods and steps away, clearing my view of the room.

In front of me stand four young girls and five young guys, including my siblings, watching me. My eyes immediately fix on the floor, too intimidated by them.

Hurt by their words, embarrassed by my state, and shocked at the news, I stand, turn around, and rush up the stairs. An overflowing sense of being unwanted and lost hits me as I run down the hall and up into the attic.

Abigail's words echo in my mind: Everybody should be entitled to choose the members of their flock. I assume she means family, since blood doesn't mean a thing to her.

The message is loud and clear. I'm no longer welcome in this house or this family, Big Guy, especially since You took Grams.

CHAPTER FIVE
Cooking Time

I wake up, expecting to find the white walls of my dorm room. Instead, I face a bare, wood wall. Startled, I sit up and analyze the cluttered space filled with old furniture and cardboard boxes. My eyes finally settle on the light blue sofa where I lie, identifying it as Grams. Yesterday's memories crash back, and I realize it wasn't a figment of my imagination, but I'm still not brave enough to accept it as my new reality.

Dry paths of tears line my face, my only companion while I cried myself to sleep last night. Now they threaten to join me during this early time of the day.

What am I going to do?

But what would I be able to achieve? At sixteen, finding a job where I can support myself will be nearly impossible, and I like having a roof over my head.

My stomach growls loudly, and I quickly wrap my hands around it, hoping to calm its protest at the involuntary fasting. After hiding myself in the attic, I didn't dare go downstairs to fetch something to eat.

The early morning hour gives me an opportunity to fill my basic needs while my siblings still sleep. Afterward, I can analyze my options and find more reasonable ideas with a full stomach.

And, it will also keep me distracted from the terrible news I found out yesterday.

A blanket falls at my feet when I stand. I pick it up, knowing it wasn't there yesterday during my pity party. To my utter surprise, I find a lump on the floor near the stairwell. Curious to the new addition in the attic I tiptoe my way over to it. Shocked, I find Zach lying on his back, his chest raising and falling rhythmically, sound asleep in a sleeping bag.

My heart lifts at his presence. At least he made sure I didn't disappear into thin air.

Not wanting to wake him up, I swiftly and silently sneak all the way down the stairs to the first floor. After making sure no one is there, including a certain little mutt, I go to the kitchen, finding the fruit basket that caught my attention yesterday. With great disappointment, I realize its contents are made of plastic.

No, no, no, I silently whine. *Oh God, I need food!*

My hopes lift when I recall Archie arriving yesterday with two groceries bags. Quickly, I open the fridge, picturing a dish of scrambled eggs with bacon and a side of hash browns. A disappointed sigh, followed by a groan, escapes me at the sight of several cartons of milk, bread, ham, and some bananas with black skin. My hopes of a nutritional breakfast go up in flames when I open the freezer, only to find boxes and boxes of frozen food.

Ewww! What does that even taste like? No wonder the kitchen is spotless. They never cook here.

Disheartened, I close the freezer with a loud bang and analyze my options with the ingredients, sadly determining two choices: venturing to try the frozen food or make some French toast.

Not a lot of… Wait. What do we have over here?

My eyes focus on a bag on the bottom shelf. Stepping closer, I reach for the bag and find a note on top of it.

Samantha:

Sister Josie asked us to give you this. She specifically told us to tell her little minion to make her proud.

Dr. M and O.

A million questions go through my mind.

Sister Josie spoke with them? What's inside? And who is O?

With my hopes raised, I open the contents of the bag anticipating a batch of her cookies or maybe some of her famous jam. To my great disappointment, I find flour, eggs, butter, nuts, chocolate, and other items needed to cook.

Trust Sister Josie to make me work for my food.

If I weren't starving, I'd be touched rather than discouraged. But at least this widens my breakfast options. My mind goes through the different recipes I can cook based on these new ingredients.

I can put the eggs back on the menu! Now, what else? Those black bananas could transform into banana nut bread! It will take a little longer than I expected, but it might work.

I hunt through the kitchen, searching inside the cabinets and drawers for the items I need to make a decent breakfast. Being in the kitchen, doing something I love, brings a sense of tranquility and comfort. Focusing on the task ahead of me, rather than on the next step in my now unpredictable life and on the awful news, seems simpler.

I choose to focus on Sister Josie's recipes, working through all the steps required to create delicious banana bread, smiling when I purposely add more nuts than expected and picture my nun friend chastising me about the quantity.

She'd probably even throw a tantrum about it. I snicker to myself, covering my mouth to stop the giggles.

With the mixture in a pan, I place it inside the preheated oven, adjusting the temperature and quickly create the glaze that will bring the taste of the bread up a notch. The glaze's secret ingredient sets this bread at a higher quality level than others I've eaten.

My mind goes into an auto-defense mode when I finish and focus on what I need to do next for my breakfast.

Rather than eat starch and sweets, I should focus on something with a higher nutritional value. I make a list of the inside of the fridge, smiling when I realize all the ingredients for a ham omelet are available.

After removing the ingredients from the refrigerator, I slice the meat while enjoying the smell of the banana bread. It makes my mouth water and my stomach growl again for the hundredth time.

We've made it this far, little one, you can hold for an extra minute.

Considering what I've gone through, I deserve a cup of chocolate as a small treat for surviving one of the worst days of my life and decide to add it to the menu.

Almost there!

I enjoy the sense of control I get while cooking, smiling when everything seems to come into harmony, noticing how all the chips fall into place. My timing with the omelet, the hot chocolate, and even the bread seems impeccable. Before I know it, a cooling banana bread with the glaze already on top sits on the counter, along with a perfect omelet I know will make Sister Josie proud. The hot chocolate sings to my growling stomach, ready to subdue my hunger.

After setting the mug and the plate with my food on the small bar, I return for the fork and make my way out of the kitchen, ready to sit on one of the stools and eat.

My right-hand flies to my heart, dropping the fork in the process, when I notice three sets of eyes staring at me.

A young girl stands in front, wearing a purple silk pajama set. She greets me with a wave of her hand. Her long, blond hair, tied in two ponytails, curl at the ends as if she put a curling iron through them.

Behind her stands a man, his muscular arm going around her shoulders. He stands two heads taller than her. He gives me a friendly smile, showing me the perfect contrast of his pearly whites against his golden-brown skin.

Next to them, an Asian girl yawns, her arms stretching above her head while her red t-shirt rises, revealing her small, thin frame. Slowly, she brings her arms down, her hand stopping to scratch her messy black hair, pulling back some of the loose tresses to reveal an innocent face and a set of black eyes curiously studying me.

I stare at them, frozen in place.

"Morning, Sunshine!" the blond girl kindly says with a thick, southern accent.

I guess this might be Barb, the girl who proposed different options rather than agreeing with Abigail last night.

Intimidated by their gaze and the guy, I nod in acknowledgement.

The Asian girl's eyes fix on my breakfast and a small whimper escapes her lips. It seems she also woke up with an appetite like me.

"Would you care for some breakfast?" With my eyes set on the girls, I manage to get the words out of my mouth before my tongue decides to glue itself inside.

"Yes, please," replies a male voice behind me, scaring

the bejesus out of me.

I spin around with a jump to find two boys.

Thank You, Big Guy, for me not holding the food plate. The last thing I would like is to see my handiwork wasted because of my nervous state.

I glance at Archie, recognizing him as the one who spoke, but my attention then sets on the guy next to him. I recognize him as the bearded guy who arrived yesterday with Dr. Morris.

My heart skips a beat when his black eyes scan me up and down, stopping when they reach and lock with mine. A strange sensation runs through my body, starting from the tip of my toes and slowly traveling upward, leaving a warm tingle behind. I fight against the impulse to divert my gaze and instead settle on studying the rest of his handsome, tan face and dark hair, momentarily wondering if he has some Latin heritage.

Oh my, what a cutie-pie.

After a few seconds of openly gawking at him while the color rises to my face, I allow my instincts to flow freely and bring my eyes down. He and Archie both wear plaid pajama bottoms and a t-shirt.

They step aside, creating a small gap for me to go back to the kitchen. With my arms glued at the sides of my body to avoid touching them, I return and stop near the stove, trying to steady my breathing and my rapid heartbeat.

I can do this, no biggie. People similar to creatures from heaven. Easy peasy lemon squeezy, as Grams used to say.

"Somebody should eat the one I made before it gets cold." My voice shakes as I pull eggs out from the carton and do a mental calculation of how many I'll need.

The commotion that follows startles me. My eyes widen when I glance over my shoulder to find the Asian girl grabbing the omelet plate, while Archie steals some from the side. The tall guy hands the cup of hot chocolate to Barb. She sips it and then offers it back to him.

In my peripheral vision, I catch a hand inching toward the banana bread. Instinctively, I slap the tanned hand away. Too many years in a kitchen with Sister Josie taught me to defend my cooking against little thieves.

"It needs to cool down," I state with the commanding tone of the elderly nun.

"Ouch, damn!"

I freeze when I realize who I hit. Oh, my Lord! Did I just slap the hand of a guy?

I step back, my mouth falling open, unsure if I should apologize or continue cooking.

"Can we help?" Barb approaches the kitchen counter while the tall guy trails behind her.

I breathe in, trying to calm myself. What would Sister Josie do?

Ha! Easy! Order them around.

"We need to slice more ham," I shakily tell Barb. "And I'll need a bigger pot. Fill it with milk and put it on the stove," I order the big guy without facing him. "And you," not wanting to make eye contact, I point to the spot where I slapped the Latin guy, "please take some plates out and set the table."

"Aww, exactly like her siblings, bossing us around," Archie chimes behind my back.

Everybody chuckles, except me, oblivious to what he means. Instead, I keep quiet and focus on my current work, cracking and whisking the eggs, while mentally calculating the extra pans I'll need to cook the omelets.

"You should throw in another four eggs. Lyra, Oliver, Zach, and Abigail will join us shortly," the Asian girl comments after removing the eggs from the shelf.

I stare at her, believing she might be kidding me.

"Nothing like the smell of warm bread to smoke out a sleepy crowd from under the covers," Barb adds, giving me a small wink.

I follow her orders and add the extra eggs.

"Kellan, baby, can you bring the bread closer? I don't trust Archie's hunger or Joy's fast reflexes," Barb mentions after the tall guy finishes putting a pot on the stove with milk in it.

The strong, tall guy steps closer to the counter and guards the bread as if it was a child, giving the rest of the crowd a glare. I wouldn't dare come close if it means facing him.

The image of an old story comes to mind. I smile, picturing myself as David facing the big giant. Yeah, Goliath can keep it.

"Samuel, can you make some coffee?" Archie asks.

Keeping my eyes down, I follow the Latin guy, who walks toward the pantry and searches inside.

"I can't find any," he replies with an accent difficult to place.

"It might be inside the fridge," offers the deep voice with the German accent.

I quickly turn around, finally able to match Kellan to it. I return my eyes to the pan. "Is the ham ready?"

Barb comes closer and places the cutting board with the ham next to me. Knowing it will take too long, and with my nervous state, I'll fail at cooking a perfect omelet, I make an executive decision, and throw the ham into the frying pan, changing the menu from omelet to scrambled eggs.

I check the milk and drop the chocolate bars inside.

"Do you need me to stir it?" Kellan steps closer to me, intimidating me as he towers over my head.

I nod in response, knowing whatever sound comes out of my mouth would be considered a squeak. He immediately gets ahold of the spoon and stirs the mixture.

"Archie, make yourself useful and go wake up Oliver," Barb commands.

O as in Oliver, the one responsible for the goody bag, then.

"Ugh! Send a rescue party if I don't return in five minutes," he answers, but obeys, walking toward the garage door and disappearing through it.

"Who the hell keeps coffee in the freezer?" Samuel asks.

"Zach," everybody answers in unison.

I chuckle at their perfect synchrony. The kitchen

suddenly becomes quiet, making my giggles sound loud.

"What did I do now?" my brother asks, arriving in the kitchen, his dark hair mussed from sleep. He brings the unwanted attention to him.

"Coffee in the freezer?" Kellan brings him up to speed.

"How many times do I need to tell you it helps preserve the flavor and freshness," Zach answers with a yawn. "What's for breakfast?"

"I need to plate soon," I inform them, using my Sister Josie's impression when I notice the eggs will be done shortly.

"Here." Samuel steps closer, bringing a stack of plates and spreading them onto the counter.

"Scrambled eggs with ham, hot chocolate, banana nut bread, and coffee." The Asian girl sits on the kitchen counter, her head shifting back and forth as she smells the food, her eyes expectant and her thin lips smiling widely.

After putting the eggs on the plates, the guys and girls take them to the table.

I deposit the dirty utensils in the sink and then focus on removing the banana bread from the baking pan and placing it on a plate to slice.

When I walk out of the kitchen, three new people sit at the dining table.

At one end of the table, Abigail sits, her sleepy eyes watching the garden door, ignoring me. Next to her sits a gorgeous girl, the rays of sun reaching her pale skin. Her aquamarine eyes come alive when they settle on the plate I hold. She turns toward my sister, her dirty-blond braid swaying with the movement.

"It smells wonderful," she declares, closing her eyes and taking a deep sniff. "One of these days I'll bake one."

Archie covers his mouth. However, a snort filters through. The guy sitting at the other side of the table stands and pats him on the back, making me believe Archie might be choking until I notice his shoulders shaking with laughter.

"Lyra, please don't," the Asian girl pleads. "The firefighters were not happy with your last attempt."

The guy patting Archie's back stops to run his hand through his dark-brown hair and momentarily closes his eyes, frustrated.

"Joy!" he warns the Asian girl, who sticks her tongue out at him in response.

"Oliver?" Joy replies back innocently.

"Everybody take your seat." He lets the discussion die.

My brother quickly appears next to me, depositing a pot of freshly brew coffee on top of the table.

"Here, Samantha, let me help you." Zach turns and offers to take the banana bread plate from my hands, which I release. To my surprise, he places it at the side of the table where Oliver now sits, ignoring Joy's and Archie's protest about the new location.

The table quickly fills in, leaving one open seat at the middle. I sense all eyes following me, waiting for me to join them. Samuel stands and moves the chair out, momentarily startling me until I realize he pulled it out for me.

"Thank you," I mumble, not daring to meet his eyes.

After I sit, he gently pushes the chair back in, helping me get closer to the table.

Such a gentleman.

Oliver waves his hand toward the food. "Okay, dig in."

Everybody grabs their forks.

"Wait!" I stop them. Every single eye returns to me expectantly. I divert my gaze while my face warms, probably turning a lovely shade of red, but I continue, "We need to say grace."

Abigail snorts and gives me an evil eye. I sink lower in my seat. My eyes itch, a sign of tears coming. Nervously, I direct my gaze to the plate in front of myself and bite my lower lip.

"Abigail, thank you for offering to lead today's prayer!" Oliver turns his head toward my sister, his brow furrowing as he singles her out.

Silently, everybody puts their forks down on the table, and their attention focuses on me. I make the sign of the cross and put my hands together, closing my eyes.

"Dear Lord, we thank You for the food we are about to receive. Please bless them and bless us as well," Abigail says coldly, momentarily pausing. "We would also like to take this time to thank You for allowing strangers to become family and hoping for family to become stran—"

"Amen!" Zach immediately cuts her off.

Startled, I open my eyes, full of disbelief. I stare at

Abigail, who holds Oliver's glare, silently challenging him.

The meaning of her words and the intention behind them sting deeply. What did I ever do to her? I barely know her, and yet I don't hold anything against her. Or, at least I didn't.

It appears during the last three years of my absence she evolved from ignoring me to outright insulting me to my face.

"I-I-I've lost my appetite." I stand, the chair screeching loudly against the wood floor. Keeping my gaze on the floor, I speed walk out of the dining area.

"You crossed the line, Abigail." Oliver snaps at her before I reach the stairs. I pause, curious as to what kind of power he holds to talk to my sister in such a way. "She doesn't deserve to be treated in such a manner."

"Abbie, she was opening up to us," Barb explains.

"Zach, you know what Grandma thought about her knowing anything about the Phoenix School," Abigail defends her attitude. "I'm doing her a favor. The less she knows and mingles with us the better. It'll be safer this way."

Woah, woah, woah. What is the Phoenix School?

"Abigail, I believe you didn't understand me last night. I will spell it out for you. Samantha holds a higher priority than Calvary," Oliver warns her. "If necessary, we will abort the investigation until we resolve this situation."

"What do you propose we do with her?" Abigail challenges him.

"Before deciding, we need to explore all the available

options," Oliver answers calmly. "But pushing her away and mistreating her isn't one of them."

"Considering her situation and experience, she only has a few of them. I reviewed her information and drafted the report you requested yesterday." I identify Kellan's accent.

What information is he referring to?

With my interest spiked, I quietly inch closer to listen better. My heart thunders in my chest, and I hope not to be discovered eavesdropping.

"I propose searching for something familiar and subtly introduce..." Kellan continues.

"She can be homeschooled by Grams's sister," Abigail rudely cuts Kellan off.

Homeschool?

"No," Zach answers. "Secluding her with Aunt Anne will be a setback. We need to continue with our decision and get her in touch with the real world."

They decided it? Or Grams decided? They shouldn't take credit for her decision.

"The situation was different when we allowed the application for her dancing course in Spain. She doesn't deserve to be rewarded after being expelled," Abigail retorts, annoyed.

"We should probably ask her directly what happened," Barb speaks up. "Kellan mentioned the accusation doesn't fit her character. We need to be fair, Abbie."

"Do you want to talk fair? Do you know how expensive pointe shoes are? Or the dancing course in

Spain? We allowed her to do what she loves and wants, while staying out of her way. We already deal with a lot trying to get through college while helping Oliver's uncle in the Phoenix School. At this rate, she will probably graduate from university before we manage to do it ourselves, and we're four years older than her," Abigail expresses in frustration.

Again with the Phoenix School.

Lyra speaks up, "I understand it's hard, but we can work—"

"Work around it?" Abigail sounds sarcastically amused.

I can't take it anymore. I need to cleanse my mind.

Instead of going up the stairs and hiding in the cluttered attic, I go out the front door and quietly shut it behind me.

When the cold October wind hits me, I wrap my arms around my body protectively. I remember too late about my bare feet when they touch the pavement, but I don't want to risk going inside and listening to them anymore.

Besides, a couple of minutes shouldn't be a problem.

I leave the driveway without a destination in mind, breathing in the October air.

"Inhale, exhale," I repeat while walking down the sidewalk. Creating a physical gap between my problematic family and me allows my mind to come up with a solution without allowing my emotions to control me.

I don't want them to know what a big loser I am. Yesterday, the group caught me crying my eyes out. The hydraulic factory will only get me so far. I need to keep myself composed and strong when I face them again

To be on the safe side, I increase the speed of my stride in case they notice my absence and come after me, hoping to buy a couple of extra minutes to calm down. Usually, putting things into perspective allows me to realize if I'm overreacting.

I walk slower and close my eyes, not allowing myself to get distracted.

Grams died, and my siblings need to take care of me. As far as I can tell, they inherited a pebble inside their shoe. But, let's face it, things could be worse. My problems seem minuscule if I compare them to people living on the street or in a war zone. I may not know where I'll be tomorrow, but deep down, I know Zach and Abigail won't throw me out on the streets. Grams would probably come down and haunt them in their sleep. At least there will be a roof over my head and food on the table.

My tummy rumbles at the reminder of food, protesting at this last statement.

Well, soon there will be food in my system. Let's think of it as a temporary setback. My world won't crumble at this. My next step should be…

"Watch out!" a high-pitched call snaps me out of my inner turmoil.

What the heck?

CHAPTER SIX
Darcy

I open my eyes to see a bicycle coming toward me. My hands fly up to shield myself as the front tire crashes into my leg. My palms against the handlebars stop the rest, minimizing the damage. However, the force of the impact throws me to the ground.

Oh my, Big Guy!

A wave of pain travels through my leg, followed closely by another in my butt, and I close my eyes and clench my teeth. My hands quickly find the injured spot on my leg and rub it as if trying to dissipate the pain from it. Worried about a severe injury, I move my leg up and down, assessing the damage, and yelp when pain radiates from it. Luckily, I don't detect any broken bones or sprains, but there will be a nasty bruise in a few hours.

I turn to face the rider, ready to give him a piece of my mind, and stop when I find a girl around my age staring worriedly at me. Her green eyes keep darting from my face to the spot where my hands rub, while her red-haired ponytail sways from one side to the other with the slight shake of her head. She lets go of the bike, allowing it to crash loudly against the pavement.

"Oh, my God! I didn't notice you there," she apologizes, pulling the headphones from her ears and kneeling at my side.

"Don't worry. I'm okay." I speak through clenched teeth. My injuries might not be permanent, but they do hurt.

"Are you sure?" She steps closer to me, her hands stopping inches from mine, unsure of where to put them.

"I'll live." I test my leg again, pointing my toe and then relaxing it. "I've had worse."

"Worse than being run over by a bicycle?" Her eyes widen in surprise. "Did a car hit you before? Or a motorcycle?"

"Not exactly." I don't want to elaborate on the many times Brittany *accidentally* hit me.

"Still, it was my fault. My brothers are right! I'm an accident waiting to happen," she explains in a shaky voice.

"We could also chalk this incident up to my streak of bad luck." I chuckle, remembering the last twenty-four hours. "I should probably stay in bed for the rest of my life and hope the sheets don't kill me." I joke, trying to ease some of the tension from the poor girl's mind and distract myself from the pain.

"With my luck, I'd probably fall out of bed and manage to injure the entire innocent population of creatures within a ten-mile radius with the ripple effect of my fall," she compares, frowning.

We both laugh at our pathetic situation.

"My name is Darcy." She extends her hand, which trembles slightly.

"Samantha." I take it and shake, letting it go after a few seconds.

"Nice to meet you, Sammie." She places one of her fingers to her mouth and bites her nail. "Sorry for hitting you. A song distracted me, and I momentarily forgot to keep my eyes on the road."

"You could blame me as well; I forgot to keep my eyes open while I was walking," I confess, adding a small roll of my eyes and a shrug from my shoulders.

She grins, though her eyes study me as if evaluating whether or not I'm lying to her to ease her guilt.

Well, since nothing appears to be broken, bleeding, or sprained, I might as well go home.

"Let me help you up." She stands and offers her hands to help me up. I take them, ready to place my weight on my good leg. However, her strength surprises me as she pulls me to my feet. She might be a few inches shorter than me, but she packs some muscle.

She stands next to me and puts one of my arms across

her shoulders. It takes me a couple of seconds to figure out what she wants me to do. Am I supposed to use her as a crutch?

"I can still walk, you know." I smirk at the concern on her face.

"Oh!" She blushes, the color similar to her hair, and lets me go without looking at me.

"But thanks, Darcy, it was nice to meet you." I give her a small, encouraging smile, afraid she thinks I'm making fun of her.

When I turn around to orient myself, I find myself like a hamster inside a maze, with no clue which way I came from. I'll bet the rodent's sense of direction surpasses mine.

"No, no, no," Darcy steps in front of me. "How many fingers am I holding up?" Her hand lifts in front of my face and she holds up three fingers.

Seriously?

"Four," I joke.

Her face pales. She drops her hand and reaches for her back pocket, pulling out a cellphone.

"Darcy, I'm kidding! There were only three fingers, all right?"

"Phew! Don't prank me with health issues. For a moment, I thought I gave you a concussion," she says sternly while returning her cellphone to her jeans. "I was about to call 911."

"Not a concussion, but I can't seem to find my way home." I turn around, hoping to find a clue to lead me back to Grams's house.

"Amnesia?" she asks.

"Nope." I chuckle, realizing she might be accident-prone if she considers all these options.

"When I fell, I lost the direction I came from…" I face the other side of the street and focus on the surroundings, scratching my head as I try to identify something familiar.

"First time around the area?" Darcy picks up her bike from the sidewalk and comes up next to me.

"Yeah! Every house seems the same here."

This will take longer than anticipated. If Zach and Abigail notice my absence they'll think I ran away.

"Do you know the street name?" Darcy asks.

"Solar Drive?" I answer, hoping she recognizes it.

"North or South?"

Confused, I glance at her.

"The street. North Solar Drive or South Solar Drive?" she explains.

"There are two?" I smack my forehead, surprised at this new piece of information.

Shoot! What if they set up a search party with strangers and police officers involved because little Samantha ran away from home after she got kicked out of school and found out her Grams died?

"I assume it's probably South since you're barefoot." Darcy points out, bringing me back to reality.

"Seems reasonable, although I don't know how long I've been walking." I wring my hands nervously, worrying it might be North.

Her eyebrows raise, and her eyes widen. "Are you nuts? Walking barefoot can be dangerous! What if you hurt yourself with some rusty metal and get tetanus and die? Or cut a major artery with a piece of glass?"

Wow! She can be melodramatic. Although, being a dancer, I should take better care of my feet.

She guides me to turn right.

I match her stride. "I left the house in a rush and forgot my shoes. But, I was being careful of where I step..."

"You got run over by a bicycle because we were both distracted. Imagine if I broke your toes."

Touché.

"I should take you to a doctor to make sure you don't have internal bleeding," she continues with her nervous rambling, studying me with her green eyes.

"If I feel ill, I promise to call my uncle. He's a doctor," I answer, hoping to calm her worries.

"Are you sure?" She turns, analyzing me.

"Yes!" I reply.

"No x-ray needed?"

"No! I told you I..."

"Really? Because you're walking funny."

With a sigh, I scratch the back of my neck and tilt my head toward the sky, remembering how Brittany made fun of my *duck walk*, a mixture of over-using my toes and exaggerating the movement of my hips. I do it involuntarily, a side effect of all those years dancing, the same as how I bend down and unconsciously do a plié.

It's probably exacerbated because of the sting from the dog bite and the hit from the bicycle.

"Not your fault, only a bad habit I picked up over the years from training in ballet," I explain.

"You dance!" She eyes me with a tinge of envy.

I shrug, not giving it any importance.

"Are you any good?" she inquires. "I would love to dance! But coordination is not one of my strong suits. Two left feet. I blame my dad for it."

When she pulls a face and points at her toes, I chuckle.

"I am not bad." I don't want to acknowledge Miss Johnson's praises for my talent, because after watching all those ballet-videos on YouTube and studying the movements from the dancers, I consider myself average. "But it does have its side effects."

"Well, boys will find it cute, the whole hip moving action you've got going there." When she attempts to mimic my stride, it ends badly when she bumps her knee on one of the bicycle pedals, tripping herself. I grab her arm to help stabilize her so she won't end up on the ground like I did.

Big Guy, I understand what she means about her coordination issues.

"Be careful! Next thing you know, I'll be the one taking you to the hospital," I joke. "Good thing I know a doctor."

"Then we can share a CAT scan! Wouldn't you love to see our brains?" she chimes excitedly.

Big Guy, she makes it sound as if we're about to get our nails done together.

"Darcy, I believe it takes a little more than getting hit by a bicycle and tripping over your own feet to get a CAT scan." I giggle, noticing her face falling when I minimize the injuries.

"According to my brother, you need to consider the location and the force of the hit." She lifts one finger then the other, emphasizing each point. "Taking a hit to the head isn't the same as a hit to the leg. Consequences vary depending on the sensitivity of the area."

"And yet, I can still walk even though I got hit in the leg. We can assume I'll live." I cross my arms. "Sorry to burst your bubble, but no CAT scans for us today."

She purses her lips and slightly shakes her head, reluctant to accept my answer.

We turn down a block, and Darcy guides me through the maze of streets while pushing the bicycle at her side.

"What was on your mind before I ran you over?" She questions, probably too uncomfortable with the silence.

"You didn't run me over. We crashed," I correct her.

"Whatever." She stays quiet for a few seconds. "Boy, home, or school problem?"

Hmm, if we throw in the family drama I can safely say, all of the above.

"School problem." I choose the safer topic and a less painful one than talking about Grams.

"Bad grades?" she inquires, her eyes set on the ground.

"Last minute transfer," I lie, ashamed to confess I got expelled.

Sorry, Big Guy, I'll say a Hail Mary before going to bed.

"Oh! Which school will you attend?" Her head snaps toward me, her eyes shining with hope.

"My family is still reviewing my options." Yeah, I'll add another Hail Mary to the count with another white lie. "So far, it could be homeschooling, public school, or a boarding school in Alaska."

"You're kidding, right? Boarding school? In Alaska?" She laughs, giving me a slight shoulder to shoulder touch.

"They might not be serious about the Alaska part, but boarding school is the most feasible option."

She pulls a face at my answer. "Maybe you'll get a penguin as your roommate?" She jokes, lifting her eyebrows, lightening the seriousness of the situation.

"No! Penguins live in the Southern Hemisphere, not in Alaska." But I chuckle at her idea.

"Okay." She rolls her eyes. "Then with a polar bear. Do you like the scent Au Parfum du Salmon?"

Oh, well. Might as well get used to the idea.

"I'm used to boarding school." I shrug. After twelve years, what is a little more time in the joint? "Then again, it probably beats the public-school option."

I glance at her, expecting to find her holding back laughter, but her face remains serious, her eyes fixed forward. "One of my older brothers tells me horror stories about drug dealing in the halls and shootings. Can you imagine metal detectors at the school entrances?"

"Those schools are probably far away, like on the other side of the country," I comment, but stop when she shakes her head.

"Unfortunately, the closest school has that record. If I had to attend there, I would probably drop out. I prefer to be ignorant and breathing over brilliant and dead body. But, some public schools can be nice. Just not the ones near us."

My mouth hangs open. Back at Saint Magdalene, I caught rumors about public school incidents. Somehow, I placed them far away. Knowing it's this close breaks the illusion of safety.

"Don't stress yourself." She assesses me. "You appear to be a good girl. That school is the last option in public schooling here in the area."

If she only knew how, after yesterday's incident, I'd been kicked off of the good-kids list. My breath hitches as I realize my current dilemma.

"Would you consider homeschooling to be the best option?" I ask her opinion since she knows the area better than me.

"No!" she answers immediately, her head turning toward me. "Well, it's not a terrible option, but not the best one for me. At least, the school I go to allows me to spend time outside of my family, which helps my clumsy self socialize with people and do things without my brothers making fun of me the whole time." As she shrugs her shoulders, the bike wobbles slightly, one pedal coming close to hitting her in the leg.

"Where do you attend?" I ask, realizing she rejected all the options I presented.

"I go to a private school near here. My mom works there as a teacher," she explains.

"Do you like it?"

"It's okay." Her head tilts from one side to the other, one corner of her lips pursing, not fully convinced. "I believe this option works better with my life. I get to go home every day, and it's safer than the public schools around here. But, as with any high-school, you can't escape the drama and problems." She shrugs her shoulders.

I analyze her answer while a pang of sadness hits me in the chest, remembering Grams will no longer be here waiting for me at home after school. Instead, it will be my siblings. Would I like to live in a house where every single day I get mean comments from Abigail?

On a more positive side, Zach did seem calmer and friendlier this morning. Plus, I need to consider what Miss Johnson mentioned, about getting in touch with my family.

Whatever remains of it.

"However, the real question is, what would you like to do?" Darcy's eyebrow rises as she glances at me. "You'll be the one living with the final decision,"

My steps slow down, giving some serious consideration to her question. Abigail and Zach will make a decision based on what works with their current schedule. But what about me? Shouldn't my opinion count?

"Here we are, South Solar Drive." Darcy stops walking and points to the street sign.

I study the road, hoping to locate the missing tree in

the yard, but find nothing. I shake my head. "It's not there." I doubt at this point my absence will go unnoticed, the odds no longer in my favor. "We should try North Solar Drive." I wring my hands together, studying the other side of the road, hoping one of the trees will magically disappear.

A song interrupts our discussion, and Darcy's hand flies to the back pocket of her pants to remove her cell phone. She releases an exasperated sigh after reading the caller ID.

"Mom!" she answers. "No, I should be back soon." She stops talking and listens to the other side, shaking her head. "Potter can help you out." She closes her eyes, annoyed at the answer. "Ugh! You over pamper him! When I was his age, you recruited me to work in the kitchen."

Darcy pulls her head away from the phone when the voice on the other end of the line gets louder.

"Mom, you created an army of minions at your disposal, and yet you always ask me." Darcy makes another face. "All right, I'll be there in ten." Her answer appears to be the wrong one because her expression turns sullen. "I'm in the middle of something. No! It's not a boy. Ugh! Okay, two minutes."

Annoyed, she hangs up the phone and returns it to her pocket.

"Would it be okay if we stop at my house first?" she asks apologetically, her cheeks turning red. "My mother wants me to help her with a few chores."

"You can point me in the right direction, and I'll get there," I offer, not wanting to get her into trouble at home. After all, she's been nice to me...well, besides the small accident. But I find talking to her refreshing and easy compared to the girls at school.

"Please, come home with me. I need somebody to bail me out of child labor." Her eyes plead for my aid. She seals the deal when she pouts her lip.

"Okay," I agree.

Can things get any worse, Big Guy?

CHAPTER SEVEN
The O'Flannagan's

I follow Darcy through the streets, even more lost than before. She increases the speed of her stride until we arrive at one of the house clones, the door marked with the number 261.

She opens the fence that leads to the garden and drops off her bicycle then hurries to the front door where I wait. We enter into a small hall that runs down the center of the house, dividing it in half, the stairs just a few feet away from the door, however, she turns left through the dining room, giving me no time to study the house decorations in her haste state, and I almost bump into her once we reach the kitchen and Darcy stopping suddenly. At the central counter stands a red-haired woman, her wavy hair held back by a clip behind her head. She wears an apron, which covers part of her pear-shaped figure.

With her attention focused on a cookbook in front of her, she scratches her eyebrow. In the process, she accidentally pushes down her reading glasses

"I need your help, honey. You can begin with separating the eggs. Yolks in the crystal bowl, the rest in the mixing bowl." She points at the set-up laid out in front of her without moving her eyes from the cookbook.

Darcy pulls a face, grossed out by her given task. "Can't I help you with something else?"

"No. You need to learn how to do it properly." Darcy's mom retrieves a kitchen scale from the counter. "And no eggshells this time," she warns, pulling out baking trays from beneath the counter.

"But they're gross, and there's too many," Darcy whines with a higher pitched voice, sounding childish.

A quick peek at the counter reveals three cartons that hold a dozen eggs each.

"Don't start with me, young lady. You need to learn. Otherwise, you'll fail my class," she warns.

"Great. My mother will fail me. I'll be the laughing stock at school." Darcy's face turns sad.

"You won't if you learn how to do it right," her mom fires back, her attention on the baking pans as she lays them on the counter.

"I can help," I offer, trying to be useful and end the discussion.

Darcy's mother's head snaps up. She takes her glasses off, noticing me for the first time. Her eyes, the identical shade of green as Darcy's, travel from my face to my feet and widen when she notices my bare feet.

"Really?" she asks.

"No problem, easy peasy lemon squeezy." As I sing-song Grams old saying, a pang in my heart reminds me of yesterday's news.

"Perfect," Darcy happily agrees, not giving her mom a chance to dismiss me.

She pulls me closer to the counter, releasing my hand when we stand in front of the prep area.

"We need to wash our hands first," I insist, following Sister Josie's teachings about the importance of hygiene while cooking, especially after my hands touched the ground when I fell.

When I walk to the sink, I sense their eyes on my back, following me. I glance over my shoulder and catch Darcy's mother mouthing a silent question to her daughter, which Darcy answers with a shrug of her shoulders.

"I'm Samantha, by the way," I introduce myself, ashamed to forget the basic rules of etiquette. Sister Josie would chew my head off if she ever hears about it.

"Nice to meet you, Samantha. I'm Mrs. O'Flannagan, or Darcy's Mom." She gives me an awkward smile, then eyes her daughter who keeps her attention on me to avoid her mom's stare at all cost.

"Nice to make your acquaintance, Mrs. O'Flannagan."

Tension fills the space between her daughter and her. Trying to ignore it, I approach the table with the eggs and take the first one, carefully cracking it in the middle. With one half of the shell, I balance the yolk from one shell to the other, allowing the egg white to fall inside of the mixing bowl. My hands tremble slightly, their stares making me nervous.

"What will you cook, Mrs. O'Flannagan?" I ask, hoping to distract them, afraid my shaky hands will mess up the next egg I crack.

"Meringues," she answers, mimicking a Spanish accent. She comes closer and studies the results of my work. "Mrs. Smith planned a tea party in the afternoon, and she requested a big order."

She assumes I know Mrs. Smith.

"Oh, sounds nice," I answer noncommittally.

She studies the bowl with the egg whites and gives me an approving nod.

"Darcy, come here and help Samantha." She flaps her hand at her daughter, signaling her to stand by my side.

"Why ruin something good, Mom? I don't want to mess up her—"

"Now, Darcy! I need to speed things up. Get the second mixing bowl from the top counter," she commands in a *don't mess with me, young lady* voice. "I'll go and wake up Anakin and Bennedick. Your father expects them in the market soon."

Mrs. O'Flannagan leaves the kitchen without another word.

I turn around to find Darcy dragging her feet to the counter where she pulls out the mixing bowl. She then shuffles to the sink to slowly wash her hands.

"This will take, like, forever," she complains while drying her hands.

"It's easy." I show her the way I balance the egg yolk from one shell to the other.

"Um, remember? Accident waiting to happen? My crazy mother believes I can do this." Defeated by the small challenge, her arms drop to her sides and she tilts her head upward.

Noticing the despair in the girl's eyes and the happiness disappearing from her features, I remember an old trick. It might not solve her clumsiness problem, but it will help her with the task her mother set for her.

"Can you get a clean plastic bottle?" I ask her.

"Why?" She stares at me as if a nut got unscrewed in my brain.

I give her a mischievous glance. "You want to pass the class?"

"Yeah!" Her back straightens at my words.

"Then get it," I command while continuing to work.

From the pantry, she removes a bottle of water, opens it, takes a few gulps, and pours the rest in the potted spice plants that rest in the windowsill. She washes the bottle, dries it with a clean paper towel, and hands it to me.

After making sure no water remains in the bottle, because it could ruin the meringue, I signal for Darcy to come closer.

"I'll share a little secret, and it will speed up the job." I purposely crack one of the eggs and pour the whole thing into the bowl, making Darcy gasp when the one yolk floats on top of the whites. With a yoke in the mix, it ruins the whites for making a meringue. She stares at me wide-eyed. In return, I give her a wink.

Pressing the sides of the empty bottle together, I collapse it and put it on top of the egg yolk. I gently release the pressure of my hands, allowing the container to return to its original shape while sucking up the egg yolk in the process.

When she sees the result, her hands fly to her mouth and she giggles.

I put the bottle over the yolk bowl, turn it upside down, and give it a small squeeze, releasing the yolk into the bowl.

"It only took you like, half the time," she says in amazement, still studying the bowl of egg whites.

"It's easy, even if it's cheating," I reply, worried I might get her in trouble with her mom.

"Nu-uh. The woman said, 'separate the egg,' and as far as I'm concerned, we achieve the same result." She dumps the egg white in my mixing bowl.

I glance up questioningly.

"An extra precaution in case I screw up, I don't want to ruin the whole lot if the yolk breaks," she explains, making me giggle at her honesty.

We work together. At each step, Darcy asks me a question about the process, which I happily answer. By the time we crack the last egg, she's mastered the art of separating eggs with the help of a plastic bottle.

When we finish, her mother still hadn't returned. Darcy eyes me, grinning mischievously. "I believe we can make a run for it?"

I shake my head, not wanting to get her in trouble.

"We could help her," I suggest, pointing at the cookbook.

"You know how to make meringues?" Darcy asks, full of disbelief.

"It's not complicated." I remember the last time I helped Sister Josie. There isn't a lot of science involved if I recall correctly.

I read the recipe in the cookbook, checking the ingredients and making the necessary adjustments based on the number of eggs we used.

Wow! Mrs. O'Flannagan didn't lie when she mentioned it was a big order.

We follow the recipe. Darcy acts as my assistant, handing me the measured ingredients I request. I give her a step-by-step tutorial of the steps as I perform them and ask her to do some of the extra jobs, like preheating the oven and preparing the oven trays. Meanwhile, I mix the ingredients as Sister Josie taught me, enjoying the effect of how the mixture expands to a beautiful white, puffy consistency. I tilt the bowl to one side, making Darcy shriek when she notices the angle and then gasp when the mixture stays steady at the bottom of the bowl.

"Now we need a pastry sleeve with a flat tip." I search

the counter for it and turn to her.

"Care to explain that in English?" Her eyebrows draw together, studying me as if I asked her a question about astrophysics.

"It's a pastry tool like a bag with a metal tip used to decorate cakes," I explain patiently.

"Oh! One of her little toys." She cheers, recognizing the item, and pulls it from one of the drawers.

I put part of the batter in the pastry sleeve and expertly create the shape of the meringue. I work the rest of the tray while explaining to Darcy the secrets for a perfect one. She does the second tray and jumps up and down when she replicates the same result.

We place the trays in the oven, reducing the temperature before setting the bake time on the clock.

When I turn around, Mrs. O'Flannagan stands off to the side, her stare fixed on the two of us.

"I leave you two to crack eggs, and when I return, I find the meringues in the oven?" she questions in disbelief, her eyes widening when they settle on the oven before slowly moving to the sink where we stacked the dirty bowls.

"We followed the recipe, Mrs. O'Flannagan," I explain, ashamed and worried I overstepped my boundaries when I remember I'm not in Sister Josie's kitchen. Internally, I kick myself for being so thoughtless. "I hope they turn out all right." I add in a small squeaky voice.

"The size and shape were beautiful," Mrs.

O'Flannagan confirms, regarding me. "You would have gotten an A plus in class and extra points for tutoring Darcy."

I smile, happy to know I didn't mess up.

"You, Darcy, on the other hand..." She points toward the plastic bottle.

No! We forgot to remove the evidence! My palm flies to my forehead.

"Not exactly what I planned when I request your help, but I'll give you extra points for creativity and speed. Probably a B."

"Yes!" Darcy raises her right fist. "Nailed it!"

I bite my lower lip, amused when her mom closes her eyes and pinches her nose at her daughter's hopelessness.

A sweet aroma fills my nostrils, and my long-ignored stomach announces its presences with a loud growl, making Darcy chuckle. "Hungry?"

"I haven't had breakfast," I confess. My cheeks heat when my stomach growls again.

"We have some cereal if you like." She walks to the pantry and opens the doors, revealing a stack of different kinds of boxes to choose.

"Darcy Austen O'Flannagan! Offer your friend something better." Her mother comes into the kitchen and pulls food out from the fridge. "Would you like some fresh fruit, some yogurt?"

I glance at Darcy, lifting my eyebrows after hearing her second name. She shakes her head and looks down and away.

"That sounds great, Mrs. O'Flannagan." I answer. "Can I help you?"

"You've already helped with the meringues. The least I can do is get you breakfast." Darcy's mom sets four empty bowls on top of the counter.

"I can help you wash the dishes," I offer while picking the last of the dirty utensils and taking them to the sink.

"Sherlock doesn't like when somebody messes with his department," Darcy answers.

Right, Watson?

I expect to see her smiling, but her face is dead serious.

"Mom decided to get creative during her pregnancies," she explains. "Instead of food cravings, hers were *literary* cravings. Therefore, she took the name or last name of one of her favorite characters and then the last name of the author, ending up with Anakin Lucas, Legolas Tolkien, Sherlock Doyle, Bennedick Shakespeare, Potter Rowling, and Darcy Austen."

"Don't criticize my creativity," her mother defends her choices. "They're unique."

"And, a total dork alert. The only one who doesn't get hell is Anakin." She shoots daggers at her mother with her eyes. "At least not from the geek squad who lust after his name."

"I love your name, Darcy," I tell her with sincerity, trying to ease the tension that skyrocketed between Mrs. O'Flannagan and her in the past thirty seconds.

"Until you get to read Pride and Prejudice." Darcy

rolls her eyes.

"Sherlock, Legolas, Bennedick, and Potter stink then?" a male voice asks from the kitchen entrance.

I freeze in place, my tongue sticking to the top of my mouth.

Slowly, I turn around to find a guy around eighteen years old, sizing me up. His serious, dark blue gaze moves from my head to my feet as if trying to figure out who this strange girl is.

He combs back his mussed, black hair with one hand, his lean arm flexing, showing the evidence of muscles under his t-shirt. The superiority of his attitude, together with his serious demeanor and his studying glance, makes me believe this guy could be either Sherlock or Legolas.

Intimidated, I divert my gaze to the kitchen floor.

"This was ringing, Mom," he mentions while stepping inside the kitchen. "Mr. Morton activated the neighborhood alarm."

I dare a glance to catch her son handing a phone to Mrs. O'Flannagan, who puts her reading glasses on. Her nose scrunches while she reads a text message.

"Oh, Lord! They report a missing teenage girl with black hair, hazel eyes, and tan skin," she reads.

Guilty, I peek at Mrs. O'Flannagan, only to catch her son scrutinizing me.

"The granddaughter of the late Mrs. Morris," she finishes.

I hold my breath while all their gazes fall on me.

The neighborhood alarm? *Oh shoot, things are about to go*

south, Big Guy.

However, on the plus side, they didn't call the police, yet.

"Samantha Melbourne," he states. His handsome eyes gleam and he smirks with success, like he solved the mystery of the missing girl.

Yeah! This O'Flannagan brother is Sherlock.

"Oh!" Mrs. O'Flannagan examines the message and then contemplates me, her face full of questions.

But the words refuse to leave my mouth, too intimidated by her son.

"She got lost, Mom," Darcy tells her. "I was helping her get home when you called."

If I wasn't utterly embarrassed by the whole situation, I would thank Darcy for the explanation.

"Why didn't you say something before?" Mrs. O'Flannagan demands, her head snapping toward her daughter.

"You didn't let me explain! I barely put my feet inside the house before you ordered me to crack the eggs." She crosses her arms defensively.

Mrs. O'Flannagan scowls at her, unaccepting her explanation as a valid excuse.

"We need to inform her family about her whereabouts. How worried they must be not knowing my daughter brought you here," Mrs. O'Flannagan continues.

If only.

"She lives close. I can take her," Sherlock proposes.

"I'll go with you," Darcy offers, probably taking

advantage of the opportunity to allow her mom to cool down and avoid her lecture.

"Yes, please do. I'll send a message to Mr. Morton immediately." Mrs. O'Flannagan brings the phone up and stares intently at it, as if solving a physics problem.

"Ask one of the twins to help you. Last time you erased all your contacts," Sherlock calls while leaving the kitchen and going out to the hall.

I give one last glance to the fresh fruit lying on top of the counter, my stomach again protesting the sudden change of events. Once again, I was close and yet the opportunity slipped from my fingers.

"The meringue should be done in little less than an hour," I remind Mrs. O'Flannagan, not wanting our work ruined by this distraction. "Thank you for letting me help out."

Mrs. O'Flannagan comes closer and pulls me into her. Being touched is such a foreign gesture for me. The nuns almost never hugged. Her warm gesture comes as a surprise, her action freezing me in place.

She met me a little over an hour ago and yet she treats me as if I was a lifetime friend to her daughter. Is this normal?

"You're welcome to help anytime, sweetie," she says, pulling back with a soft smile.

"Bennedick, Legolas!" Darcy screams from outside the kitchen. Leaving Mrs. O'Flannagan, I join Darcy at the bottom of the stairwell. "Mom is trying to use her cellphone!"

A loud thunder of footsteps comes from the stairs as if the house is on fire. A pair of boys, identical twins, reach the lower level. Like Sherlock, their hair is black, but they share the same green eyes and freckles as their sister and mother. I step to one side of the hall to get out of their way and avoid being run over.

"Well, hello, gorgeous," one of them says, stopping to contemplate me. He gives me a playful grin before inching closer.

Afraid, I step back, moving closer to Darcy.

"Mom. Cellphone. Stat!" Darcy orders, bringing the twin back to the emergency at hand.

"Let's go, Samantha," she grabs my hand and pulls me to the door.

Before leaving, my heart accelerates when I notice a twelve-year-old boy coming down the stairs. His messy black hair and sleepy green eyes regard me with curiosity for a moment. Except for the missing scar and glasses, he's a dead ringer for Harry Potter.

I leave the warmth of the O'Flannagan house and walk the streets to return to my siblings and their friends.

What kind of welcoming reception waits for me at home, Big Guy?

CHAPTER EIGHT
Change is Good

The red door of 249 North Solar Drive stands in front of us. My heart beats at full speed, a sense of déjà vu choking me: the door, me, and the promise of a lecture. This time, I ring the bell, hoping Zach answers it since I'll fair better with him than with Abigail. When the doorknob turns, I hold my breath and pray for the best.

Please let it be Zach. Please let him be the one to answer. My sister opens it, her face unreadable. I can't catch a break.

"Samantha, oh thank God!" She reaches out, surprising me with a hug.

Stunned at her reaction, I don't know if I should put

my arms around her and return the hug or run for the hills and hide. Before I can decide, she releases me.

"You had us worried sick! What happened?" Her eyes travel the full length of my body, studying me.

"I-I-I..." I stammer, still confused at her unexpected welcome.

"I bumped into her near the park," Darcy explains. "She got lost."

Bump being an understatement.

I glance at Darcy who keeps a straight face, never faltering while she explains. However, the mischievous glint in her eyes betrays her. I struggle not to laugh at the whole display.

"We were heading this way an hour ago, but we got detained," she continues the act without breaking character. "I apologize for any inconvenience and worry our small detour caused you and your family."

"Thank you, Darcy, for helping me find my way home," I tell her before I giggle at her act, guessing Abigail would not find my reaction amusing.

"Yes, thank you, Darcy, and..." Abigail fixes her gaze on Darcy's brother.

"Sherlock O'Flannagan." He extends his hand. A smile spreads on his lips, while he appears to be slightly star struck.

My sister takes it and gives him a brief, coy smile. She bats her eyelashes. "Abigail Melbourne."

Oh, my, Big Guy! Totally unexpected.

My sister's behavior comes as a shock. She usually

behaves like a tomboy, but right now she resembles more of a girly girl.

Glancing at Darcy, I notice her open mouth, appearing as surprised as me with this whole interaction.

"Thank you, Darcy and Sherlock, for making sure she got back home safe." Abigail's eyes remain locked on his. She lets go of his hand and twists a short lock of her hair around one of her fingers.

Heavens! She is totally flirting with him!

"Anything we can help you with, Samantha knows where we live," he tells her. He steps back, misses the step behind him, and almost falls.

"Smooth, Sherlock. Now who's the clumsy one?" Darcy mumbles underneath her breath.

I bite my lip to hold the giggles back.

"Are you all right?" Concerned, Abigail takes one step forward and extends her hand, stopping before she touches him.

"No problem." He gives her a reassuring nod. "Darcy, we need to leave. Mom still wants us to help her with some errands."

"Okay. Samantha, see you around. And, good luck with everything." She steps down and waves good-bye before catching up with her brother.

"Bye, Darcy! Goodbye, Sherlock!" Abigail calls, putting extra emphasis on the boy's name.

She waves her hand with a big, silly smile on her face. Before they reach the end of the block, I catch a few lines as Darcy sings loudly, "Sherlock and Abigail, sitting in a tree..."

Abigail and I walk inside the house and the sound dies when the door shuts behind me.

"What's wrong with you?" Abigail stabs a finger against my chest, her dark side coming out as she drops the whole sweet sister act. "We've been searching all over for you!"

Now, this is the kind of reception I expected.

Before I can explain the situation, my sister turns around and leaves me by the door, walking into the dining room. I trail behind her to find Joy sitting in front of a computer at the dinner table with Lyra next to her.

"Lyra, text everyone and inform them she returned. Joy, call Oliver and tell him he doesn't need to drive to Saint Magdalene." She barks the orders as a general to her soldiers. The worst part is, both girls follow her directions. She pulls her cellphone from her back pocket. "I'll inform Uncle Jonathan and call off the neighborhood alarm."

She steps out to the garden.

Once again, she acts as if I'm not in the room. Then again, there's no point in trying to smooth things over. Might as well take this opportunity to search the kitchen for some leftovers of the food I prepared earlier while the other girls work on their new assignment.

My heart falls when I find the impeccable state of the kitchen and all the dishes washed. Luckily, when I open the fridge, I find half of the banana bread still waiting for me.

Thank You, Big Guy!

Hungrily, I pull it out along with the carton of milk. I serve myself a big chunk along with a glass of milk, happy as I finally take a bite. My taste buds water when the sweetness of bread makes its way to my mouth. Eyes catching on a binder that rests on top of the counter near one of the cabinets. It wasn't there this morning. My interest spikes when I read the title on the spine: Samantha Melbourne.

Well, since my name's on it, there shouldn't be a problem if I read it.

Inside, I find a summary of my life at Saint Magdalene: grades, achievements, misconduct reports, details of each of my school years, friends, roommate information, and a full report on Brittany's conduct and suspicions of bullying.

I don't need to go into a lot of detail. I know how it ends. I flip it to the last page, expecting to find yesterday's event and finding something different instead.

"Samantha Melbourne Psychological Analysis by Kellan Russ." My eyes focus on the first paragraph. I sit down on the floor, pulling the binder closer to read.

"Samantha lived most of her life in an overprotective environment, limiting her knowledge of what to expect from the world.

"Academically, she proved to be one of the brightest amongst her grade, but several of the teachers pointed out she performs poorly in group activities. Her social skills would be considered below average with no known lasting friendships, causing her to seek safety and confidence from elderly figures.

"Her contact with the opposite sex has been near to none apart from her brother when she visited during summer and Christmas breaks. She avoids at all cost interacting with males, and if necessary, she gives short or wordless answers, projecting the appearance of fear.

"During middle school, her dancing teacher suspected some fellow students took advantage of her and physically attacked her. When confronted, she never confirmed it, blaming most of her injuries on dancing accidents. Considering the evidence disappeared during her high school years, the school opted to shut down the investigation.

"She finds escape in her dancing, spending her free time in the ballet studio, perfecting her moves or studying dance videos.

"Once she sets her mind on a goal, she works hard to obtain it, though she prefers the safety of what she knows, avoiding taking risks or trying new things.

"She developed a strong aqua phobia after a car accident which resulted in her mother's death.

"Her nature could be described as an attentive, kind, and well behaved kid. However, due to her lack of social abilities, her leadership skills are non-existent."

In summary, I am a socially inept push-over who is afraid of boys and water.

Great!

The report continues, but the sound of footsteps nearing the kitchen distracts me. Not wanting to be caught red-handed, I close the binder.

"Joy," Abigail calls out, stopping a few steps away from the kitchen. I stay put but keep my ears open. "Any news about the boarding school for Samantha?"

My attention snaps to this new line of conversation. I clutch the Report in my lap and focus on their discussion.

"They accepted her, but under probation because of the last incident," Joy replies after a quick click of the keyboard and mouse.

"Excellent," the clap that follows my sister's cheer feels kind of insulting. "Can she begin on Monday?"

She won't allow me to stay for Grams's church services or give me a chance to mourn her.

"If we can get her the books and uniform, she's good to go," Joy informs her. "They already emailed me the list of items we need to get."

"Lyra, can you help us locate them?" Abigail asks.

"Sure, email the list, and I'll work on it immediately. Should I get the items shipped here or to the boarding school?" Lyra questions.

"It'll be easier to send it straight to school. It will save time and money," Abigail confirms confidently. "Also, book her a one-way plane ticket and a round trip for Uncle Jonathan. He'll be taking her there."

Unbelievable!

"Are you sure about this, Abigail?" Joy asks. "Shouldn't you check with Zach first?"

"We got her in a school without pulling any strings. We can follow up the job we offered to help the Phoenix

School and perform it without any distractions. If everything works out, we can solve the situation at Calvary before the end of the school year and continue with our majors. How can he say no to this?" She sighs with relief.

My sister didn't even bother to consider what I want, or what makes me happy. She only contemplated Zach and herself. *What a selfish girl, Big Guy.*

"A trip to Fargo it is. The next direct flight leaves tomorrow morning," Lyra notes.

"Can we get them in one leaving today?" Abigail amends. "Uncle Jonathan already asked for the day off to search for Samantha. It will be easier for the hospital schedule."

"I don't believe the red-eye will suit your Uncle or the price. It will be easier and cheaper if we wait until tomorrow," Lyra argues. "Have you considered Archie flying them there?"

My breath hardly reaches my lungs as the drowning sensation returns. Only this time, there isn't any water involved, only the weight of my sister's decision to change my life without consulting with me first. Again, my nervous tic starts up, and before I know it, I need to pull my hand away from my mouth to stop chewing my nails.

"I forgot he can fly," Abigail agrees happily. "Joy, text Archie. Tell him to go to the airport and prepare his plane. We'll cover the gasoline fee for his trip to North Dakota."

What? North Dakota?

I rise from the floor with the binder still in my hand.

Joy's head turns to where I stand, her eyes widening in

surprise. "Abigail?"

Abigail ignores her friend's call. "Lyra, please work on the booklist while I bring her suitcase down."

"Abigail?" Lyra notices me and tries to get my sister's attention, nodding her head in my direction.

"Problem averted. Samantha returns to school, and we can continue with our job," Abigail remains coldly oblivious to her friend signals.

"Abigail!" Joy and Lyra speak at the same time while staring at me.

"What?" Abigail snaps out. She follows Joy and Lyra's eyes. Her face flushes and she juts out her chin, her hands clenching into fists of anger.

Breathe in, breathe out.

The binder in my hands suddenly weighs a thousand pounds. Until now, other people decided how my life should go. Nobody bothered to ask me what I wanted. And now a few measly words sum up those twelve years.

Do I want to continue being a socially inept push-over who's afraid of boys? Or should I allow myself to get out of my comfort zone and interact with the world outside? To learn how to survive before life pushes me into it and I fail miserably.

Opportunities like this don't come often, I can choose to let it go and keep living like I did, or stand up and fight for myself.

Change is good.

"I'm not going," I state, the words faltering at the end.

"Yes, you are!" Abigail commands. "It works perfectly

with everybody."

I give her a small shake of my head. "What suits you, doesn't mean it suits me," I correct her timidly.

She lets out an exasperated sigh and turns around, ignoring me. "Lyra, did Archie answer yet?"

My stomach feels as if somebody set it on fire. Since the moment I arrived, she never asked me anything, and when I finally voice my opinion, she ignores me? Not anymore!

"Don't be a bitch, Abigail!" I yell before I clamp my hands over my mouth.

Jeez, I need to add another Hail Mary to the count. I'll make it a Rosary for good measure.

Immediately, a pang of regret hits me for calling my sister the "b" word, but honestly, she deserves it after the way she's treated me.

Her back stiffens.

Lyra and Joy stop working, their expression full of surprise, their heads silently moving from Abigail to me.

My sister turns around and approaches me. From my peripheral vision, I catch Joy urgently typing on her cell phone. "You'll be the pretty little dove Grandma loved, and go to school in North Dakota," she commands between clenched teeth, controlling herself from exploding.

Well, Grams is no longer here, is she?

I purse my lips and shake my head, holding her stare, challenging her. I did not trade Brittany's bullying for Abigail's.

Enough is enough!

"You can't make me," I state bravely, even though my legs threaten to buckle under me.

"Fortunately, I can, since Grams appointed me as your legal guardian." She crosses her arms over her chest, which only makes me madder.

Her attitude fuels my determination. The pain of Grams's departure, mixed with the rejection from her and Zach, pushes me one step closer to blowing up.

"I may have to go," I warn, mimicking her same cold tone, "but don't expect me to behave."

Her nostrils flare, but she holds her breath for a few seconds before inching closer and whispering, "Just obey, Samantha, and for the next school year I promise to find a place closer to home and with ballet in their curriculum."

What? This new school doesn't teach ballet? Does she know how much this affects my training and my mood?

"Now, put some shoes on and bring your suitcase down from my room. I'll make the arrangements for you."

I resist following the order. Instead, I cross my arms and prepare myself to confront her.

Big Guy, she might have an army of little soldiers obeying her without any question. Luckily, I'm not one of them.

"Why do you so desperately want to get rid of me?" I ask, ignoring her last command.

She sighs but keeps quiet.

"What did I do for you to treat me like this?" I speak aloud the question that haunted me since I overheard her hate talk yesterday evening.

She continues to ignore me.

"I might be innocent, but not stupid, you know." Anger feeds my bravery. "How can I know how the world works if you shove me back into a bubble? I need to learn, and I'd rather do it sooner than later."

I slam the binder on top of the counter, showing her I know about the report. Her eyes momentarily widen at the evidence.

"Joy. Anything?" Abigail continues as if I didn't say a thing and turns around.

"Why have you always pushed me away?" I demand.

She might ignore me, but she will hear me out before my anger turns into something worse.

"We're sisters, Abigail. Talk to me." I walk closer, softening my voice, "What did I do wrong?"

She stiffens in place, her back straightening as her head snaps in my direction.

"Don't go there, Samantha," she warns, acknowledging she heard me. "Please go to school," she sounds weak, and almost sad. "Let me keep my promise to Grams."

"I want to stay here with my family and get to know you. I'll bet Grams would have loved it." I reach out to her. "Please, Abigail?"

She turns around, her face like ice, the color drained from her features. "You'll be safer in North Dakota, away from us and our crazy lifestyle." She stares down at the kitchen floor, chewing the inside of her cheek as she prepares her next response. She sighs. "There is no room in my house for you."

A few years back, Brittany used to release her frustrations by using me as a punching bag. She loved to sucker punch me, her fist painfully hitting my soft belly, pushing all the air from my lungs. At this moment, Abigail sucker punched me with her words.

There's room for them, but not for me, her blood.

"You could at least allow me to mourn Grams and attend some of her funeral services before shipping me out," I whisper, frustrated, not daring to look at my sister or her friends.

Before I cry, I leave the kitchen with whatever dignity I have left. I pass the living room, turning around to the entrance to head upstairs and prepare for my trip to North Dakota.

I stop, noticing a group standing in the reception area: Uncle Jonathan, Samuel, Barb, Kellan, Archie, and Zach. Their eyes watch me with pity.

Great, I got an audience!

My head snaps down, while I keep my arms close to my body.

Don't cry. Don't cry, I command myself.

I continue my way to the stairs, stepping to one side to avoid colliding with anybody. However, a pair of arms goes around my shoulders, stopping me and pulling me into an embrace.

"There will always be room in my house, Samantha." I glance up and find Zach holding me. His hazel eyes search mine. "If you still want to stay with me."

For a moment, the air finds its way back into my lungs, the pain of the sucker punch easing.

The sincerity of his smile and the way he waits expectantly for my answer shines like a small ray of hope illuminating my dark and lonely future, especially since this is the first time I've witnessed him standing up to Abigail on my behalf.

"Yes, please," I whisper, nodding my head.

His smile widens and he squeezes me.

His eyes momentarily leave mine, and he scowls straight ahead. "This is her house as much as yours or mine." I assume his words are meant for Abigail, but I don't dare to confirm my assumption. "Grams also appointed me as Samantha's legal guardian."

It seems the audience arrived at the house a while ago.

"Zach," Abigail argues. "She can't stay here with everything we committed to do and without her—"

"Abigail, don't turn your back on her," Barb interrupts. "I would welcome my sister with open arms if she asked for my help."

"Barb, we can't compare one situation against the other," Abigail answers.

"Why is it different?" Samuel questions her, stepping closer to the stairwell and blocking my escape path. His eyes narrow at my sister. "Besides the fact you kept her a secret from all of us?"

"Because of the past," she snaps, jutting her chin upward.

"Hers or ours?" Archie asks, crossing his arms.

"Both," she straightens her back, crosses her arms, and defies Archie with her eyes. "She sees the world in a different way than we do. Our lifestyle wouldn't suit hers. Her reality doesn't come close to ours."

"Abigail, four years ago all of our lifestyles couldn't be more opposite from one another," Joy replies. "Each of our reality varied according to our upbringing, social position, or situation in life. Ironically, no matter how different each one was, we all managed to find a destructive path. Thanks to the guidance and trust of some people and your grandmother, we managed to shift it to a constructive one."

"Now it's our turn to help her." Uncle Jonathan steps up, "Angela would hate to know you turned your back on a member of her flock. Especially her little dove."

Abigail rolls her eyes when she hears Grams's nickname for me.

"Kellan, your report clearly states we needed to slowly introduce her..." Abigail replies, seeking refuge in the dreadful report.

"Her willingness to accept change and take risk should be considered a big leap. If anything, we need to take the opportunity and guide her. Otherwise you might face a setback," Kellan declares.

"The school which Abigail proposes has an amazing curriculum," Lyra speaks up, bringing over a printed brochure of the school. She offers it to Zach for review, but he shakes his head, not taking it.

"How about we compromise?" My sister uncrosses

her arms, moving her head from one side of the room to the other, studying her audience. "She goes off for the rest of her junior school year while we work on the Calvary job, and then, I'll take another year off college and take care of her during her senior year."

Again! Big Guy, I should probably go out of the room and let the adults discuss my future.

"She clearly stated she wanted to stay here," Samuel reminds her, his eyes searching for my approval.

Okay, Big Guy, thank You for making sure somebody pays attention to what I say.

"What she wants and what she needs are two different things," Abigail defends her point of view.

"Angela!" Archie shouts, bringing his head upward as if talking to the ceiling. "It finally happened! Karma does exist" Archie jokes, earning a drop dead glare from my sister. "Did you bite your tongue while you said that?"

Kind of disrespectful for Archie to speak in such a manner considering how my Grams passed away this week.

"Abigail!" Zach stops her. "What she wants is what she needs, and you know it."

"Her timing sucks!" Abigail's defenses come up again.

"Well, according to you, the time has never been right since Grams died," Zach answers, angered.

Big Guy, am I misinterpreting things? Because it kind of sounds as if Grams died a little longer than a week ago. But that can't be right. I got an email from her this past weekend.

"Either we were too young to handle such a big responsibility, or not the proper role model for her to follow. And now we use the Calvary excuse," Zach snaps back, pointing a finger at her.

How old could they get in a one week period? See, something doesn't add up.

"This stops now. Time for us to accept our responsibility, or before you know it, we'll miss the opportunity to know how amazing and talented our sister is!" he replies.

Didn't Zach hate me? What changed his opinion about me?

"Zach!" Abigail brings her hand to her heart, her face contorting with pain as if he stabbed her in the back.

"No, I'm putting my foot down on this," he warns her. "She stays, and that is final!"

The rest of the group appears shocked at Zach, except Uncle Jonathan who I notice gives him a thumbs up behind Abigail's back.

When I don't hear any further argument from Abigail, I glance at her, noticing her giving a small, reluctant nod, accepting the new plan.

"Archie, ask Mrs. Donahue if we can borrow her driveway for a few months. We'll need the garage to store some of the items from the attic." Zach's gaze returns to me. "Kellan, we need to call Oliver's uncle and ask if he can assign one of his guys to help us create a big living space. Samantha's returning home."

I don't want to complain, Big Guy, considering things appear to be going my way. But something doesn't make sense and my logic senses are tingling. When did Grams die?

CHAPTER NINE
The Market

After some awkward glances from everybody, Uncle Jonathan asks me to go upstairs to get dressed.

I remove my suitcase from Abigail's room and take it to the attic. Most of my wardrobe consists either of school uniforms, ballet gear, or a few skirts I made during sewing classes. I pull out my only pair of jeans, knowing they've seen better days. Their color has washed out, and they no longer fit properly. I match them with a white, long sleeved shirt, one from the school uniforms, and get dressed.

The finishing touch to my simple wardrobe consists of the last pair of black flats I own. The other pair needs to be thrown away due to water damage.

When I return, the area is now conveniently empty except for Uncle Jonathan who waits for me at the bottom of the stairs.

"Samantha, would you care to join me to buy some groceries?" he asks.

I nod, excited at the proposal.

Earlier, I wished to stay with my siblings. However, considering the tension I created, escaping for a few hours while letting things cool down sounds like an excellent plan.

And a chance to try to make sense of what happened.

We leave the house and silently walk to his car. He opens the passenger door and gestures for me to get in. Once I settle into the seat, he closes the door, walks to the other side of the car, and slips into the driver's seat.

"Seatbelts, hun," he reminds me while he puts his own on. I follow his lead, earning an approving nod from him.

He turns the car on and drives away from the house.

"How about we go to the Farmer's Market? Get some fresh ingredients?"

I shrug and offer a small, nervous smile. With him, I don't get as intimidated. Being older probably helps, but still, I don't know him well enough. I manage to untie my tongue and give him an answer. "Sounds good, Doctor Morris."

Chuckling, he focuses on the road. "You can call me Uncle Jonathan, Samantha. After all, we're family."

"Okay, Uncle Jonathan," I respond and bite my lower

lip, liking how the words roll out of my mouth.

"See? It sounds better."

I nod in agreement, finding it comforting to be able to rely upon another family member who protected me from Abigail's harshness.

"I apologize for pulling you out of the hospital today," I mention, knowing my behavior cost him precious hours with his patients.

He shakes his head, cutting me off. "Yesterday, I planned to have the day off, since I needed to take care of an important matter today."

"More important than saving lives?" I ask, surprised.

"Saving lives is important, and I love my job, to the point of being considered a workaholic," he replies. "Unfortunately, I neglected other aspects of my life, family being one of them, and I need to remember family needs to be a priority."

Oh!

"Believe it or not, I'm happy you returned home, Samantha." He turns and quickly glances at me. "I look forward to getting to know you better, since you're staying with the rest of them."

Well, at least he has a more positive attitude about me returning home, despite the circumstances.

"I don't believe Abigail shares the same sentiment," I mumble.

He stays quiet for a few seconds, his gaze attentive on the road as he thinks over his answer. "Abigail needs to improve the way she expresses her feelings, but you need to understand she worries. She wants to keep you and Zach safe."

Sure she does.

"She has a very particular way of showing it," I respond politely, not wanting to disagree but finding it hard to believe after our last encounter.

"You'll learn in time to read her moods and will understand the reasoning behind her actions. You need to trust me on this one, little dove." He winks at me while he expertly parks the car.

Maybe, I will. Maybe, I won't. Only time will tell.

He gets out of the car. I follow, opening my door and stepping out. I freeze when I notice him walking around the vehicle, heading my way to open my door.

Sister Agatha will send me straight to the chapel if she ever learns about this incident.

For a moment, I consider sitting back down and closing the door so he can achieve his original goal, but I'm already out. It would be awkward. I'm still undecided on how to proceed when he reaches for my door and closes it.

"Sorry, next time I'll wait for you," I cringe with mortification.

His eyes sparkle when he catches a glimpse of my blushing face. "No need to apologize, Little Dove. You'll learn soon enough the ways of the South."

He takes my arm and gently puts it in the crook of his, leading the way toward a coffee shop.

"Would you be kind enough to join me for coffee and

a muffin?" he asks while opening the door to the shop and gesturing for me to enter first.

The smell of coffee and sweets suddenly wakes up my stomach, which growls hungrily. The glass of milk and small piece of banana bread I ate didn't even cover half of the caloric intake I usually eat for breakfast, and after yesterday's lack of food, my stomach has a legitimate reason to protest.

"Of course," I answer, trying not to sound as desperate as my stomach.

A young lady at the counter takes our orders. I decide to ask for a hot chocolate and a big piece of apple pie. Uncle Jonathan orders a black coffee and a blueberry muffin.

We sit in one of the booths located at one end of the cafe while we wait for our order.

"Now, I believe you might have some questions about, well, everything. I can try to answer some as best as I can." Uncle offers.

My mind quickly processes the long list. The first and most important one pops into my mind, and I blurt out, "What happened to Grams?"

My mind hasn't wrapped around the concept of Grams moving to a better world, especially since I never got a chance to say goodbye to her. I still loved her, despite the small time we spent together.

He clears his throat and focuses on his hand. "After your last visit, her health decayed. We ran some tests, and the results came back with the terrible news about cancer."

My hand flies to my mouth, drowning the gasp while he regards me expectantly.

I recall how she appeared weaker the last time I saw her, but I blamed it on her growing age. Now I know it was the illness doing its terrible work on her body.

Oh, Big Guy.

"She hoped with chemotherapy and radiation she would get better. She didn't want to burden a thirteen-year-old girl with this terrible news and decided not to tell you," he continues.

I suck up some air and hold it for a few minutes while the news sinks in.

Grams had cancer.

"She wanted you to remember the times you two spent together with her being happy, strong, and healthy. Not sick and weak."

Now I understand the reason she didn't want me to come home during the summer and Christmas breaks, and yet, by not telling me about her illness, she robbed us of the time we could be together making some new memories and getting closure.

"Unfortunately, her cancer was an aggressive one, and she passed away a few months after being diagnosed," Uncle Jonathan explains.

Excuse me, what? That was three years ago. My mind practically explodes with this new piece of information, considering all the emails we shared these past three years. *Then who answered my emails all those times, Big Guy?*

"Why didn't they notify me when she died?" I grab a

napkin to clean the falling tears.

"She knew her death would be a big blow for Abigail and Zach. She expected, once they got in better shape, they would be there to help you cope with it," he soothes after noticing my tears.

Once again, my siblings became her priority, and I was left to fend for myself on the sidelines. What made them so special they deserved to live with her and not me?

"I know she asked your brother and sister to slowly inform you about her illness since the outlook didn't look promising," he explains. "She hoped the news of her departure wouldn't take you by surprise and affect you as bad as your mom's death affected them."

Big Guy, seems the plan did not go as she expected. The news not only took me by surprise, but we can add betrayal and anger to the whole situation.

"When were they planning on telling me? Ten years after she passed away?" I ask, furious. "Or, wait, how about when I mysteriously appear at their doorstep?" I add sarcastically, making a tight ball of the small napkin I used for my tears.

He shakes his head, his lips in a tight line. "Samantha, what Angela asked them to do was not an easy task," he whispers. "I don't know all the details of what she expected afterward. You need to ask your brother and sister directly."

And expect them to tell me what? The truth?

"I doubt they'll be honest with me," I lash out at my uncle. "After all, for three years I thought Grams wrote me news, words of encouragement, recommendations, only to find out it was all a lie!" What did Grams expect when she came up with this crazy plan? "I'll bet they enjoyed reading about my insecurities, my questions. They probably got together and shared a good laugh before answering me."

Uncle Jonathan catches my hand and keeps a strong hold on it. "Never for one moment believe Zach would take things lightly," he says, getting my attention. "If anything, those emails gave your brother a better perspective of who you are and allowed him to get to know you better."

Then Zach is the one who answered my emails. *Oh no, Big Guy! Please tell me he didn't read my questions from when I got my period.*

"He wanted to tell you sooner and bring you home, but Abigail thought they were too young to bring up a thirteen-year-old girl when they had barely turned eighteen." He releases my hand from his.

"She still doesn't believe this to be the right choice," I reply, remembering the discussion from the house.

"She worries about you and Zach."

Sure she does. I'll bet she spends sleepless nights thinking about her stranded sister safely locked up in a boarding school full of nuns while she can go out and party with her friends.

"Correction, she only worries about him and herself," I state.

Uncle Jonathan flinches at my words. "Abigail grew and changed significantly during the last few years," he answers cautiously. "But she still believes she isn't the proper role model for you."

Well, we can concur on that point.

"But Angela didn't agree with her, otherwise she wouldn't have left your custody to her and Zach," he reminds me.

Big Guy, please do me a favor and ask Grams what outcome she foresaw?

Our order arrives, and the waitress puts the plates down, smiling professionally during the whole process. This small break gives me time to process the news of Grams passing away awhile ago. It will take time for reality to sink in and work on getting closure.

And, get to know my siblings.

As soon as the waitress leaves, Uncle Jonathan looks expectantly at me. I take a sip of my hot chocolate before asking, "Can I visit Grams's grave?"

I don't know what to expect, but I hope to pay my respects and begin the grieving process.

"I can take you after we go shopping if you would like," he offers, which I gratefully accept.

Uncle Jonathan takes a bite of his blueberry muffin, while I think over my next question. "Who are the people in the house?" I realize how rude I sound and correct myself. "I mean, they seem nice. Do they live there?"

I assume this last part since they came down for breakfast with their pajamas on and Barb asked Archie to go wake some of them up.

He grins, changing the somber mood. "They're close

friends. They met your siblings a few years back. They supported each other through some tough times and grew very close. You could almost call them family."

Wow, Big Guy! How freaking perfect! They consider strangers family, unlike me, their own blood, who they need to be kept far away like a stranger. Also, if they grew so close during all these years, how come none of them knew about my existence? Am I some dirty little secret that needed to be kept hidden?

I sip on my hot chocolate, not happy about the answer to this question either. I eat a spoonful of the pie while trying to calm down. It tastes stale, most likely because of my angry mood, which is a pity because of all the hard work the baker put into it, only for me to not enjoy it.

"They support each other, Samantha," Uncle continues calmly, noticing my change in attitude. "They take care of each other."

"Sure," I reply sarcastically, attacking the pie with my spoon to break it into little pieces.

"They didn't know about you, Samantha. Angela thought it would be better this way." He takes my hand, stopping me from destroying the pie. "However, they consider you a part of their family now, and they will take care of you. If you still wish for that."

I shrug, dropping the spoon and pulling my hand from his touch.

"The majority now lives together in the house." He leans back in his chair, his brown eyes still analyzing my face. "The girls sleep on the second floor while the boys have rooms in the basement, and they share the common area."

Of course, it is. Everyone gets a room and a bed except for me, who ruined their plan and got kicked out boarding school.

"Where will I sleep?" Anger spikes through me, guessing the few things Grams gave me and the items stored in my old room were thrown away or donated.

Not even something for me to keep for old time's sake.

"Zach will make sure to set up a room for you," he replies.

Jeez, let me get this straight. Instead of assigning one of the girls to relent their room, I'll get the crumbs. I'll bet Harry Potter's cupboard room under the stairs will be considered a penthouse compared to what I'll be left with.

"It helps if all of them live under the same roof while they work together on the assigned project, since it requires their full attention," he explains.

"The project assigned by the Phoenix School?" I remember Abigail briefly mentioning it during our discussions.

He nods cautiously.

"What is the Phoenix School?" He momentarily stiffens at my question.

"A particular kind of school." He gives a nervous smile, his hand reaching for his cup of coffee and bringing it to his lips.

I replay in my mind some of the conversation I

eavesdropped on, making the answer he gave me more confusing.

"High school or college?" I ask, trying to understand since Abigail mentioned helping the Calvary school and returning to their majors.

He sighs.

"The Phoenix School," he says slowly, "is a nonprofit organization, aimed at helping young people."

I notice how he avoids giving me a straight answer. "Help them how?"

"To help teenagers back to a healthier lifestyle while helping others," he explains.

Healthier lifestyle?

"Is it rehab? Like AA and drugs?" I ask, horrified, not wanting to presume my siblings and their friends are junkies.

"Not entirely. When they enrolled, their issues were more in regard to their attitude." Uncle Jonathan stops and takes a sip of his coffee. "Your Grandmother got involved when Abigail and Zach attended there when they were sixteen. To her great relief, she noticed how their program managed to steer her grandkids to a healthier lifestyle."

I believe Abigail still needs some additional help with her anger issues.

Confused, I ask, "What did they mean about pulling some strings to help me get into school?"

His eyes go momentarily wide while he keeps the forced smile in place. "Nothing to worry your pretty little head about."

"Why?" I press the matter, noticing how Uncle Jonathan evades the answer, making me more curious about the subject. Tell a girl to forget about it, and the more curious and obstinate she becomes.

He shrugs and takes a bite of his muffin, wordlessly telling me the discussion is over.

"What is the Calvary job?" I move to the next question without dropping the subject, which appears to make him uncomfortable.

He raises one eyebrow in surprise. "You need to discuss this with them. I only know the general idea of the project."

Still, I can't make out anything from it because of his broad answers.

"Are you done eating?" He points a finger down at my pie.

After its deadly encounter with the spoon, it no longer resembles a pie but a pile of crumbs. I nod and drink the rest of my hot chocolate.

"Excellent." He stands and drops a tip on the table.

I rise, and he offers me his arm once again.

We walk out and silently make our way to the Farmer's Market across the way. The stands located at each side of the walkway of the park leave a small pathway for the customers to travel. I stay close to my uncle, not wanting to be lost among the people. Vendors step a few feet away from their tables, offering samples of their products and presenting their merchandise. They ask if they can help us find something while assuring us of the high quality of their products.

The smell, the noise, and the big crowd overload my senses, making me quite aware I'm out of my element.

Every time I get close to a stand, I shy away, finding myself surrounded by customers or a salesperson trying to show me stuff, which makes me momentarily forget what I want.

Uncle Jonathan patiently follows me, letting me wander through the stands, always staying one step behind.

Oh, Samantha, grow a backbone, will you? I scold myself as I hurry away from another stand.

After walking through several of the stands, I choose one that appears to offer most of the items I need: vegetables, fruits, dairy products, and spices. My mind immediately comes up with different ideas of what I can prepare with this bounty. But I stop, telling myself I need to make a cooking plan, otherwise I might overbuy, and then a lot of the food will spoil.

"Hello, gorgeous, could I interest you in some of the merchandise? Vegetable? Fruit? Or maybe some delicious meringues freshly baked and prepared by one of the best chefs in town?" My head snaps up at the words. I recognize the familiar, green eyes studying me, his freckled face smiling. I smile back at one of the O'Flannagan twins, glad I chose what appears to be their stand. He winks and offers me one of the final products of Darcy's and my morning project.

"Bennedick, stop flirting with the customers!" A hand appears out of nowhere and hits the back of the twin's head. "Mother will be furious if she finds out you sold Mrs. Smith's order to someone else."

Bennedick flinches and rubs the sore spot, glaring back to where the assaulter stands. I bite my lower lip, holding back the giggle daring to escape.

"She'll be happy to know the baker tasted her final product, numbnuts," he retorts.

An unknown face appears from behind the counter, but I can safely guess he's the O'Flannagan kid I didn't meet at the house, considering he shares Darcy's red hair and Sherlock's blue eyes. His face appears older than the rest of his siblings, placing him around his early twenties, which I assume makes him the oldest of the lot.

And jeez Louise, he is cute! There must be something wrong with me. How come every single guy I meet seems to be attractive?

Easy, I've been boy deprived for too long. My teenage hormones are creating a revolution in my system, killing any living neuron inside. Free us! They shout. We can smell testosterone, and we want out!

My communication system shuts down, again, with my tongue automatically gluing to my mouth like all the previous times when I need to provide an answer to a guy. Apparently, a perfect system designed to make me appear like an idiot.

"Did I finally meet the miracle worker who achieved the impossible? Darcy in the kitchen without burning anything?" he jokes, his eyebrows shooting upward while my stomach goes in the opposite direction.

I stay as quiet as a tomb.

"You know my niece?" Uncle Jonathan steps next to me and thankfully distracts them from my predicament.

The siblings share a surprise look.

"Dr. Morris at your service," Uncle introduces himself.

"Anakin O'Flannagan, and this is my brother Bennedick," the older one introduces himself and his sibling. "I've only had the pleasure of meeting your niece now, but she helped our mother this morning with an errand."

"Oh! No wonder we couldn't find you." Uncle turns to me with surprise. He lifts his eyebrows, entertained at my inability to speak.

I nod, wishing I could elaborate more.

"I wouldn't mind tasting one of the final products," Uncle Jonathan accepts, stretching out his hand.

Bennedick hands over one of the nicely packed boxes with a dozen of the meringues inside. When Uncle Jonathan reaches for one, Bennedick signals he should keep the whole box.

Uncle Jonathan pops one into his mouth, his eyes full of surprise when he tastes it. His gaze travels from the box to me.

"You are an excellent cook, Samantha," he comments after swallowing, gazing at the box, tempted to eat the second one.

"There wasn't anything really complex in the recipe, Uncle," I answer, shrugging and ignoring the observant eyes of the O'Flannagan brothers as best as I can.

"It's not difficult, but it does require a certain level of knowledge to get the right consistency," Anakin acknowledges, but I keep my focus on Uncle Jonathan.

He raises one eyebrow, regards Anakin with a slight close-lipped smile. "I suspect she likes to minimize her abilities."

"Being humble is a good quality for a beautiful girl," Bennedick speaks in my defense. My face comes alive at his comment, probably a lovely shade of red. "Like a beautiful blush," he finishes with a chuckle.

I try to cover my face with my hand, as if that will help. *Oh, Big Guy, please make it stop and return my cheeks to their standard color.*

Through my fingers, I catch Uncle Jonathan's shoulders slightly shaking with amusement.

"I told you to stop flirting with our customers," Anakin reprimands his brother. However, there isn't the same amount of conviction in his voice as the last time he said it, and a lack of a small blow in the head.

"Dad likes it when I do. Says it improves the sales," Bennedick defends with a chuckle. "He encourages it, which is why I always end up in the market with you."

"Please excuse my brother, he got the short end of the deal brain wise when the cells split in half with his twin," Anakin diagnoses.

"But, I got the good looks." I dare to glance at Bennedick and catch him winking at me. "Don't you agree, Samantha?"

I can't help it; I giggle. They're identical twins.

"I mean, Legolas is rather charming," he continues, encouraged by my laughter. "But how can you deny the power of an attractive personality?" He smiles widely and gestures at himself.

I roll my eyes at him and bite my lower lip.

"How can we help you today?" Bennedick's brother cuts his flirting short and goes back to business mode. "See anything interesting to take home today?"

Uncle Jonathan puts his hand on the small of my back, silently encouraging me to make my order.

I focus on the essential items we need to at least survive breakfast and lunch, increasing quantity accordingly for the number of people in the house. Based on this morning, I got the impression they appreciate good, homemade food.

I make my order, imagining an older woman takes it and not a couple of handsome guys. My eyes lock on the ingredients to avoid breaking the spell and letting the mute system activate.

"Do you deliver to the home?" Uncle Jonathan asks when I finish and he realizes the size of the order.

"We usually don't, but since you live relatively close to our house, it shouldn't be a problem. As long as we can deliver later in the afternoon," Anakin offers confidently.

"Plus, Mom likes Samantha. She couldn't stop bragging about her all morning." Bennedick places some of the items I ask for inside of a box. "She would skin us alive if she knew we denied you this small favor."

"Excellent," Uncle Jonathan responds as he pulls his wallet from his back pocket and pays for the items.

I'd like to complain about him covering the fee for the food, but my current economic situation regarding cash equals zero.

"I'll catch you later, gorgeous," Bennedick tells me, followed by a wink.

"And, Darcy will probably like to go." Anakin cuts Bennedick's flirting off. "She mentioned something about checking for any permanent damage?"

I laugh out loud at this.

The boys share a glance and then divert their gaze to Uncle Jonathan who seems as confused as them.

"We bumped into each other this morning," I explain, momentarily forgetting my audience.

"Well, she said she worried about her friend," Anakin comments.

We spent less than two hours together, yet she tells her brothers we're friends.

My heart swells up at the simple thought, making me believe the report might be wrong and there's hope for me in the friend department.

"But, avoid mentioning your uncle's profession. She'll never leave your house if she knows," Anakin suggests, coming closer.

I bite my lip and shake my head, remembering her obsession with all the medical tests.

"I apologize about not informing you ahead of time," Bennedick jumps in, leaning closer to me. "On behalf of the rest of the family, we ask for your forgiveness for her future behavior. Keep in mind we're not all as crazy as her." He turns both ways and loudly whispers, "Except for Legolas. He is a total wacko. Don't let his handsome face fool you." He winks at me and returns to his place.

Uncle Jonathan and I leave the O'Flannagan's stand laughing while waving goodbye to them.

"Interesting. You made new friends?" Uncle Jonathan asks with a happy glint in his eyes.

Taking this opportunity, I explain the whole encounter and how I ended up in the O'Flannagan home helping Darcy. I made sure to clarify how my absence resulted from me getting lost and not because I planned to run away.

After listening to the whole story, Uncle chortles and confesses that the whole experience was an eye-opener for Zach, probably giving him the courage he needed to finally put his foot down, knowing he counted on his friends' support.

For a moment, I get lost in my uncle's confession, until my eyes travel to a flower stand near where the car is parked. With a heavy heart, I remember our next destination.

"Can we get some flowers for Grams?" I ask him.

"Of course, we can." He steps closer. "Which ones would you like to take her?"

"White roses," I immediately answer, knowing how much she loved them because of their significance.

A white rose means either unity or purity.

"Eleven white roses please," Uncle requests from the attendant.

He pays for the bouquet, and I carry it, enjoying the smell of the flowers. Its gentle fragrance brings back the memory of Grams's perfume.

I smile as I inspect one of the rose buds, its petals not yet ready to open and face the world, but preparing to make its big entrance. I count the roses, realizing he asked for eleven flowers and not a dozen. I shake my head at the odd number.

When we reach the car, Uncle opens my door, closing it once I settle in my seat. Before reaching the other side, he pulls his cell phone from his back pocket and makes a call. I imagine he's checking on one of his patients and patiently wait the few minutes it takes for him to finish and gets inside the car.

"Ready to visit Angela?" he asks, and I nod.

Not really, Big Guy.

CHAPTER TEN
Second Chances

During our quiet drive to the cemetery, my mind goes back and forth through my memories of Grams. My strongest contain her constant encouragement for my ballet career. Since I was little, she always told me how a dancer is a creator and a storyteller, enlightening me to the world of possibilities this form of art holds.

Other memories remain fresh in my mind, like the times we spent together in the kitchen. We enjoyed baking different recipes and trying new ingredients. I picture myself like a secret double agent who would share Sister Josie's little dark secrets, and afterward spill Grams's tricks to the nun.

Most of the time, mixing both of their knowledge proved to enhance the final product. I know they would have been great friends if they ever had the chance to meet.

We arrive at the cemetery, and Uncle Jonathan parks the car in one of the lanes next to the graveyard. I remember to stay inside and wait for him to open the door. I find his lips pulling upwards at one corner, knowing I kept my promise. He stretches his hand toward me; I put mine inside of his and allow him to help me get out.

I take the flower bouquet, stepping away from the car.

Uncle Jonathan closes the door behind me, and I wait for him to join me. When he reaches me, he puts his hand on my back, gently guiding me through the maze of tombstones until we finally reach the one marked:

In loving memory of
Angela Morris
"Always believe in yourself"

My breath catches in my throat at the sight of the stone and tears flood my eyes, finally acknowledging she's gone. The grave kills the small, lingering ray of hope which didn't allow me to accept reality. Three years ago, I never imagined our next encounter would be like this.

"I'll give you some time alone," Uncle Jonathan offers as he signals for me to give him the bouquet. Sullenly, I release it, leaving me empty handed and with nothing to offer her or to keep myself busy.

I don't know what to do. Should I talk to her? Would

she even listen to me?

As a Catholic, I believe there's life after death in what people like to refer to as heaven, but speaking to a rock feels kind of weird.

What if Grams is busy and doesn't listen to me? *How does it work, Big Guy?*

I settle on acknowledging all the good things she did during her lifetime, knowing she wasn't perfect, but she always gave her best and made decisions following her heart.

At some point, did she regret sending me to boarding school for such an extended period of time? Or once she knew the cancer treatment wouldn't work, did she wish she could go back in time and handle things differently?

But, alas, I can't continue wondering and analyzing the 'what ifs' of the whole situation. She made a decision and stood by it until the end. I should trust her judgment on this one.

With a sigh, I kneel, sitting on top of my calves. The cold, damp grass touches my feet where the flat shoes don't cover. I close my eyes and concentrate on all the lovely times we spent together, trying to find the evidence she loved me in those memories. I focus on her smile when she picked me up from school to spend time at home and on her tears when I returned to school.

I lose track of time, not knowing if I arrived a few minutes ago or one hour ago. However, a voice behind me takes me by surprise.

"Can we join you?" I turn to find Zach together with

Abigail. I nod and move to one side of the grave to open the space for them to pay their respects to Grams.

They sit next to me. Abigail wears sunglasses to hide her eyes, making it hard for me to read her emotions with her cold face. I glance at Zach, finding his mouth pulled down. His eyes focus on the tombstone in front of us.

They probably want to spend some time with her privately. I'm just in the way, like always.

A hand gets ahold of my arm and gently keeps me in place when I shift my feet in front of myself to stand.

"We failed you terribly, Grams." Zach's voice breaks the silence. My gaze settles on his face, noticing how his eyes fill with unshed tears, evidence of the longing and how her death still affects him greatly. "Before you died, you asked us to take care of Samantha and to keep her happy. We strongly believed keeping her in Saint Magdalene was the best option."

Seeing him all teary and slightly broken puts my system on high alert. My initial instinct wants to inform him things at Saint Magdalene were not bad, but I stop because it would be a lie.

I liked dancing and spending time with some of the nuns, but in reality, it only helped to keep me entertained while weeks passed, waiting to hear news about Grams, hoping the next email would finally mention the day we could see each other again.

"But, it should have stopped awhile ago. We should have come clean with her sooner."

Yes, you should have! Preferably when they heard she

had cancer, thus I could say my farewell in person and not to a piece of rock three years later.

"I remember the time you asked me to drive you to Saint Magdalene when we found out about your illness. How your face lit up when you watched Samantha laughing and joking in the kitchen with a nun, while her dance instructor told you about her great dancing potential," he says, his eyes focused on the tombstone. "Right there, you decided not to tell her about the cancer to avoid worrying her about your sickness."

When did she go to Saint Magdalene? Was her illness already evident? Did she know the treatment failed, or did she hope to make a full recovery? And why did Miss Johnson never mention anything?

It only adds more questions to the already long list.

"Afterward, you told me you expected a change to come to all of us, and you worried about Samantha. You asked us to please keep her safe and protected when it happened," his voice trembles slightly at the end, while a tear falls from his eye. And as a chain reaction, they bring out mine. "I thought you meant about the change that came with your departure and her growing up. But it only proved to affect Abigail and me since we kept Samantha in the dark. I finally understand protecting her doesn't mean storing her away in boarding school and taking the reins of her life from afar, but rather to let her grow and make her own choices while guiding her. As you allowed us to do." Zach stops speaking and bows his head. "You were right, it was time for a change."

"We promise you." Abigail's voice takes me by surprise, my head turning by instinct in her direction. Her features remain cold, but the trail of a fallen tear still glistens on one of her cheeks. "We will do our best to keep her safe."

I bite my lower lip, noticing how Zach glares at her, guessing it's because she wanted to take the easy road and keep her promise to Grams by shipping me to North Dakota.

At least he's willing to try. *But, Big Guy, should I trust him?*

He became my Grams behind the emails in the last three years. If the essence of what I noticed in those words remains, there might be a shot at building some kind of relationship, even if it started out based on a lie.

Could I say the same from Abigail?

Ha! Nope!

Clearly, she can only tolerate my existence if I live in a different state. But, I made up my mind to stay. I don't want to be the girl in the report any longer. Time to stop blaming others and step forward with the challenge. After all, my future depends on it and I won't allow Abigail to stop me this time.

Big Guy, if I managed to survive twelve years with Sister Angertha, I can put up with Abigail a couple of years.

"And, you guys are not alone." A masculine voice at our back startles me.

My head snaps up to identify the speaker and I find the rest of their group behind us, standing together with

Uncle Jonathan. I don't recognize all of their voices yet, but I believe Oliver was the one who spoke.

Each of them holds a white rose from the bouquet. Uncle Jonathan comes closer and hands us each one flower. I get the small rosebud I singled out earlier.

"I was not lucky enough to get to know your Grandmother closely, but the stories my uncle and you guys tell me show me a small glimpse of how wonderful she was." Oliver comes closer and deposits the flower on top of her tombstone, then returns to his previous position.

"She always welcomed us into her home, listened to our problems, and tried to help as best as she could. I will never forget what she did for me," Barb's voice breaks at the end. After clearing her throat, she steps closer and puts her flower right next to where Oliver left his.

"She always found a way to crawl into our hearts," Archie adds and steps closer to the tombstone. "And to our stomachs." He chuckles at this last part and the others join in the laughter while he deposits his flowers.

"She made us face our demons." Samuel mimics the others.

"And, encouraged us to work together as a team." Joy follows up with her flower.

"Taking advantage of our strength and helping each other through our weaknesses," Lyra continues.

"To achieve our dreams," Kellan finishes. The two of them approach the tombstone to deposit their flowers.

Jealousy inches inside my heart, wondering what

special kind of super power they had for Grams to welcome them into her life while keeping me at a distance, practically abandoned at Saint Magdalene.

How did they end up knowing Grams?

From all the information Uncle Jonathan told me today, I can conclude they were some troublemakers and ended up at the Phoenix School where they met my siblings. Which means, during a couple of my vacation breaks, Grams already knew them. How come we never met each other?

Was she testing them to check if they wouldn't corrupt her little dove before introducing us?

"I would be honored if I managed to be a fraction of who she was." Abigail wipes away a tear that escaped her eyes.

"She was a beautiful lady, a loving mother, and a kickass grandmother," Zach continues with a small smile on his lips.

The twins bring their flowers, Abigail's hand slightly shaking as they place them next to the others, decorating each side of the top of the tombstone with the white roses Grams loved. A small gap remains for the flower in my hand.

The last twenty-four hours have been terrible, but after all, I was an unexpected arrival, taking everybody by surprise, especially those who didn't even know I existed.

Clearly, Grams spent time with this team. I know she wouldn't allow them to approach Zach and Abigail if she considered them a bad influence. Their words indicate she cared for this group, opened her door and heart for them.

And yet she kept me afar, her own granddaughter. Which doesn't make sense. Protect them from me or vice versa? Or maybe she hoped to personally make the introductions but the Big Guy had other plans in mind.

There are too many unsolved questions I may never know the answer to. But taking my frustration out on them for Grams's decision would be wrong on my part.

Could I trust them? Uncle Jonathan's words from the coffee shop come back.

"You could almost say they are family."

I'll assume Grams took them under her wing. After all, she did include them inside of her flock.

I glance at each of them, their eyes watching me expectantly. If anything, they made me feel welcome during breakfast, allowing me to open up at my pace, searching for me when I got lost and fighting for me when Abigail turned her back. They don't know me, but they didn't reject me.

And now they support me in the cemetery, by not allowing me to grieve alone and showing me a small glimpse of the way Grams behaved with them.

As for Zach, he hides behind excuses for his behavior, but at least he made sure to keep an eye on me through the emails. How can I deny him an opportunity to rectify the situation, after I constantly ask our Lord for forgiveness for all my indiscretions? It won't be easy but before giving up on my blood family, this is the least I can offer.

Life is not perfect. People are not perfect. We are

human, and error is part of our nature. People learn from their mistakes and try their best not to repeat them. Zach made his mistakes, as did Grandma, but I can't blame them entirely for it.

Had I ever voiced my opinion regarding wanting to come and live with them? Nope.

I need to acknowledge my errors for staying at Saint Magdalene for twelve years; it was easier to allow others to take hold of my life and even blame them for it.

Do I want my life to be the same? No.

This wake-up call works both ways.

Hitting Brittany's nose might be a small blessing after all. *You do work in mysterious ways, Big Guy.*

As for Abigail...

Sorry, Big Guy, but part of the reason I stay is for the sheer pleasure of bugging her with my closeness. Yeah, yeah, I know it's mean, but hey, she started it.

I step closer to the tomb with the small rosebud in my hand. Gazing upward, I find all eyes on me.

I replay their memories, describing Grams, comparing my image with their kind words. I already lost her; I won't allow my stupid pride to distance me more from my family.

"I wish I'd known you better, Grams," I acknowledge, finding my voice. "But I can find a little piece of you in each one of them." I give a small smile.

Studying each of them, I recognize leadership, compassion, love, bravery, teamwork, intelligence, toughness, and a potential family.

I vow to find your legacy in each of them, and hopefully continue your fantastic work. I promise internally.

I bring my flower down, closing the gap. Reflecting on top of the tomb, the union of all of us, and the meaning she always said signifies the white rose.

Bye, Grams.

A tear escapes my eye. Immediately, a pair of arms goes around my neck, taking me by surprise as they pull me close. When I glance upward, I find Zach holding me close to his body.

"Aww, not fair, I want in," Barb expresses with her distinctive Southern accent. Her words are followed by a small push, her face appearing next to Zach's.

"Group hug!" Archie announces, and immediately there's another push in the group, letting me know he also joined in. His proposal is met by chuckles, followed by more pushing and shoving.

I giggle as I find myself at the center of a nine-person group hug.

"Abbie, the flock sticks together," Barb calls out before one final push in the group, which makes me guess my sister finally joined in the hug.

"She might be the glue this group needs to work together as a team," I catch Uncle Jonathan's murmur. "I will keep an eye on them, Angela, and try to keep them on the right path. This is my promise to you." When I spot him through the crush of bodies, his hand rests on top of the tombstone as if sealing his words with a handshake.

"Now, Samantha, I should probably check to make

sure your injuries are minor after your small run in with the bicycle." Uncle says as he steps back. "We should do this before your friend comes and asks for a full report when they drop the groceries at home."

The hug quickly breaks once my uncle's words set in, all of their eyes on me, some with curiosity burning in them, others full of worry.

Way to break the moment, Uncle Jonathan!

Now they'll want to know the full story regarding the small incident with Darcy.

Oh, nuts! I should give him a heads up about my little encounter with Rasputin since he will inspect my leg.

Let's add a new characteristic to Samantha's report: accident magnet!

Way to make a good, first impression...

CHAPTER ELEVEN
Calvary

Thank God for hospitals and doctor-patient confidentiality. Uncle Jonathan was not happy to find the little bite on my leg. He insisted on cleaning the wound; although, it didn't show any signs of infection. He put a bandage on where my little assaulter bit me and promised to subtly investigate if Rasputin was up to date with all his shots. Right now, I cross my fingers hoping to avoid returning to the hospital, especially to get rabies shots. I remember somebody mentioning those hurt terribly.

He wrote me a prescription for some light medication in case I showed any signs of infection and made me promise to call him if I feel ill, no matter if it regards the wounds or any other kind of ailment.

It seems the least of my worries turned out to be the hit I received from Darcy's bike, only a good old bruise which will recover on its own. I find it funny when he hands me a doctor's slip to calm down Darcy's nerves. I put his note in one of my pants pockets.

When I leave the room, I was not expecting to find the whole crew staring expectantly at Uncle Jonathan as if waiting for a major diagnostic about a life and death surgery. They kind of overreact for a bump, a dog bite, and, well, the almost drowning experience, which I skipped mentioning in our conversation.

"Everything seems all right with her," Uncle Jonathan announces with an upturned face. Some of them appear to breathe more calmly as if they didn't witness how I walked into the room on my own half an hour ago.

Jeez! They could easily give Darcy a run for her money.

"I prescribed her some pills for the pain and as an extra precaution, in case she develops a minor infection, some antibiotics," he explains. However, a bump would not justify the use of the medication,

Subtlety, I clear my throat, reminding him to avoid mentioning yesterday's injury.

"For some small cuts and scratches, she got," he adds with a conspiratorial glance.

I nod, acknowledging the explanation regarding the bandage in case somebody asks.

"Is her throat all right?" Zach questions eyeing me and

then our Uncle. It seems he didn't miss my not too subtle throat clearing. "There might be some after effect after yesterday's incident."

My head snaps toward his direction, quickly shaking my head warning him to keep quiet. I don't want to return to the room for my Uncle to examine my throat. After the nerve-wracking couple of days, I want to return home and relax.

"I am okay, Zach," I reassure him, touching his arm, getting his attention. "Let's go home," I propose with a small smile.

"She is fine, Zach," Uncle Jonathan intercedes, getting ahold of my brother and directing him toward the exit, followed by the rest of the fellows and girls. "Only a bump," his reassurances calming them and allowing us to leave the hospital.

The team splits into different cars. Uncle Jonathan needed to stay behind at the hospital to check up on his patients and therefore I leave with Zach, who isn't bad considering all my other options, besides I feel more comfortable with him.

And thank you, Big Guy, for Abigail riding in a different car.

The drive from the city to the house takes around twenty minutes. I get lost in my head trying to come up with a solution for my education situation. I most certainly don't want to drop out of school and neither do I want to lose a school year, especially because of Brittany's bullying.

Homeschool could be an option, not the best one since I need to work on my socializing issues, but a better one than the public school if what Darcy mentioned is true.

"Penny for your thoughts?" Zach asks, bringing my attention to the present.

"I was considering what my school options are," I comment with a sigh, watching the city passing from the window.

"I wouldn't worry about it," he replies confidently.

Well, you wouldn't, since it doesn't directly affect you.

I turn to catch his expression.

"We will make sure you finish your school year," he answers my unspoken question, his eyes watching the road.

"With the incident at Saint Magdalene, I don't believe any school will accept me," I respond, knowing how this mess will permanently stain my almost perfect school record. Doubts will always go through people's minds, trying to figure out if I cheated or not.

"Samantha, either you got excellent at cheating overnight, or the other girl lies. My bet is the second option," he states, not a trace of hesitation in his voice.

I scoff.

"What? You are too smart and good natured to cheat, Samantha," he continues, taking a quick glance over my direction.

I don't know if I should take this as a compliment or not.

"Maybe I cheated for twelve years and managed to go unnoticed this long," I challenge his opinion of me.

"Nah, I bet if you squish an ant you go straight to the confession booth and ask the good Lord for his forgiveness," he guesses with a chuckle.

What? I am not...

I open my mouth to retort.

Wait... I did do it once. Although the bee asked for it, after it stung me, ergo meeting its creator. Plus, being six years old and learning about the Ten Commandments kind of fell under the sixth commandment. I still remember the priest laughing and afterward explaining to me how things worked.

Zach glances over at me, his jaw dropping when he catches my guilty expression and laughing.

"See, I knew you didn't have it in you," his smile widens after I confirm his assumptions, "I am right about the other girl cheating."

I shrug my shoulders.

"Does it matter?" I question him. "I can no longer prove what happened." I accept my reality, knowing I lost my window of opportunity the moment my fist met her nose.

"Yes, there is," he replies confidently, "you can always take a test and prove them wrong,"

I did propose this same option to Sister Agatha.

Ha! Told you Big Guy, great minds think alike.

"Nobody would believe me now," I say disappointed, returning my gaze to the view outside the car window.

"Abigail and I discussed other school options while you visited the market." He returns to our previous topic.

Well, I already know what Abigail had in mind

"After some discussion, we decided you should try out Calvary School," he proposes.

Calvary?

The first image that comes to mind are horses and guns.

"It's a private school, located near where we live, but unlike Saint Magdalene, Calvary is a non-religious, co-ed school. On the positive side, it's considered one of the top high schools in the state, with an excellent ballet program in their curriculum, even better than Saint Magdalene..." With each sentence he says, my heart speeds up, since it sounds like the perfect school.

My mind, however, brings me to a complete halt.

Why would they accept a student with a cheating and violent incident in their school file?

"Why would they allow me to enroll, Zach?" I stop from getting my hopes up, realizing my predicament. "The semester already started. Plus, I don't believe they will overlook the reasons I got kicked out of school." I raise my eyebrows.

He slowly nods, understanding the problem.

"I know for a fact they accept students once school has started," he answers. "Plus, we aren't giving them a choice, either they accept you, or we leave," he emphasizes, his eyes focused on the road.

Either they accept me, or they leave?

"You mean you attend there?" I ask full of disbelief since they are four years older than me; at least, Abigail and Zach are. Why are they even in high school?

"We all do," he answers slowly.

Calvary plus Phoenix program, wait...what?

"Don't you attend college?" I ask remembering what Uncle Jonathan told me, "Or, do you work at the Phoenix School?"

"We volunteered to help the Phoenix school investigate an internal situation at Calvary." His eyes and nose crinkle when he quickly glances at me. "For us to help them, we asked for a sabbatical from each of our majors." He smiles. "And it's perfect timing with you returning home if you ask me."

Yeah, exactly what crossed my mind when I punched Brittany.

I roll my eyes, making him laugh.

"We talked with the principal and we agreed on Monday you will join us when we go to school. Admissions will perform an aptitude and a knowledge test. Based on the results, it will be decided which grade you'll attend," he explains.

"You mean if they accept me?" I correct him.

"No, as I said, you will stay with us. However, they need to define if you belong in a freshman, sophomore, junior, or senior class. There is a chance you'll share classes with different levels based on your scores," he responds.

"But would they accept somebody with my school file?" I ask full of disbelief.

"Probably not. However, the Calvary principal is interested in our help,"

Help? I wonder if I can get some of the answers Uncle Jonathan declined to answer.

"What exactly are you helping them with?"

He sighs and glances over.

"Don't tell Abigail I told you, or she'll bite my head off," he warns.

Bite your head off? Apparently, I was wrong about Abigail only being mean to me. Welcome to Abigail's blacklist.

"There are rumors running around for the last couple of years about extreme bullying cases where kids got seriously injured, even one suspected case of suicide. The school doesn't know if it's the students with the competitiveness, or the teachers trying to keep with the high standards, possibly a little bit of both. Right now, the administration requested our help to infiltrate the student body and investigate." He sighs.

My mouth goes dry, considering all the years I faced this issue. Luckily for me, my bully and I came to an agreement, which minimized the physical attacks. But no agreement could take away the fear to figure out which mood Brittany woke up with, or the daily stress to make sure to get both our schoolwork done with her expected high standards. My nervous biting tic always acting up when grades came in hoping for an A or B+, because anything lower and it would be a sucker punch session for me.

My big question is: how did she manage to get a good grade when tested...huh? It seems I already know the answer to the question, since I experienced it. Wonder who of my classmates provided her the answers? Or the actual test?

"Perhaps it is not the right school for me then," I comment not daring to experience all those feelings once again.

"Why would you believe that?" Zach asks full of surprise. I divert my gaze, ashamed to turn around and face him with the cruel reality. I keep quiet, letting my silence provide him the answer. "Oh! Then Kellan's report..."

"It's true," I cut him off.

At this moment, I wish for some of Abigail's toughness. Never in Brittany's life would she even dare cross paths with my sister. Her first attempt would probably have ended with the same result I accidentally did.

"Samantha. Why didn't you tell me?" he asks, concerned.

Wait what? *Oh, Big Guy, time to open Pandora's box!*

"Because you never spoke to me," I answer, his head snapping toward me, surprised by my tone of voice, "Technically, I was speaking with Grams," I call him out on the lie he fed me for the past few years.

His face changes to a bright read, and he bites his lower lip.

"Yeah... about that," he slowly says, "Grams asked me to keep up with it once she passed away until we told you the truth," he explains.

Oh, you plan on taking the easy road and blame it on Grams. Pitiful!

"I apologize for letting it go on for so long," he mentions, "but the more I wrote to you, I became more intrigued about you."

Excuse me?

"Look, squirt, let me be honest. I never gave you a chance when we were younger."

Gasps, what a shocker! I sarcastically think.

"And, I accept the full blame for it. Before my eyes, you always appeared as my baby sister," he confesses. "Besides, nothing of what you said or did appealed to me because you only talked about ballet, pink colored things, or nuns,"

Okay, point taken, but my life circled around those items, Big Guy. What else did he expect me to talk about, the weather?

"Besides, you reminded me of mom," he adds, saddened. His hand runs across his hair. "Happily dancing around, smiling exactly like she did. You acted as if you never experienced our loss, and in my stupid, little kid's mind, you needed to be sad, like Abbie and I."

You want to speak about fairness. You got to spend time with Grams when I didn't.

"Plus, we were busy coming up with our next evil plan to regain Gram's' attention," he replies with a sad chuckle, his hand returning to the steering wheel, his knuckle turning white. "We were a couple of jealous little brats."

Yes, you were. At least, I should count my blessings;

they never took it out on me.

"But while helping Grams type her answer when she became too ill to do it herself, I realized you grew up. I could help you with your questions, guide you and," his sober mood improving, "I love reading your theories of Sister Angertha's next excuse to bench you in the chapel."

Oh, I had tons of them! And no matter how much I tried to avoid the bench, I manage to get myself there.

"And Grams used to love to read about Sister Josie's threats in the kitchen. I remember her crying from laughter when we read the part where you smurfed the rice for all the girls' dinner."

Big Guy, I still blame Sister Josie for putting the wrong label in the container.

"You became a real person to me. I started relating to your struggles, wondering if you managed to achieve the difficult step Miss Johnson asked for. Proud to learn you aced the Biology test you spent days studying for. Like us, you had problems, but you kept your head up high and faced them straight on, not allowing them to bring you down.

"You kind of became an addiction after Grams passed away because I could find happiness in your words and memories of her smiling with your stories," he comments. "When I was younger, I envied you for being happy. Once I got to know you better, I didn't want to lose what I like to call mom's amazing spark."

Big Guy, are those crickets I hear in the background of my mind? Because I can't come up with a sarcastic comment.

"But, I wasn't fair and honest," he adds. "Instead of getting to know you through emails, I could have met you in person. I cowardly hid behind a computer and kept quiet instead of confronting Abigail, and I regret it. I hope you can find it in your heart to forgive me."

It's not like I can erase time.

"Time will tell," I answer while shrugging.

"Time and actions, which I plan on working on," he declares confidently, giving a small nod.

At least, we can agree on this.

"But now, back to our previous topic, as far as I recall you never mentioned to Grams, me, about being bullied. Otherwise, we would have put a stop to it," he comments full of regret. "How long did it go on?"

Do we really need to talk about it?

Ashamed of how long I allowed it to go, I turn my face away toward the window, not wanting to go into detail.

"You should have told us, Samantha. We would have taken care of it."

Says the guy who I didn't see in the past three years.

I doubt anybody would believe me; after all, Brittany Murphy is the daughter of a congressman, and the nuns' favorite student.

"You don't know how hard it is to talk about it."

"I am getting a better idea right now. We attended Calvary for almost a month, and no one tells us anything."

I look at him straight in the face.

"I understand them. I never told anyone about this

girl, because of the repercussions I'd face once she figured out I snitched," I explain. "Tattling to a teacher doesn't guarantee the problem will be solved. Bullies always act differently in front of them, the only way for a teacher to believe you is catching the bully red-handed and even then, the bullied might end up being blamed."

"This is the reason why instead of being teachers undercover, we act as students trying to get more sympathy from them to trust us or become targets," he explains, momentarily diverting his eyes from the road.

"I'll bet you were never bullied in your life." He shakes his head answering my question. "Or any of the others experienced it."

He stays quiet, taking his time to answer.

"Not by another student, but some different kinds of bullying," he explains.

"For a student to open up about his or her problems with their friends, there needs to exist a certain level of confidence. You need to earn their trust. Otherwise, they will never talk about it," I state, based on experience since I never talked with anybody about my issues, but then again, my friends list was limited to Sister Josie and Miss Johnson. Right now, confessing to Zach proves to be harder than expected and I am only giving him a small glimpse.

We keep quiet for a little while Zach drives, but appears to be contemplating our conversation.

"You might be right, Samantha. This school could be hard for you. We can always review other options," he finally accepts after a few minutes. "Or we can always drop the investigation."

"No!" I cut him off.

How bad can things be if a school reaches out to an outside organization for their help investigating this situation? Simple. Very bad. However, Calvary's concern to act and not turn their back on the students speaks greatly of the institution.

Besides, as a bullied student, I can't find it within me to selfishly ask my brother or their team to back down so they can take care of me, knowing kids my age are getting seriously hurt or come to a point of despair where the only solution they find is suicide.

What if I keep my head low, while they continue with their investigation? We could kill two birds with one stone.

"They need your help, don't back down because of me."

"What exactly do you propose then, Samantha?" Zach asks, confused.

"I should at least try it. Brittany will not attend Calvary and there's always the choice of homeschooling if I don't get a good feeling about it," I suggest, although internally the thought of Brittany being miles from me brings a sense of relief I was unaware of.

"Nobody will bother you. We will make sure of it," he promises.

Big Guy, I'll believe You when I see it.

We keep quiet for several minutes, each one trapped in our own thoughts. I find the irony amusing, all those years of being bullied might come in handy to them.

"Perhaps I can help you?" I offer.

"No!" he immediately shoots back shaking his head. "This investigation is ours, you need to focus on studying and doing your homework."

"What I meant is, I'll keep my eyes and ears open and inform you if I notice something out of the ordinary," I explain.

"Okay, I believe I can accept your offer. However, you need to promise me if anything happens you will tell us," Zach steers his eyes momentarily away from the road, "you need to trust us, okay?"

I nod, agreeing with his proposal.

He returns his eyes to the road; I focus on my surroundings realizing we reached the maze.

Having a plan in place regarding housing and education problems brings a sense of relief. My new issue, which makes me nervous, are the tests they'll perform on Monday.

What if I score lower and end up in class with the freshman?

Oh dear, talk about putting some stress on me. The North Dakota plan sounds like an easier choice. After all, they accepted me, no questions asked.

When we arrive at the house, I notice a group of people I don't identify talking with Oliver and Abigail.

"Samantha, can you please wait inside the house? I need to discuss some things with the guys," Zach asks me after parking the car. He pulls out his cell phone and sends a quick text out.

I agree, while I analyze the newcomers, their features appear older, probably around Oliver's age.

The door of the car opens, and I am met by Archie's handsome face, his hand stretched ready to help me out.

"You and I need to have a serious talk," Archie warns with a frown while I get out.

What did I do now?

His request and serious manner takes me by surprise. For a moment, I'm tempted to lock myself inside of the car and wait for Zach to come to my rescue.

"Nothing bad, I promise." His frown melts, his eyes sparkle, and he nods toward the garage door.

CHAPTER TWELVE
Proper Introductions

I walk through the garage door and into the kitchen to Rasputin's reception. The little beast jumps toward me, challenging me for a second round of our fight. I cowardly hide behind Archie, using him as a human shield against the two-millimeter-long teeth.

Lucky for me, Archie grabs the little pooch.

"A Doberman trapped in the body of a Chihuahua," he laughs at his joke earning some licks on his face from the little beast.

"Eww," I say, making him laugh harder.

"I believe you two need a proper introduction," he comments stepping inside the kitchen door with me following behind him.

Rasputin doesn't seem enthusiastic about me returning to his territory, growling his opinion.

"Now, now, Rasputin. I know this might be confusing, but your instinct about her not being Abigail is correct." As if the dog understands Archie, he stops and turns his little head toward his owner. "This is Samantha, and she is a friend," he points at me, "and she appears to be nicer than her sister because she can cook," he loudly whispers to the little dog, making me smile at his poor attempt to keep his voice down.

He steps closer with the little menace; I take a step back not wanting a second bite mark. One is more than enough.

"Samantha, this is Rasputin," he slowly comes closer as if not trying to frighten me, "and since you both live here, you need to get along and play nicely." The little dog cocks his head to one side, analyzing me, his little nose moving, sniffing me. "No attacking her, Rasputin. She appears to be kind of shy, but I believe she will warm up soon enough to us."

I chuckle at his pet talk, not knowing if it is intended for the little one or me.

"Pet him," Archie mouths the words. I shake my head, and he mouths, "Trust me."

I slowly bring my hand up, letting the dog know what I intend to do, observing its reaction, ready to pull it away in case it decides to bite me again.

It inches away from my touch but doesn't show any

signs to attack. Archie pats his lower jaw, distracting the little menace from my hand, allowing me to reach the top of its head.

The little dude appears happy, closing its eyes while enjoying the gesture, not caring whose hand it is. I move my hand from its head to the back of its ears. The dog keeps his eyes shut and moves his head to the other side, encouraging me to scratch the neglected one. I could bet if it were a cat it would be purring this instant.

"He is officially our guard dog and tends to be overprotective," Archie explains, "but once he knows you he is a sweet little thing, aren't you?"

The little dog moves its head upward and licks my hand, his scratchy little tongue moving in my palm.

"He won't attack you again," Archie assures me. "In fact…"

He stops, bends down, and puts the little dog back on the floor.

He points toward one of the kitchen cupboards and indicates me to open it.

Obeying, I find inside a bag of dog treats. Archie nods indicating to me to pull it out.

As my hand touches the bag, I immediately feel Rasputin's little paws on my leg. When I glimpse at him, he stands on his hind legs, happily turning around as if dancing.

I laugh at its cute display. I take one of the treats, making the dog jump up and down. When I bend down and put the treat within its reach, it greedily takes it and eats it.

"Now, he officially pledged his allegiance to you," Archie explains with a light voice. "Which is more than I can say for the rest of the birds in the house."

Did I hear right?

"Birds?" I ask, wondering if I walk to the boy's room will I find a parrot.

Archie grins.

"We like to refer to ourselves in such a manner," he explains. "Since we are a flock." He makes some air quotations at the last word.

Really? Birds? I believed only Grams referred to us in such a way.

"It's not farfetched. You only need to find the right kind of bird for each of us. I've always imagined Barb as a peacock, Joy as a hummingbird, Lyra an owl, Zach a nightingale, obviously, the condor would be me, and Abigail as a vulture," he chortles at his joke. "Although, your Grandmother insisted on calling her a swan, which is totally crazy!" He throws his head back and laughs.

I raise one of my eyebrows, surprised at his frankness. He's criticizing my sister after all.

"Although, your grandmother was right on calling you her little dove. You appear innocent and fragile," he steps closer. "It suits you."

Great! Back to the naïve thing again.

I don't know if I should take this as a compliment or criticism. However, the way he says it makes my cheeks go warm.

At this moment, I thank Rasputin for scratching my leg, distracting me from his amazing hypnotic blue eyes. I pick him up and scratch behind his ears. He raises his head preparing himself to lick my face, but I pull back.

"No, no, not the face," I calmly stop him. The dog obeys and keeps his little tongue to my hand.

The little rat can be quite smart, I realize.

"About yesterday, I apologize for his behavior," Archie shuffles his feet from one side to the other and for a moment has trouble facing me. "I didn't know he bit you, until today,"

So much for doctor-patient confidential agreement, right Uncle Jonathan?

"Dr. Morris didn't say anything," he corrects me as if reading my mind. "I knew after Lyra asked me about Rasputin's shots, which he has all of them, by the way."

At least I can find comfort in knowing I will not become a pin cushion with the rabies shots.

"He was simply defending us," he pleads making my heart ache, seeing him suffering for the little guy. I can't take it.

"It's okay, Archie," I manage to find my voice. "I understand."

He smiles widely, his apologetic eyes coming to life. "Let the record state, you finally spoke my name today." He raises his arms. "I beat Samuel, Woo-hoo!"

What the…? I shake my head.

"No, I didn't." I chuckle at his outburst.

He stops and stares at me, his joyous mood replaced

by suspicion. "You've spoken before mine the name of He Who Must Not Be Named?"

I laugh at the face he pulls and at his Harry Potter reference.

"No, I spoke your name yesterday when I thanked you after the pool incident." His silliness breaks the ice on my muteness.

Oh, apparently, the solution to free my tongue relies on guys being goofy. It worked for Bennedick in the market and now for Archie.

"You did?" He gapes in astonishment. I shouldn't be surprised; I did mumble it. "Now, the important question. Have you spoken his name?"

I shake my head.

"Perfect, you should keep it like that. It will drive him mad." He chuckles. "Or make sure you say the others' names before his, okay?"

I roll my eyes. The last thing I want is to make enemies.

The voices coming from the front door interrupt us. I put the little pooch down and when I stand Archie puts both of his hands together silently pleading to drive his friend mad. Smiling, I shake my head before going out of the kitchen to figure out what the fuss is all about.

Zach steps through the front door carrying a box full of fresh fruit. "Uh, Samantha? Did you buy the whole market?"

Yes! The groceries arrived!

"Only a few things to keep us fed for breakfast and

dinner," I explain while getting out of the way to allow him to go to the kitchen. "Why? Is it a lot?"

"This is the first out of eight boxes," he comments dropping the first box on the kitchen counter. "Archie, go out and help."

My brother picks up Rasputin and disappears through the garage door while Kellan comes in with another box overflowing with vegetables, behind him Barb steps in carrying a small loaf of bread.

"Thanks, Kellan and Barb," I say excitedly, reviewing the lovely tomatoes threatening to fall when he puts the box down. I smell them enjoying the sweetness of it, my mind picturing a delicious spaghetti and meatballs platter. Deciding we'll have it for dinner.

"You are more than welcome," Kellan happily responds with his German accent.

"A little help," Bennedick steps in, balancing a gallon of milk with one hand and at least three cartoons full of eggs. Barb reaches him and takes two of the three cartons of eggs.

"Hello, gorgeous. I met your twin out there. I propose an agreement where Legolas and…"

"I told you I am not her twin," Abigail steps in carrying the one bag of meat I ordered, "I'm her older sister."

She steps closer and deposits the bag on top of the counter, standing next to me. Bennedick's head turns from her to me searching for differences. I know, Abigail and I can't deny the family link, but my eyes are hazel like

Zach's, hers are green. My skin tone is a little tanner; my hair is long and black while hers is short with highlights. She is taller than me; I am skinnier than her. She appears older than me, but I wouldn't point out the last two differences straight to her face.

"Probably not identical twins, but you could easily pull off the fraternal one," he comments, still analyzing us.

"Zach already covers that position," she snaps at him.

I restrain myself from laughing as Bennedick steps back, intimidated by Abigail's attitude.

"Well, Legolas likes them feisty," he jokes, making Abigail grunt in annoyance and abandon the kitchen.

"I like beautiful girls with long hair…" he continues, his attention fully on me, leaning closer to his side of the counter, coming closer to me.

"Stop flirting, numb nuts, and make yourself useful." Darcy steps in, rescuing me from her brother's attempt at courting. Or at least, I believe that's what he's doing.

"Bad timing, Austen, I was ready to woo her with my handsome face and witty charm." Bennedick responded, annoyed at his sister. "How about we both—"

"Do you even listen to yourself? Nothing of what you say ever works." She chuckles, pushing her brother to one side. "Now, go and help unload the rest of the truck. I need to discuss some serious business with Sammie here."

"Always ruining the fun, Austen." Bennedick steps behind his sister, puts his hand on his ears as a phone and mouths the words, "Call me."

I laugh lightly, while he disappears from my view after

he winks at me.

"See, I told you. Brothers can be a pain in the ass," she comments shaking her head.

"I don't know, I guess so?" I chuckle.

Darcy's eyes widen, staring behind me. I turn to find Zach, looking amused at me.

My blood goes straight to my cheeks.

Oh, great!

"Sorry, Zach," I apologize realizing my face resembles the tomato I hold in my hand.

His face softens and shakes his head, letting the comment slide.

"You attend Calvary, right?" Zach asks my friend breaking the awkward situation I managed to get myself in.

"Yes!" I notice how Darcy's voice sounds chirpier. "You are a Senior there?"

He nods, a broad smile on his face.

Wait. Does Darcy attend Calvary?

"Zacharias Melbourne." He steps closer and stretches out his hand, introducing himself.

"Darcy O'Flannagan." She takes his hand and shakes it, her eyes meeting his. "You might share some classes with one of my brothers."

"Sherlock?" Zach releases her hand from his hold.

"The one and only," she agrees nervously biting her lower lip.

"He is cool. Hey, Samantha! You might share classes with Darcy," he comments excitedly.

Darcy's head snaps toward me, her eyes silently

conveying a hundred questions.

"We might," I respond shrugging and smiling, guessing she might be a junior as well.

"That is ... Amazing!" She runs to my side and puts her arm around me. The force of her embrace pushes me a step backward. The sting of the bruise and the little bite in my leg making me wince. "Mom will flip over this! You need to be my partner in the cooking class. I don't care who I need to bribe... wait! Are you taking cooking classes? Please say yes." Her excitement is contagious especially when she puts her hands together in a pleading manner, making me laugh at the whole display.

When I glimpse at Zach, I realize he's the one with a thousand silent questions.

"If my schedule allows it," I agree, getting on board with the excitement after learning I know another person going to Calvary.

"Oh." Her face falls, together with her arms.

"I'll try my best," I offer hoping to bring her previous mood back, "I'll need to take the tests for admissions to define my schedule..."

"You can totally borrow my books, and check out the topics we already covered," she goes back to the excited mood, "or Sherlock could tutor you."

"Thanks, I really appreciate it," I reply with relief, knowing what I could expect for the test.

"Come on, we need to unload the truck, but afterward we could..." Darcy pulls my arm, dragging me with her unknown force toward the dining area.

"You girls should stay here and unload the boxes. I'll help with the rest," Zach suggests while he moves to the kitchen exit.

I notice his eyes traveling from my friend's head all the way to her toes, which I assume means checking Darcy out, before leaving.

Nah! Probably my imagination.

"You never told me Zach is your brother," she whispers while she unpacks the fruit box.

Was I supposed to?

"I guess you also know the rest of them. All the students talk about them since they entered three weeks ago.," she continues while searching for a spot to put the fruit she removes from the box. I go to the fruit basket, remove the plastic fruit, and bring it closer to her. "I mean, they became the famous group with all their amazing skills, not to mention their good looks," she mumbles, probably not wanting to get caught like I did.

"I suppose so," I say while taking out the tomatoes from the vegetable box and putting them in the sink.

The wood creaking in the entrance alerts me of somebody heading their way toward the kitchen. I signal Darcy who continues talking not noticing me.

"You know, Sherlock practically…"

"I met with my Uncle today," I interrupt her and change the subject to avoid putting her in an awkward spot.

Friends look out for each other, right Big Guy?

"The Doctor?" This seems to distract her from the

previous topic. "Do you need a Cat-scan? X-Rays? Can I come?"

I chuckle and pull from my pocket the doctor's slip, handing it over to her.

She reads the note, a frown appearing on her face together with a disappointed pout, probably at the lack of testing needed.

"Where do you want this last box?" Samuel steps in, carrying a box full of what I believe contains sugar, flour, and other items I need to bake cookies and some other desserts.

Archie trails behind him, with a relaxed appearance, raising his eyebrows reminding me of his previous favor.

"Over there, please," I point toward the open space on the other side of the kitchen, "and thank you, Sa—"

"Wow, Samuel, be careful. I'll bet Samantha doesn't want anything to break there," Archie interrupts me, glaring at me.

"I don't believe there is anything breakable there," Darcy mentions, analyzing the items inside the box Samuel carries.

"Darcy, let me introduce you to Archibald," I continue, earning a huge smile on his part. He stretches his hand and shakes Darcy's, "and this is…" I glance at Samuel, his brown eyes gazing expectantly at me.

"Did you meet the others, Darcy?" Archie interrupts me once again, directing my friend to the kitchen exit. "You should also join us, Samantha." He pulls me with his other arm.

"I was about to wash the tomatoes…" I comment trying to get loose from his grip.

"We need to thank the O'Flannagans for bringing the groceries and introduce your friend to the rest of our group," he tells me while walking to the exit. I turn to find Samuel trailing behind us.

We join the group outside, who gathered near the empty truck parked in the driveway. Standing next to it is Anakin, Bennedick, and Sherlock. Oliver talks animatedly with the older O'Flannagan brother while the rest speak with the other two.

The conversation dies when we arrive; all eyes fix on us. I freeze in place, my mind going blank.

"Is everything all right?" Anakin asks, full of concern. "Did we miss anything from the order?"

I somehow manage to shake my head.

"Okay. I guess that will be all then," Anakin smiles. "I'll leave you our business card in case you need anything else. Give us a call, and we will bring it by." He hands the card over to Oliver.

"Samantha practically bought the entire store. What else could she need?" Bennedick jokes, making me blush profusely. I am not sure if he knows ten people live under the same roof.

Sherlock gives his brother a smack on the back of his head.

"If mother heard you, she would believe you speak Blasphemies," Anakin mentions, making us laugh.

"We'll keep in touch," Oliver assures them while

shaking Anakin's hands.

"See you at practice, dude!" Bennedick comments, high-fiving Archie's hand.

"Totally," Archie responds.

"See you in class," Sherlock glances at Lyra, Kellan, and Archie, his eyes stopping at Abigail's, his ears turning red. "And in the halls," he practically tells my sister.

How come they didn't recognize each other? Perhaps they don't share the same classes.

"Bye, Sherlock," Abigail replies in her flirty voice.

I feel sorry, knowing Abigail's show must be part of the investigation, which means it could be an act, but who knows, there is a slight chance she might find him attractive.

"It was fun to meet you all," Darcy assures to the whole group. "Hey Sammie, do you want to stop by the house and fetch my notes?"

Again, being in the spotlight freezes me.

"I can bring them," Bennedick and Sherlock offer at the same time. They glare at each other, shooting daggers with their eyes.

"I can go with you guys and pick them up," Zach suggests, breaking the silent discussion between the brothers. "It would give us an opportunity to go over your speech for the debate team, Sherlock."

"Excellent, we can walk over then," Darcy proposes.

"Bye, bye, everybody," Anakin says, putting an end to the small gathering and shaking his hand while entering the cabin of the truck.

The O'Flannagan clan leaves together with Zach.

"Samuel, Joy, Samantha, and Archie can you please stow away all the groceries? Barb, Kellan, Lyra, Abigail, and I need to go and run some errands, and we'll bring dinner on our way back," Oliver orders while we head back to the house.

My head snaps up.

"I-I-I…" I can't seem to get the words out.

Not backing out, Samantha. I can do this. After all, I'll be living with all of them, might as well get used to it.

I breathe in and try to picture his secure attitude.

"I planned on cooking dinner, Oliver," I explain, noticing Archie's chuckles. "Are spaghetti and meatballs okay?"

"Sweetie, it sounds delicious!" Barb comes closer. "We don't want to burden you by cooking for ten people."

"I don't mind, Barb." I shrug my shoulders and fight my instincts to divert my gaze.

"I'll help her," Samuel offers.

"Thank you, S—"

"Joy and I will help, also," Archie interrupts me again.

"You three? Together? In the kitchen?" Kellan asks full of disbelief, his eyes widening at the suggestion. "Samantha, I recommend keeping a fire extinguisher nearby." He adds while laughing, Oliver joining in.

"Thanks for the heads up. I'll leave the slicing and dicing to them, then." I decide, keeping in mind his recommendation, glancing over my shoulder at my little army of minions.

Sister Josie would be jealous.

"Then, consider a first aid kit as well," Lyra suggests, amused.

"I don't think it will be necessary, Lyra," I reply, realizing a little too late my mistake.

Archie beams, his blue-eyes appear to twinkle, proud of himself for annoying his friend Samuel who gives him a furious glare.

Oh, joy!

Wait, Samantha, be careful.

"I'll bet Samuel, Joy, and Archie will be fine," I reply studying closely Archie's reaction, knowing I dodged the bullet of earning an enemy.

Samuel laughs out loud, Joy chuckles, and Archie's jaw drops to the floor, appearing betrayed.

I don't know if the rest knew about this little game Archie started, judging by their laughter they seem to be somewhat informed.

Big Guy, please tell me I did the right thing?

CHAPTER THIRTEEN
The Sound of Cooking

A sense of being overwhelmed washes over me, my palms flying to my forehead while wide eyed, I analyze the kitchen counter, covered to overflowing with boxes of food.

Perhaps I did go a little overboard with the shopping.

Then again, I need to cook for ten mouths, five of them men. Judging by the size of Kellan, they can probably eat two or three times my serving.

Continuing where I left off, I wash the tomatoes, planning to optimize time by boiling them on the stove while I sort the mess.

"What exactly do you need us to do?" Joy comes

closer to stare curiously at one of the big boxes.

"We need to unpack, sort and store everything. How about we separate, fruit on one side, vegetable on another, dairy…" I answer. It's going to be a lot easier to find a space to store it based on quantity and sizes.

"Cool." She steps up to the first box and removes its contents.

"Do you know where I can find a pot to boil this?" I ask her while I open one of the cabinets.

"Not really," she replies while she opens one of the drawers. "I rarely help in the kitchen and avoid it at all costs until I smell food."

"You should try the one closer to the stove." Samuel comes closer and reaches it before I get there. "Voila." He pulls one out from the cabinet and hands it over to me.

"Thank you." I lower my eyes to escape from his handsome gaze. I take it, avoiding touching his fingers.

I bring the pot over to the sink and fill it with water.

"Did I hear right about today's menu being spaghetti and meatballs?" Samuel walks over to lean against the counter.

I bite my lower lip and nod.

"I can help you with the noodles. Do you know where I could find them?" He joins Joy, sorting through the items she pulled out of the box.

"The flour might be in the box you helped carry in, and we'll need some eggs." I place the pot of water on the stove and reach for the tomatoes to dump them in.

The kitchen becomes soundless. I turn to find my

small army of cooking minions frozen in place.

"We'll make the pasta?" Archie asks, full of disbelief. "You've got to be kidding me."

"Sure, it's not hard," I answer, stating the obvious.

The three of them immediately laugh.

"No, really, Samantha. Where did you hide the noodles?" Samuel unpacks one of the boxes, still searching.

I shrug and continue my work turning on the stove. If they don't believe me, good luck finding them among all the groceries. I know there aren't any.

Once I get the first chore going, I move to the next one sorting out the groceries.

Continuing with Darcy's job, I locate the fruit and vegetables, making sure to leave the ones I intend to use for today's salad. I do the same for the meat and dairy items.

When I finish, my helpers sadly conclude I was not joking.

"It appears we will be making pasta," Samuel says, accepting defeat.

I look at Joy and Archie.

"You two will work on the salad," I instruct, splitting the chopping chores between the two of them. I then focus on Samuel. "We will work on the pasta. I need flour, eggs, a bowl, plastic wrap and olive oil."

While he works to gather the items, I turn my attention to cleaning and sanitizing an area of the kitchen counter where I intend to create the pasta. Samuel comes over carrying the flour and the eggs.

I quickly check my tomatoes and turn off the stove to allow the remaining heat to cook them, loosening the skin.

Time to get hands on.

Following Sister Josie's lessons, Samuel helps me measure the flour and gives me the ingredients I request, while I work on mixing the items the old fashion way, creating a big ball which needs to be kneaded.

"Can I help?" Samuel's eyes intently study the way I move my hands, mixing all the ingredients to create a lump.

"Wash your hands first," I command and split the mass into two batches.

After he returns from the sink, he steps to one side and takes the lump I offer.

"We need to bash it, squash it, reshape it, pull it, stretch it and repeat over and over." I explain, while I show him exactly what I need him to do. "This creates the perfect pasta consistency,"

"Basically, we need to beat the crap out of the lump?" Samuel comments.

For a moment I remain speechless, while comparing both. I pull my hand up to block my giggles, but stop when I notice them covered in flour. The whole interaction becomes comical, making Samuel and Archie join in the laughter. Embarrassed, the color raises to my ears.

"Then Joy will be better at the job," Archie proposes, followed by a loud, "Ouch! See?"

When I turn around Archie rubs a spot on his arm, glaring at Joy. She, with a small smile on her face, innocently cuts the small tomatoes.

Lyra's proposal regarding the first aid kit might not be as farfetched as I originally thought.

"No fighting kids," Samuel warns, amused. "I want Oliver to take it easy on us tomorrow."

"Ugh! Don't remind me," Joys complains.

Take it easy on them tomorrow? What are they planning?

After a few minutes, my arms ache with the burn of the kneading, but I continue, noticing how the dough's texture changes from the rough and floury sensation to a smooth and silky one.

"Never thought of kneading as a form of workout," Samuel tells me.

I chuckle when I notice a small film of sweat forming on his forehead.

"Don't tell me a little dough is killing you?" Archie comes to our station and glances over Samuel's shoulder at the dough ball. "I always believed your arms had more force in them after all those long hours of training,"

"How about you give it a try?" Samuel moves to one side and points at the ball with his hands covered in flour.

Archie wrinkles his nose in disgust before he smugly responds, "Nu-uh, according to our fearless leader, Samantha designated me to the salad department."

I shake with silent laughter. Not wanting to engage in their discussion. I go to supervise my salad minions.

"Archie, can you cut the lettuce a little smaller please?" I instruct him when I notice the big chunks.

"Ha! It seems your job doesn't meet our fearless leader's quality standards," Samuel teases Archie. Archie stomps back to his station, his smile disappearing to be replaced by a frown.

I check Joy's work and give her an approving nod. Her eyes light up. She focuses on Archie, who clenches his jaw when she does a small happy dance and sticks her tongue out, taunting him.

Worried any further comments from me will make things worse, I return to my pasta making activity.

"Mine is almost done," I grin happily. "Can I see yours?"

"I'll show you mine if you show me yours." Samuel laughs and the others join in.

What? Confused, I turn to him. Perhaps this is an inside joke?

I let it slide and inspect Samuel's dough, smiling widely when I notice his excellent work. I take the plastic wrap and set both balls of dough in it, close it, and place it in the fridge.

"Are we done?" Archie asks excitedly.

"Nope," I answer. His face immediately falls. His frozen food must not take this long to prepare. "Now, you two will work on the meatballs." I point at Samuel and Archie. "Joy will help me with the sauce."

"No way." After one peek at the ground beef, Archie's face contorts with disgust. "It looks gross."

The guy who gets licked on the face by a dog complains about being gross?

"You can chop the onion while we work on the rest," I concede. "But please make tiny squares this time."

Joy chuckles, bringing my attention to her. "Joy, please grate the Parmesan cheese." I turn my attention to my last minion. "Samuel, can you please chop the green peppers into small pieces?"

He brings his hand to his forehead and salutes me army style.

"Sir, yes, sir!" he adds, making Joy laugh.

I smile and focus on the tomatoes. After peeling and blending them, I separate out a small portion I'll need for the meatballs; the rest will be used for the sauce. I then focus on the meatballs, thanking the Big Guy for the decorative spice rack. I add salt, poultry, and Italian seasoning together into the ground meat.

"Guys, what is the status on your tasks?" I ask, hoping to get an answer. Instead, I'm met by laughter.

I turn to find Joy holding the sides of her stomach and snorting loudly, touching Samuel's arm to draw his attention to Archie, whose eyes show a red rim around the whites while tears streak his handsome features.

My hands fly to my forehead surprised at the whole display.

Oh, Big Guy, I broke Archie.

Joy pulls her cellphone out of her pocket and swiftly takes a picture of Archie before he can cover his face.

"What the fuck, Joy!" he yells.

"Language!" I immediately correct him, my swear system on high alert. "No swearing in the kitchen!"

This only turns Joy and Samuel's laughter into plain out guffaws.

"I'm done playing cook. I'll go and take Rasputin out," he replies furiously, dropping the knife on top of the cutting board with a loud clank.

"No, you'll stay right here," I order, remembering Sister Josie's teaching, "And finish your work."

The laughter immediately dies. Archie turns around, his brow furrows and his red, watery eyes narrow.

"This was not part of the deal," he responds.

"Are you planning on eating?" I ask as calmly as I can.

"Obviously." He comes closer, towering over me with his height and attitude. But, I won't allow him to intimidate me

"Then finish your work." I point at the cutting board. "Afterward, you can go and walk Rasputin."

"No." He crosses his arms and shakes his head, his lips pursed and his eyebrows raised.

"Then, nobody eats." I mimic his pose and stare straight into his eyes. "If you quit, then I quit as well."

The tension in the kitchen grows.

"I can finish his—" Trying to ease the situation, Samuel steps in and waves his arm at the counter with all the unfinished ingredients lying in small piles.

"No, Samuel," I cut him off without diverting my stare of Archie's eyes.

After a couple more minutes, Archie finally folds, and

without a word, returns to his cutting board.

The pit of my stomach weighs down, remembering how much I hated when Sister Josie challenged me in such a manner, and now I acted just like her. Worst part, his reaction could be partially justified. Archie only acted on instinct after he became the laughingstock of Joy and Samuel. Worst part, Joy took a picture of it.

"Joy, please delete the picture," I order, trying to control myself, my shoulders heavy with guilt.

Without a word, Joy takes her phone out and obeys.

After a few minutes of silent work, Archie walks over and loudly puts the cutting board down next to me, the onion chopped to millimeter pieces. Without a word, he turns around and goes out the garage door.

"When did Samantha turn into Abigail?" I catch Joy whispering to Samuel.

"Bossiness is in the Melbourne genes," he responds.

That does it. Tears pool in my eyes, clouding my vision.

I clean my hands with the first available cloth and leave my station, going outside to the garage. I patiently wait for Archie. After a couple of minutes, he comes out, carrying Rasputin and his leash.

His eyebrows rise when he notices me, stopping mid-stride. He probably didn't expect the nagging, bossy girl from the kitchen to come and find him.

"I'm sorry, Archie. I didn't mean to treat you in such a way." I step closer to him, wringing my hands behind my back, my nerves on edge. "But, I learned from my cooking teacher to never quit once we started a chore."

"I should be the one to apologize for my reaction. I was cutting a freaking onion. What did I expect? To grow rainbows out of my eyes?" He smirks, fractionally easing the weight on my shoulders. "I wasn't mad at you. I didn't appreciate being Joy's and Samuel's buffoon. Or her taking a picture of me in such a wretched state."

"It was rude of her," I agree.

"Truth be told, I would have done the same if she was the one crying and chopping the freaking onion." He winks at me, laughing.

"Then, we are all good?" I bite my lower lip.

He examines me, weighing his options. "Only if you promise next time we cook, onion duties go to somebody else." He extends his hand.

"Okay," I agree, nervously taking his hand to shake it.

"Excellent! Now go and finish the goddamn spaghetti and meatballs. Otherwise, the team will chop my head off." He tilts his head toward the kitchen door.

"Language!" I correct him.

"We're no longer in the freaking kitchen," he dares me, raising his eyebrows as his smile widens, taunting me to retaliate.

Choose your battles, Samantha, my internal voice cautions me.

I shrug and decide to give him a break.

When I return, I find Joy and Samuel working with the meatballs and making small balls out of the mixture.

Without a word, I wash my hands and continue with

the sauce.

By the time Archie returns, Zach arrives with him. I focus on flattening one of the pieces of dough. Samuel stands by my side, waiting patiently for his turn at it.

Who knew out of all the team he would be the one who shows the most interest in learning?

I released Joy of her duties after she finished putting away the rest of the groceries and now she sits on the couch watching television.

"Smells wonderful." Zach comes closer and inspects the pot with the sauce and the meatballs inside. "Mrs. O'Flannagan says hi, and expects to see you in her class," he informs me. "But I believe Darcy will be wishing upon a star tonight for it to happen." He chuckles.

"Like Samantha needs cooking classes." Samuel points at the counter where I show him how to flatten the dough. "She could practically teach the class."

"I wouldn't mind learning a little more," I respond below my breath after handing him the rolling pin. Besides, I'd love to share a class with Darcy and her mom.

I pull another pot out and fill it with water. Adding some basil leaves in it, along with a little olive oil and salt, I place it on top of the stove, next to the sauce and meatballs.

When I check Samuel's progress, I identify in the background the song of the movie *Sound of Music*. I can't recall the last time I watched it, but I always liked it. Especially the songs.

"Remember, Samantha, how you used to cry at the

end of it?" Zach asks, having also recognized the song. "And then you kept watching it, over and over..."

"No, I don't remember," I fire back, the lie sliding easily from my mouth.

Totally worth a Hail Mary, if you ask me.

He smirks, pointing an accusatory finger at me. "You so did. Grams always wondered what made you cry."

My guilty blush kills whatever argument I planned to deliver, exposing me to the rest as a pathetic liar.

Zach, Samuel, and Archie don't bother to hide their cackles, bringing Joy's attention toward the kitchen.

Archie's face fills with amusement. "Oh, then we should watch it!"

Avoiding eye contact with all of them, I focus my attention back on the pasta. Zach and Archie leave the kitchen, laughing.

Samuel points at the flattened pasta. "Can we move to the next step?"

He did such a good job.

"We cut it and boil it." I turn up the heater on the burner under my last pot.

While the rest of the food finishes cooking, we take advantage of this time to make sweet tea to accompany the meal and set the table. When we finish, Zach informs us the rest are only minutes away.

While we wait, we join Archie, Zach, and Joy and watch whatever's left of the film. I don't realize I quietly sing the songs I memorized long ago until somebody snickers. I stop, but I don't take my eyes off the screen, hypnotized by the story.

When the movie ends, I clean the tears with the back of my hand, hoping nobody noticed them.

How embarrassing if they… Archie holds a tissue in front of me, with a wolfish grin on his face. Nuts! Hopefully nobody took a picture of my hormonal display.

I take it without a word and clean my face, silently thanking him for his kindness. Getting up from the sofa, I turn, surprised to find the rest of the team gathered around the living room to watch the movie with the rest of us.

I honestly didn't notice when they returned. It seems I got lost in the film.

All eyes land on me; nobody utters a single word.

"Anybody ready to eat?" I ask, trying to divert their attention from me.

"I am." Joy immediately jumps up from the couch and runs to the kitchen.

"Me." Samuel leaves the living room, speed walking to the kitchen. "I want to know what real pasta tastes like."

"Me, too," Zach joins in, pulling Abigail by her arm to help her up from the floor.

"Smells scrumptious, darling. Better get to the kitchen quickly before our little ninja eats everything," Barb warns.

"Not if I get there first." Archie sprints to the kitchen.

"Congratulations, everybody survived the cooking ordeal." Lyra comes up next to me and smirks. "And no need for a medical kit?"

"Or a fire extinguisher?" Kellan says, pulling Barb into a hug.

"Nope, everything went fine," I answer proudly. "I believe you overreacted."

I eat my own words when I observe, wide-eyed, the chaos that erupted in my precious kitchen.

Inside Archie fends off Joy from the saucepot; Samuel helps him keep the spaghetti out of her reach. Zach and Abigail open the cupboards, searching for I don't know what; moving items from one side to other, making a mess out of my perfect arrangement.

I'll guess their warnings come from experience.

"Everybody out of my kitchen!" the words escape my mouth in an exact imitation of Sister Josie's commanding tone.

All of them freeze in place, their heads turning in my direction. Abigail's mouth drops open.

"I'll be in charge of serving." I soften my voice. "Now, go and wash your hands, or nobody eats dinner."

They close the cupboards while the rest return the pots to their original locations and quickly empty the kitchen.

"A Melbourne through and through," I hear somebody say behind me. I turn to find Oliver, a wide grin on his face. "Seems you're going to adapt quickly, Samantha."

He leaves the kitchen, laughing.

Oh, Big Guy, help me! I'm turning into Abigail.

CHAPTER FOURTEEN
Climb Every Moun...Wall

Everyone enjoyed dinner. At first, I feared I cooked a lot of food and there would be leftovers, but they proved me wrong. I swear Joy licked her plate.

By the time they finished cleaning and putting everything away, my eyes practically shut on their own. Zach offered his room for the night so I won't have to sleep in the attic again. I didn't have the energy to put up a fight; I took it gratefully.

The noise of a door closing wakes me up the next day. The clock on Zach's side table glows red with the numbers five thirty in the morning. The hushed voices coming from the small window prevents me from going back to sleep.

My curiosity spikes. I get out of bed and walk toward it, my eyes widening at the sight, making me fully awake.

Outside in the garden forming two rows stand the rest of the girls and guys, all of them wearing a white shirt, gray pants, and sneakers as if it was a uniform. I make out Archie's and Kellan's sleepy faces. Barb pulls her hair back into a ponytail while Lyra crouches, tying the laces of her sneaker.

Standing in front of them is Oliver, eyeing them sternly.

"Let's get started then." He gains everybody's attention with a clap. Without any other explanation, he stretches while the others follow him.

A nagging little voice inside me tells me, "Go with them," instead of returning to sleep. What better way to bond with them and become part of the family than working out with them?

The family that works out together stays together.

Out of my suitcase I pull out my white t-shirt and the gray pants I wore yesterday morning. I change, ignoring the damage from my run in with Darcy and her bicycle, and finalize my outfit with my gym sneakers. While I tie my hair into a ponytail, I climb to the upper level.

When I reach the garden door, I stop, impressed by the synchrony of their movements. Oliver counts aloud while they change positions.

Silently I walk over, keeping my eyes in front, ignoring the menacing pool lingering a few of feet away. Once I reach them, I locate myself behind Barb.

I focus my attention on the leader who gives me an encouraging smile. Without a word, I follow the routine he sets.

We stretch different parts of our bodies: torso, arms, legs, neck; preparing what seems like a full work out.

We start easy with jumping jacks, mixing it with squats every other ten sets. I follow his instructions not focusing on how many we do, but in doing them right, proving I can be part of this team. He then moves to pushups. Internally, I thank the long hours I've spent in the dance studio, my muscles used to long workouts.

"We will now pair up," Oliver instructs after finishing the set. "Kellan and Barb, Zach and Joy, Archie and Lyra, Abigail, you will be my partner, and Samuel, you'll partner with Samantha,"

A surprised expression flashes on every single one of their sweaty faces when they turn and find me in their group. I raise my chin up and walk to where Samuel is; his expression changes to a grin when I step to his side.

"Now, we'll do some ab exercises. First set will be done by the boys, and the second set by the girls," he explains while getting down on the floor with his back flat on the ground, his legs stretched out. "Abigail, hold down my ankles. The rest of you get into position. Sets of twenty."

At first, I hesitate to grab Samuel's ankles; after all, I would be touching a cute boy!

I breathe in and out a couple of times, to calm myself, putting attention at the lack of interest the girls demonstrate when they grab their partner's ankles, probably something normal in a co-ed world. Placing my hands on top of Samuel's ankles, I divert my eyes while my face burns with embarrassment, hoping he believes the blush is because of the workout.

When my turn comes to do the set, I try to ignore his hands on my ankles, but the warmth of his touch and the strength of his hold makes it hard to forget. I put my focus on the burning sensation in my abdominal muscles from the exercise and keep a steady breath while focusing on the sky rather than his cute eyes.

We continue the exercises, alternating positions and following Oliver and Abigail's example. After five sets, Oliver stands, helping Abigail in the process.

Samuel gets up, and I follow his lead.

"Now, we will jog to the gym," Oliver instructs, cleaning the sweat off his forehead with a towel. Ignoring Barb's groan, he turns around and jogs toward the garden exit, followed behind by Abigail. Tracking behind them goes the rest of the teams with Samuel and I at the end.

Any crazy human up at six o'clock on a Sunday morning would believe this is some army training.

Luckily, the gym isn't far away. By the time we reach it, Barb pants heavily.

Oliver opens the door, directing the rest of the group inside. He salutes the security guard standing at the entrance and makes his way to the back area, stopping at a big tall wall.

Abigail, Joy, and Kellan laugh, while Barb and Lyra

groan. Archie cranes his head upward with a smirk on his face. Zach and Samuel remain speechless.

"Today, we will work out on wall climbing." Oliver's eyes seem to sparkle, enjoying the reaction of each one of the team members.

I stare up the wall, my jaw falling open slightly when I notice the fifty foot high wall with small plastic rocks located at different places. The taller the wall gets, the larger the gap between rocks. Things go from bad to worse when, at the top end of it, the angle changes dramatically. Only Spiderman would be able to get to the top end and ring the bell hanging up there.

I now understand Barb's and Lyra's groans. I wouldn't have joined in if I knew what was coming.

This rock climbing will require an enormous effort on the muscles of my legs and arms, which still recover from the initial warm up session.

"Shotgun on being on Abigail's team," Archie immediately speaks up.

"Sorry, guys, I already assigned the teams," Oliver chuckles, raising his eyebrows. Archie shakes his head as he eyes Lyra and then glares at our leader. Would it be considered cheating since Olive made the teams knowing ahead of time about this activity?

Yes, yes it would.

"We will take a ten-minute break to get the gear and plan a strategy to ring the bell with your partner. As usual, we will assign house chores to each team according to how well they perform on the test," he concludes before taking a break to gear up.

Studying Samuel, I notice his tall and muscular frame with muscles not as big as Kellan's but bigger than my slim ones. Judging by the others' reactions, they already went through this before. For me, on the other hand, this would be my first time.

Evidently, I'm the weak link of our team.

Poor Samuel, he got stuck with the kid who nobody would like on their team.

I silently try to apologize, but his wide grin makes me believe he doesn't share my train of thoughts.

"We'll do fine," he states confidently.

And they consider me the naïve one… suckers!

"Suuuure," I sarcastically agree between my breaths, making him laugh.

"Trust me, all right?" He raises his arm to give me a pat on the back but stops a few inches away from my body. "We most likely won't be first place, but I trust you."

His blind faith and innocent behavior makes me smile. Samuel chuckles, glancing over his shoulder locating the rest and afterwards steps closer to me.

"And I know Barb and Lyra's upper body strength is practically zero," he whispers with a mischievous expression on his face.

"How can you tell mine is better than theirs?" the question escapes my mouth before I can stop myself.

"Because a little bird told me you've danced ballet for quite some time now." He winks at me. The gesture sends tingles to my tummy.

What else does he know about me?

Before I formulate my next question. Samuel tips his head to one side, indicating for me to follow him. We reach the area where they hold the rock-climbing gear. He patiently shows me how to put the equipment on, and how to make safety checks for the harnesses while he puts his gear on. I follow his instructions receiving an approbatory nod. We walk to the side where the big, fake rock stands.

"We will wear a top rope for safety reasons. The last part can be a little tricky." He points upward.

When my eyes focus on it, I raise my eyebrows.

Only a little tricky? Forgive me if I disagree.

Unless a radioactive spider bit me, I don't know how I'll ring the darn bell.

"I-I-I've never climbed," I manage to get the words out, the constricting sensation my chest leaves after confessing my lack of expertise trying to bring him back to reality.

"It will be tricky, but we'll manage." He secures the helmet on his head. "Now, since you've never rock climbed, I would recommend you use any of the holds closer to you or go for the blue ones, they tend to mark an easier path."

What does he mean with color holds and blue ones? Glancing at the wall, I notice the colorful plastic rocks. Oh! Those rocks must be the holds.

However, there happens to be zero blue ones. I turn to face him, confused.

He discreetly nods toward the back, while he puts the rope on his harness and ties it. With a quick glance over my shoulder I notice the second wall behind us, a smaller and straighter one with the bells on top of it as well and covered with blue colored holds.

I might not be an expert in wall climbing, however, I can tell Oliver didn't mean ringing the bell from the wall behind us when he gave the instructions.

"Is everybody ready?" Oliver interrupts my train of thought. I now focus my attention on our coach. "First place gets to wash the cars," he lifts one of his fingers indicating the position.

My attention spikes. Let's figure out how bad things are.

"Second place gets to sweep and dust the house." He raises another finger. "Third place gets to wash the dishes all week." He lifts yet another finger. "Fourth place will cook and do grocery shopping."

When he looks around he lifts one of his eyebrows, I get the impression he silently conveys a secret message with the rest of them, especially when a couple of heads give a nod in agreement.

"Last place gets to do all the outside chores, such as cutting the grass today, sweeping the leaves all week long. Also," he continues, "gets to clean all the bathrooms in the house and accompany Barbara tomorrow on a new shopping task."

This last part puts the rest of the teams on high alert.

Talk about motivation.

I agree on not wanting to get stuck cleaning the bathrooms, I'll make my best effort on not getting in the last place.

"Boys will be climbers first, and girls will be Belayers," Oliver announces.

Samuel hands me the other end of the rope. My hands sweat and my stomach drops southward as I think of what lies ahead. Nervously, I watch him take a few steps to locate himself behind me. He then puts his arms around me to demonstrate the pull, lock down, pinch, and slide down movement. He also instructs me on how to pull the brakes in case he falls.

Honestly, at this point, my nerves get the best of me, either because of his proximity, his breath on the top of my head, or the fact he's literally putting his life in my hands.

I repeat his instructions, making some minor mistakes. He gets ahold of my hands and patiently repeats the movements.

His hands on mine stuns me, my brain feeding me different ideas.

Can he tell how bad my hands shake? Wow, his hands are huge, they practically cover mine. How come they're warm? Could this mean anything in the sentiment department? Do I need to worry about this?

With extreme effort, I return my attention to his instructions, memorizing his words and repeating them back to him.

"Don't let go of it," he adds while doing one last

safety check to both our equipment.

I nod and hold tightly to the rope.

"On your mark," Oliver shouts, making my knees shake madly. Samuel gets close to the rock. "Get Set." Samuel turns and gives me one thumb up. "Go!"

Samuel quickly and swiftly climbs the rocks with the rest of the guys.

Each one uses a different technique for the climb, keeping the race neck and neck. Kellan puts a lot of effort into his upper body strength. Archie, instead, balances his weight better and uses more of his lower body strength. Zach, on the other hand, meticulously chooses the holds and manages to climb faster with the least amount of force. Oliver only uses the green rocks and works quickly through his selected path. Samuel surprises me with his flexibility, reaching holds others wouldn't be able to because of the distance or risk it represents. Evidently, he's in great shape, using both his upper and lower body strength.

I secure the rope the way he taught me, my hands holding the rope tightly as I keep a close eye on him.

However, Archie, Zach, and Oliver quickly lead the race, separating themselves from Kellan and Samuel.

Speed up, Samuel, I don't want to clean bathrooms.

The tide turns when they reach the angle in the wall and climbing depends more on upper body strength. Kellan passes those in the lead, making the angle appear more like a small detour. Samuel also catches up with Oliver. Oliver's strategy of choosing the green rocks proves its advantages with the holds being more within reach. Meanwhile, Samuel's flexibility allows him to reach riskier holds, and with the help of his upper body strength, he outpaces Zach and Archie.

I hold my breath a couple of times when Archie almost loses his grip and once Samuel almost falls when he attempts a dangerous movement. I swear after this my legs become jelly, but I need to keep alert for the sake of my teammate.

The race finishes with a close call. Kellan reaching the bell first, followed a few seconds later by Oliver. Samuel receives third place, Zach fourth, and Archie comes in last.

Oliver lets go of the wall, while Abigail slowly releases the line to bring him down.

What? Nobody explained this part!

Well, I imagine Barb's job to bring Kellan down will be harder than mine.

"Ready, Samantha?" Samuel screams, scaring the bejeesus out of me.

"Yes!" I yell back once my heart rate slows down to a more normal beat.

He lets go and immediately there's a pull from my end of the rope, but as instructed by him and after watching Barb and Abigail, I follow their lead and bring Samuel safely down.

The moment his feet touch the ground, I control myself from getting down on my knees and kissing it on his behalf.

"Okay, now a five-minute break for making the new

strategies." Oliver 's voice comes in between breaths. My assumptions of rock climbing being a big workout didn't fall short and actually surpassed my expectations.

"Time to switch places," he announces, laughing.

Darn it! I forgot about this small detail.

Samuel unties the knot from his side and hands it over to me. Afterward, he releases the rope from my belt along with the extra equipment. "We need to switch harnesses."

My hands shake madly, taking me twice the time to remove it and put on the one he offers after adjusting it to my size.

A hand reaches for mine and grabs it, making the shaking come to a stop. Surprised, I bring my head up to find Samuel's kind eyes staring into mine.

Jeez, now my stomach tied itself into a knot.

"Everything will be okay, Samantha." He grins. "I won't let you fall."

I nod, unable to find my voice with the nervous state. Between the wall climbing and my hands between his, I'm a mess.

"Now, the key to our strategy will be removing the ropes quickly and making the knots and safety checks fast once we move to the other wall. I need you to pay attention."

He patiently explains to me how to make the knot and how to undo it. I then repeat his teaching.

"Excellent. Now for this to work, we need to fool them, taking advantage of their distraction." He comes closer, confidently whispering his next instructions, his breath tickling my ear and earning myself a shock of goose bumps. "My view from below will be better. I'll let you know when you need to let go."

My stomach drops to the floor at the same speed I imagine my body will be pulled by gravity.

Let go? Great! I'll willingly drop to my doom. Big Guy, staying in bed sounds like a better idea at this precise moment.

"We need a keyword," he proposes and gazes expectantly at me.

I need a word that will motivate me to make the drop.

"Bathroom cleaning," I offer, making him chuckle with my choice of words.

"All right, keep your ears open and try not to exhaust yourself on this part. We need all your energy for the final one." He gives me a pat on the back.

My conscience keeps nagging me with the cheating part.

"Wouldn't it be considered cheating?" I finally dare to ask.

"It is, but believe me, the girls don't like to play by the rules." He chuckles. "Let's call it leveling the game."

I nod and take a deep breath.

"Time is up," Oliver calls out, making my legs tremble. "Everybody needs to get in position."

The game plan Samuel proposed helps to slightly alleviate my worries. Unfortunately, it still doesn't exclude me from going to great heights and then finding out how I am not, in fact, a dove.

"Ready?" Oliver's voice echoes through the room.

"Get set."

Oh, Big Guy, a little help?

"Go!"

I run to the wall and climb, mimicking what I learned from the guys during the flat part using more of my lower body strength, selecting a particular holder color, hoping I chose a beginner's route and not an expert one.

Eyes focused on the hold I intend to use, I make sure my footing is right before lifting myself. I maintain this pace, not paying a lot of attention on which position I'm currently in. I would rather keep my eyes and mind distracted from the abyss below.

"Great pace, Abigail," Oliver shouts.

"Come on, Joy. You can be faster than Abigail," Zach says.

"One hold at a time, baby," Kellan encourages Barb.

"Lyra? How about putting a little more speed," Archie complains.

"Nice job, Samantha!" Samuel screams at the top of his lungs.

I try not to let the encouraging shouts distract me. I honestly don't want to know which position I'm in.

I somehow manage to reach the angled wall and decide to take a few seconds to breathe.

"Woohoo! Go, Abbie!" Oliver's excited words sound far down now.

"Almost there, Joy!" Zach's screams come through.

The first bell rings, quickly followed by a second.

Shoot! I need to speed things up.

I sigh and continue to climb, now putting the strength into my arms.

"Joy, if the hill will not come to Mahomet, Mahomet will go to the hill," Abigail yells.

"This time Mahomet being?" Joy asks.

What…?

"Samantha, I don't want to spend my Sunday evening cleaning bathrooms," Samuel's voice barely comes through with the constant ringing of a bell.

My heart momentarily drops. It seems I can only aspire now for a fourth or fifth place.

I don't want to clean the bathroom.

Trusting Samuel's game plan, and without giving it a lot of thought, I close my eyes and let go, grabbing my rope for dear life.

The sharp stop I expected after releasing the rope never comes. When I open my eyes, I hang practically at the same position where I let go. Immediately, I descend smoothly back toward the ground where Samuel waits. Mentally, I prepare myself for the steps I'll need to perform the moment my feet touch the floor.

As soon as I reach the bottom once more, I expertly untie my rope like I'd done this for years. Without waiting for Samuel, I run to the wall opposite to the one we climbed, the one decorated all with blue holds and with no angle. I get a hold of one of the ropes and work on the knot the way Samuel taught me, so I can start the climb.

"Wait for my signal," Samuel whispers from right behind me. "I need to do the safety checks."

"What the hell?" Archie's scream momentarily distracts me from the job. "The Sams are cheating,"

"Baby, keep moving straight up. Joy, speed up!" Kellan yells with a little more force.

"Let's beat them." Samuel gives me the thumbs up.

Quickly, I climb the opposite wall, finding it way easier than the previous one with the holds closer together, and with more to choose from. It gives me the impression of climbing a ladder.

In no time, I find myself halfway through.

"Joy, Samantha's gaining ground," Abigail shouts. "Go to the one closer to you."

The bell once again rings madly.

"No, Joy, don't go there," Archie pleads.

Kellan laughs.

We can still get third place? Bring it!

"I'll go and stall Samantha," Abigail screams.

As if I needed some additional motivation to climb faster.

"Abigail, don't you dare climb the wall without the safety rope," Oliver screams.

"Go, Samantha! I can practically hear your bell ring." Samuel encourages me between all the screams.

"Lyra, go left!" Archie's voice sounds desperate. "No, damn it, your other left!"

"Language!" I scream.

"Only Samantha would correct us through this ordeal!" Zach mentions, laughing.

"Abigail, go!" Oliver orders. "Remember they need to

be fourth place."

I climb faster, taking risks in some of the holds, my hands and face sweaty, but I don't stop; focusing on beating Abigail.

"Joy, speed up. Or you get to decide which food you like better, Barb or Lyra's," Zach screams.

This was their plan all along; they intend me to cook all week?

Seems my cooking skills earned me an unusual position in the house. But honestly, right now I want to show them they shouldn't underestimate me.

"Great work to motivate Joy, Zach." Oliver snickers.

But she is not the only one, because no matter how fast Abigail is, I can now watch the bell, and I will beat them.

"What the hell, Lyra?" Archie screams, desperate. "Do you want to help Barb with the assignment? I certainly don't!"

"Screw you, Archie," Lyra finally snaps at him.

I'm about to call them out, but stop when I catch Samuel's voice.

"Go Samantha!" Samuel screams happily. "Stretch your arm and ring the bell!"

I grab the cord of the bell and pull it at the same time somebody touches my leg. However, my bell rings loud and proud.

"Woohoo!" Samuel shouts happily. "Third place! You did it Samantha! We got third place!"

"Damn it." I turn and watch Abigail, expecting to find

her fuming. Instead, she seems disappointed. "I hope you enjoy your food either undercooked or…"

Another bell sounds in the distance. We both turn to find who got the fourth place.

"Then it will be overcooked," Abigail confirms with a sigh.

"You believe I'll allow you to kick me out of my kitchen?" I challenge, making Abigail grin. "I would rather cook than wash the dishes."

"I believe Barb and Kellan will happily trade jobs with you, and won't hear complaints from the rest of us." Laughing, she lets go of her hold.

"Time to come down," Samuel shouts, and I let go with no hesitation this time, knowing what to expect.

"Excellent work, Samantha." Samuel walks to me with his palm high up when I touch the floor. I bring my palm up and high five him. "We make an amazing team!"

"Next time, I get Samantha as a teammate," Archie proposes while he lowers Lyra.

"Nu-uh. With more practice, Samantha will be up there chasing Joy and Abigail," Samuel teases. "I propose we continue with the assigned teams."

"You two cheated," Lyra reprimands us, disappointed once her feet touch the ground.

"What? You never complain about Joy climbing down to bring you the bell," Samuel laughs off. "What a wonderful way to start a Sunday."

Sunday? Oh, my Lord!

"What time is it?" I search the compound for a clock.

"Breakfast time!" Joy speaks up, raising her arms above her head and slightly jumping up and down with excitement, "and after the workout we deserve some pancakes! Samantha's pancakes," she corrects, glancing over her shoulder at Barb.

I grab Zach's arm and pull at his wrist to see the time on his watch.

"Plan to meet someone? Or need to be somewhere?" Zach jokes.

Eight o'clock! It barely gives me time to shower and get dressed.

"Yeah, the nine o'clock Mass!" I state the obvious, remembering how Grams loved to take me to this service when I visited her.

Everybody clamps down and eyes each other.

"I believe your teammate won't mind accompanying you to church!" Archie mocks, crinkling his blue-eyed gaze, his smile stretching when Samuel turns and practically shoots daggers with his eyes.

"Or you could accompany her," Lyra proposes, enjoying how Archie's smug smile magically disappears.

"I can't go inside a church." Archie wrings his hands together. "Remember, I'll probably be struck down by lightning the moment I put a foot inside."

"Your mother is not Satan," Oliver corrects him, rolling his eyes.

"No, but she might be his bride," he retorts, pointing a finger at him.

"Being a lawyer doesn't mean she married him," Zach

says, sighing.

"Well, she has been doing an excellent job doing all his dirty work for so many years and worst part, she enjoys it. Deep down I know she made a deal with him, to be on the safe side I'll stay out of a church," he explains, determined.

The devil? A deal with him? I don't like this creepy talk.

"Ugh, you can be such a baby," Joy answers, annoyed.

"I'll go by myself," I venture after nobody volunteers. Hopefully, this will bring a stop to the discussion.

"No, I'll accompany you," Samuel offers. "Allow me to give her a heads up. She needs to prepare David."

Prepare him? I don't understand. Who is David?

Hoping for an explanation, I glance at the rest of the group, but now everybody's distracted, taking off their gear and talking about a different topic. Suspicious, I eye Samuel.

"Nothing bad, I promise." He comes closer and helps me with my harness. "My mother will be excited to find me there and will insist we sit with her," he explains.

Okay…

"However, my brother gets tense in big crowds," he continues handing me the harness, "and he gets nervous around strangers."

"I promise to be nice to him," I say, trying to ease his doubts. Honestly, I'll be more nervous than him.

"It is neither your fault nor his. He was born with a slight spectrum of autism called Asperger's Syndrome," he explains. "Once he knows you and becomes familiar with you, it will be easier. If he's rude to you, don't take it personally."

Somebody once explained to me about the syndrome; however, I've never met anybody with it.

How should I act? What do I need to expect?

Probably acting like me and checking how David reacts will be my safer bet and not take anything personally.

"We'll get along fine," I say encouragingly. "How old is your brother?"

"He is thirteen," he smiles, noticing my interest.

Shouldn't be too bad, being younger should help calm my nerves.

We return the equipment and Samuel purchases a couple of water bottles and granola bars.

"When we get home, there will be enough time for a quick shower and to dress up," Samuel instructs, handing me a drink and a bar. "Eat this. Afterward we can grab brunch."

I nod and try to open the water bottle, the darn cap not budging in my efforts to twist it. He smiles, opens his, hands it over, and exchanges water bottles with me.

Lyra catches up with him, giggling. "You should warn your mother about her."

Samuel singles her out with an unfriendly glare.

I notice the amused expression on everybody's faces. "What?"

"Let's just say—" Joy begins before Archie rudely cuts her off.

"No! No! No! Let's not spoil the fun! They did cheat, now time for their punishment. I want to listen to all the details about the arrangements and the date we will need to save," Archie's lips upturned with mischief. "And Lyra, you can consider yourself off the hook now."

"Oh, she'll be completely blown away by Samantha." Barb grins.

"Hey!" Zach says.

"No, no. Time to watch our little dove's charm backfire," Lyra jokes.

"What charm?" I ask, hoping somebody takes pity on me and explains.

"You know what? I'll take her to church," Zach finally offers.

"No, we already came up with a plan. Plus, we need to work on the items we discussed yesterday," Lyra says excitedly. "If I need to accompany Barb on her assignment together with Archie, I might as well get off the hook in the other matter."

I turn to peek at Oliver, hoping he can put an end to this since he's the oldest one from the lot. He shakes his head and smiles.

Samuel releases a sigh and rolls his eyes.

Again, I'm going to be kept in the dark? Seems going to church will represent a bigger challenge than simply spending some time with the Big Guy.

CHAPTER FIFTEEN
The Lonely Goatherd

We arrive at the church with five minutes to spare, and to my great surprise, the building is very different from the last time I visited. At first, when Grams mentioned it, I imagined she meant a new coat of paint. However, it's been completely overhauled, making it more beautiful than before.

The new altar has a lighter wood tone, and the new coat of white paint allows light to reflect better, unlike the previous brown color.

A leaded glass panel replaced the wall that used to be behind the altar. Its beautiful mural, made entirely out of glass, looks expensive.

"Wow," I say beneath my breath, gazing at the exquisite masterpiece. I had gotten used to the school's dark, cold, and somber church. The changes here are an unexpected and happy surprise. I feel even more connected with the Big Guy in a church full of light.

I'll bet Grams loved the new changes, if she got to see them.

"Over here, Samantha," Samuel calls from a few steps ahead. I didn't realize I stopped walking while I studied the church.

Following the voice, my gaze falls on Samuel who I notice put a little more effort on his attire than I did. He wears modern and sophisticated clothes; the light-olive dress shirt makes his dark hair appear lighter and brings a glow to his tan complexion.

Next to him, I must look like a mess in another of my white dress shirts from school and a pastel blue pencil skirt that fit correctly when I made it during sewing class two years ago. Now, my wider hips stretch the fabric to near breaking point. I'll avoid bending or making any sudden movements to be on the safe side.

Luckily, I didn't experience a major growth spurt, too, or the skirt would be too short and unfit for attending Mass. To complete my simple attire, I added my black ballet flats and styled my wet hair in a braid. At the last minute, I grabbed a dark blue cardigan, remembering the chill in the air.

I move carefully, hoping the skirt doesn't give out. It makes walking more awkward than usual. My gait resembles more of a duck than a human.

And, Big Guy, if we add the two bruises on my leg, I believe we can all agree I'm a mess.

The church quickly fills, and only a few open seats remain. How on earth will we find Samuel's family?

We go to a large column located on one side of the altar. It partially hides a row of benches from the rest of the congregation. A beautiful, young woman and a teenager already sit on one bench.

The woman appears to be around her mid-forties. Her dark, wavy hair combed back away from her face reveals her black eyes, which remain focused on the altar. A beautiful and peaceful smile stands out on her lips. Her features remind me of Samuel.

The teenager has beautiful, caramel-colored hair and paler skin. His dark eyes focus on the lead glass window, critically analyzing it. He turns toward the woman and whispers something to her. Her attention shifts to something the teenager points at in the panel and she nods in response.

We approach them. As we walk closer, I realize she placed her purse on the bench next to her, saving a spot.

"Corazón!" She exclaims in Spanish the moment her eyes settle on Samuel. With a big smile on her lips, she waves him over. "Quickly, quickly. We might be in the presence of the Lord, but some of his followers can behave unchristian-like when it comes to getting a seat."

"Hola, Mamá," Samuel replies. I understand what he means, internally thanking the Big Guy for the few basic

Spanish lessons I took before planning my trip to Barcelona. "Ella es Samantha."

She studies me, the grin on her face frozen in place, then turns to her son.

"¿Acaso no es Abigail?" she asks, confused.

Samuel shakes his head.

The teenager approaches his mother and whispers loudly. "They are entirely different. The girl's hair is raven black and around twenty-three inches in length, compared to Abigail's, who is carbon colored and thirteen inches shorter," he states while his eyes still set on the mural wall. "Her eyes are pure hazel, quite different from Samuel's friend who has gemstone green. Her skin has a tan quality, unlike Abigail's, which is ivory. She appears to be four inches shorter and seventeen pounds lighter. Additionally, she has three freckles on her nose."

He hardly glanced my way and made a complete analysis of my sister's and my physical differences.

Even some I never noticed, Big Guy! I like him!

"How could I have missed those details," his mother jokes.

"It's understandable since you forgot your glasses. You left them at home on top of the dining table," he immediately responds, oblivious to his mother's humorous tone. He continues with his eyes still on the decorated wall. "I mentioned it twice, but you were in such a hurry to get here on time and save a seat for Chris—"

"Hi, David," Samuel interrupts him. "As always, you're very keen in your observations."

"I saved you a seat," she changes the topic, happily pulling her purse closer to herself and encouraging us to sit beside her. Like a gentleman, Samuel steps to one side and beckons me to go ahead. I end up sitting next to his mother.

"Oh, my! How utterly rude on my part. My name is Miranda," she introduces herself, her voice thick with a strong Latin accent. She extends her hand. "And this is David."

"Nice to meet you, Miranda and David." I want to address her formally, but since I don't know her last name, I decide to stick with their first names.

"David, say hi to Samantha," she addresses her other son.

"Why?" he asks quietly, his gaze now fixed on the top portion of the mural.

"Because it's polite," she answers. "She's a friend of your brothers."

I almost miss David barely whispered response, "Hi, Samantha."

"I want to thank you for bringing my son back to church," Miranda comments, bringing my attention back to her.

"Mom!" Samuel warns her.

"He offered to join me," I correct her, which is technically true.

She happily chuckles and glances over to Samuel, her eyebrows raised to silently convey a message.

"Don't get any ideas!" he warns, pointing a finger at

her.

"A mother can only hope," she jokes, making Samuel grunt when she gives a slight shake of her shoulders.

I'll bet any parent would hope for her or his son back to church.

The music from the choir signifies the beginning of Mass, stopping the small discussion arising between the two of them.

For some strange reason, I expected to find the choir seated at the church's second-floor balcony. However, they sit on the opposite side of the altar, across from us.

Perhaps they only use the balcony for special occasions.

The priest arrives, followed by two altar boys, and the mass begins.

Ten minutes into the service, Miranda gives a small groan. When I glance at her, I notice she's alarmingly pale, and a small layer of sweat covers her forehead.

I grab ahold of her arm, worried she might faint. "Are you all right, Miranda?"

"I'll be all right," she answers confidently, but judging by her sickly pallor, I can safely guess she's lying.

Samuel leans over, facing her, to analyze her features. "Mom, did you bring your pills?"

"Don't turn your back to the Lord." She slaps him on the shoulder with hardly any strength.

"And let you fall? Please sit down," he whispers to her.

"It is not the time to—" she complains.

"Neither the Lord nor the priest will mind, Miranda," I step in, hoping to convince her. "They would both understand the situation."

She concedes without an argument and takes our advice, sitting down on the bench.

"Where did you put your pills?" Samuel nervously asks once again.

"There should be one in my bag." She points at the purse at her feet.

Samuel takes it and searches inside, his hands coming out empty.

"They're not here," he says, alarmed.

"They should be. I could swear I..." She closes her eyes, looking worse by the moment.

David's gaze wanders to the ceiling, oblivious to the current dilemma, as he replies in a monotone voice, "She left them on her bedside table."

Samuels's eyes widen in alarm after hearing the bad news. "Mom, I'll drive over there and get them, you should..." He stops, his eyes focusing on David and then on me.

"But the service just started," she complains.

"And you are about to faint," he argues back.

"But David." She points at her other son. "You know how important it is for him to follow a routine."

I may not know a lot about the syndrome, but I know doctors recommend keeping a schedule and routine to reduce their anxiety.

"I can stay with him," I suggest, hoping to offer a

solution to their dilemma.

Both of their heads snap toward me and then they glance at each other.

"We could..." Samuel says.

"But you know..." she continues but stops. Her face contorts in pain and she bites her lower lip.

Samuel grabs his mother's phone from her purse, turns it on, and quickly types something into it.

"If anything happens, call me on my cell. We won't take long." Samuel hands it over to me. He input a number that I assume is his.

"David, please stay with Samantha. We will go and get mom's pills, all right?" he tells his brother.

David gives Samuel a small nod, indicating he understood his brother's instructions.

Immediately, Samuel gets ahold of his mother, lifts her up as if she weighs nothing, and carries her out through a back door I never knew existed.

The service continues, and I regularly check on David to make sure I don't detect any changes different from how he behaved previously. Once, I shift closer to reduce the gap between us. I catch the way he closes his hand into a fist, his knuckles becoming white with the effort. I scoot a little farther away, and his hand returns to normal.

Everything continues without any major glitches. It's obvious David dislikes the music. His hand clenches into a fist when the music begins and it stays that way until it comes to an end. Other than that, he stays in control.

After the first reading, a family of three comes to

stand next to our bench.

"Miss, could you please scoot over?" the tall, teenage son asks. With his big, football linebacker frame, he makes me feel miniscule. I study his parents and notice he inherited the body structure from his father.

With a quick mental calculation, I guess the only way the five of us can fit on the bench will be if our shoulders graze each other. I know I can barely bear being in contact with one of them; however, I know David won't be able to handle it.

As they begin to sit, taking over the spot we saved for Miranda and Samuel, David replies loudly, "Mom and Samuel were sitting there."

The father grunts, his eyes singling David out, displeased by the comment.

"I apologize, but my friends will be here shortly," I explain, trying to ease the man's mood.

"Since they're not here, we should be allowed to sit," the father objects.

I weigh my options to either tell the truth or lie about them being in the confession booth. "I promise you, sir, they will return any moment. They went to—"

"Son," he interrupts me to speak to his son. "Move over. I'll sit next to her."

The large man pushes his way in, making me retreat farther, and I accidentally hit David in the shoulder who stiffens in place. When I try to return to my previous spot, I find myself blocked.

"This bench is for the elderly, the ill, and the

pregnant!" David yells, covering his ears with his hands.

"My wife presents a medical condition," the father replies without glancing at us.

I take a peek at the woman. A small brace immobilizes her pinkie finger. The guy stretches the truth, since I don't believe that qualifies as an illness.

Beside me, David's head rhythmically moves back and forth, his panic attack worsening. "They should not sit there! My mother sits there!"

I can sense eyes on us, and not necessarily from the family.

"Honey, breathe in and breathe out!" I tell him, trying to calm him down, but he doesn't register my words. "Please, sir, I beg you," I plead with the father who now openly glares at me.

"And allow the idiot to get away with his tantrum? No!" he snaps back, determined.

I rise to gain a little more height, and the loud tearing sound of my skirt giving out freezes me in place.

Oh no! Not now!

My hands immediately fly to the back of my skirt. Meanwhile, my face turns the color of a tomato.

The family stares with amusement as if to say God's wrath fell upon me for the scandal.

However, the humming sound and the rocking movement in my peripheral vision comes to a stop. I glance over to find David with a smirk on his lips, his head turned toward the mural, but aware of what just occurred.

"The hole in your skirt shows your gluteus!" he states

with his monotone voice, loud enough for the priest to be aware of my current predicament.

Without taking my eyes from the rude man, I remove my cardigan and tie it around my waist, making sure the only one who got a real glimpse at my rear end were David and the Big Guy.

"You should dress more accordingly when you intend to visit the house of our Lord," the mother of the family smirks without eyeing me. I study her impressive dress; the fabric seems expensive as the cut and the logos of the thin belt confirm my suspicions. I'll bet it costs more than half... Well, I don't know, but it looks pricey.

She turns and gives me a once-over, her lip turning upward, making me more self-conscious of my clothing. The ill-fitting skirt I wear a reminder of how limited my wardrobe is. At school, either I wore my uniform, my jeans, my ballet gear, or my pants.

"I believe the Lord focuses more on actions than on wardrobe," I state, saving a shred of my dignity.

She scoffs. Apparently, she doesn't share my same beliefs.

Noticing David calmed down, I decide to let the seating issue slide. The only problem the family comfortably sits on the bench taking most of the space, leaving a gap barely acceptable for David to be comfortable.

I move to the end of the seats, intending to stand the rest of the service. However, this doesn't go unnoticed by Samuel's brother.

"We arrived first, finder's keepers!" he screams, moving closer to the edge of the bench, separating himself from the rude man, his hands going to his ears once more.

The music thankfully drowns out David's words, which become louder.

I need to come up with something, and I need to do it now before the music stops!

Music! Up?

I raise my eyes to the second floor and find the answer to my predicament.

"David, I'll bet we can get a different perspective on the panel if we go to the choir balcony," I loudly tell him, taking advantage of his fixation on the wall art to gain his interest and convince him about this new option.

He stops and glances over to the second floor.

"But, it is not for the ill, elders, or pregnant," he corrects me. "It is for the choir."

I could kick myself for referring to it as choir's balcony instead of a simple balcony.

"Exactly! You and I are not ill, pregnant, or elderly, which means we can't sit here," I explain pointing to our current bench. "If we hurry, we can save a spot for your mother and Samuel up there."

"It is for the choir, not for us," he repeats.

Think Samantha; I need to change his perspective.

"I don't believe they would mind since they appear comfortable sitting on the other side of the altar," I point in their direction, not really sure if he'll accept the reason.

"But, Mother will not be able to go up the stairs. She

should be sitting here in the designated area," he states.

A little help, Big Guy?

I remember how Samuel previously took her away. "Your brother can carry her up the stairs."

"Shhhh!" the mother of the family shushes me, irking me to the high heavens.

That does it! I can practically hear my tolerance crack.

"Plus, I believe these folks deserve the bench more than us. Idiocy is an illness that is nearly impossible to recover from." I regret them the moment the words leave my mouth.

First, because I insulted a family inside the Big Guy's house, and second as if on cue the music dies, the church becomes utterly silent, and my words travel farther down the bench than it should.

Don't make eye contact with the family!

David chuckles. Without a word, he stands, and I follow him to the entrance Samuel and his mother disappeared through earlier. We swiftly walk to the main entrance, and as if he knows the church like the back of his hand, he finds the stairwell that takes us to the balcony.

I let David pick the bench where he feels most comfortable and sit next to him, making sure I leave a gap between the two of us.

Halfway through the service, the phone in my hand vibrates. I glance at it, noticing a so-called Christopher calling. Since I don't want to intrude on Miranda's personal life, I ignore the call. The phone continuously vibrates throughout the rest of the service.

Well, it seems this Christopher guy really needs to get ahold of Miranda.

When communion begins, I finally give up and answer the phone.

"Samantha?" I listen to Samuel's worried voice on the other end.

"Samuel?" I ask, confused, and take a second look at the screen.

"Where are you guys?" he asks a little more calmly. "Is everything all right?"

"Yeah." I realize I forgot to call him. "We decided to get seats with a view." I stand and scan the crowd, finding him near the choir. "We're up on the balcony."

His head snaps upward in my direction. I wave, and his eyes finally focus on me. My stomach plummets to the first floor when his concerned expression transforms into a relieved smile. "What in heavens name are you two doing up there?"

Before I can answer him, David also stands. "We need to get communion."

"Hold on. We should be down in a jiffy," I tell Samuel.

His smile grows. "A jiffy?"

I stick my tongue out and hang up.

David leads the way, meeting Samuel when we reach downstairs, but I don't stop to greet him. Instead, I follow David to receive our communion.

As the service comes to a close, we join Miranda who sits at one of the benches at the end of the church. Samuel walks to her side and helps her stand.

"There you are, you two. Did you have fun?" Samuel's mom asks when we join her, a wide grin on her face.

"Mother, we are here to pray, not to have fun," David says, stating the obvious.

Miranda chuckles at her son's correction.

"It was a beautiful service," I answer, hoping nobody tells her about the altercation we had with the rude family.

"We should go back home, Mom." Samuel walks toward the exit. "I'll drive you in my car since I parked closer, and afterward, I'll get somebody to give me a ride here and return your vehicle," He shakes his head. "Can you believe someone parked in the handicap spot without a registration?"

"I'll bet there's an excellent explanation." Miranda gives him a small pat on the top of his hand. "I need to talk with the priest before we leave."

Samuel helps her outside and guides her to a nearby bench. Meanwhile, David walks farther away from the crowd. I stay close enough to keep an eye on him, while leaving a gap to make him comfortable. He keeps eyeing the trees and the sky. I follow his gaze, trying to guess what exactly he finds attractive.

"Oh, Lord! We had the most terrible experience during service," a familiar voice interrupts my analysis. "A couple of kids tried to kick us out of the reserved seating. Of course, Larry would not tolerate it, since my finger is still recovering after the tennis incident."

I turn in time to catch the woman showing a big

crowd her finger. Hands clasped together, I restrain myself from showing her my finger. And it wouldn't be the pinky one.

Oh, Big Guy! I might need anger management classes.

"They kept going on and on and on about nonsense. The boy started throwing a tantrum, and the girl even tried to bribe Larry by ripping her sorry excuse for a skirt to get her way, the little slut!"

Am I the little slut? Sorry excuse for a skirt? *Big Guy, I swear she's asking for it.*

"This happened all during service?" one of the women exclaims at the top of her voice. "Oh, no, she didn't!"

"Uh-huh! The priest needs to hear about this kind of incident. We can't tolerate certain kinds of people in our church. Honestly! After all the remodeling, they will bring the wrong kind of crowd back," she states. "Oh, there's Father Gomez! Father Gomez!" She waves her hand.

The priest turns after the loud woman practically screams his name, rudely interrupting him from his conversation with other members of the church. His approach halts when he recognizes the caller. His eyes roll up to the heavens as if to ask the Lord to give him strength.

"Yes, Mrs. Tribecca?" Father Gomez kindly addresses the woman. "How's your finger? Mr. Tribecca mentioned you still wear the immobilizer as a precaution?" His question brings the conversation around her to a complete stop.

Oh, my, Big Guy! Is she faking it?

"Well, you know one can never trust the doctors. They might be wrong." She gives him a fake smile. "But thanks for asking. Your concern and prayers are always welcome."

"Always happy to help, Mrs. Tribecca. Now, how else may I assist you?" He steps closer, offering her an open ear.

"You know, during service, a couple of kids—" Her gaze lands on David and me and one eyebrow shoots up, her smile turning into an ugly grin.

The priest follows her gaze and studies David and me.

Oh great! Once again, I'll be completely humiliated in public. *Please, Big Guy, let it be swift, and keep David out of her crazy rambling.*

CHAPTER SIXTEEN
The Beauty in Asymmetry

"You met David Solis?" the Priest asks in surprise. "I didn't know you were familiar with our local artist."

Mrs. Tribecca stops and closes her mouth.

"He designed the lovely mural in our church. A marvelous piece of art. Wouldn't you agree, Mrs. Tribecca?"

My mouth drops to the floor along with the woman's.

He designed that? Wow!

When I glance at David, he still gazes at the morning sky, lost in his own world, oblivious to Father Gomez's praise of his work.

"Well, yes, most certainly. However, he and that girl

behaved quite rudely during service. The girl practically assaulted…"

The priest's eyes now fall on me. He momentarily appears lost as he studies me. Finally, the corner of his mouth lifts up. "Whoa! Twice the honor today, Mrs. Tribecca. You do realize who you met, don't you?"

I doubt either of them recognize me. He probably has me confused me with Abigail.

Hopefully, her reputation follows her.

"Samantha is the late Mrs. Morris's granddaughter. You do remember Mrs. Morris?" he challenges her. "One of our greatest donors on the renovations of our church."

He knows of my existence? But, I would remember him from my last visit.

Mrs. Tribeccas's mouth opens and closes for a moment. "But my family donated a large sum of money. You once told me we were…"

"Not all donations come with a dollar sign on it, Mrs. Tribecca," he says jokingly, but with an undertone of chastisement. "Mrs. Morris brought to our attention David's talents. She also dedicated a lot of her time working with the handymen. Thanks to her excellent financial administration, we renovated a large portion of the church and stopped me from blowing it all on the altar."

His eyes sparkle and the corner of his lips turn upwards.

"Well, yes, but I believe her granddaughter didn't inherit Mrs. Morris's great passion for the church," she corrects him.

"She probably exceeded hers." He winks in my direction. "For years, Samantha worked and helped some nuns, and somebody told me she makes a hell of a devil's food cake." He chuckles. "Pardon me, Lord." He makes the sign of the cross. "She would give your lemon pie a run for its money."

It seems Mrs. Tribecca doesn't find Father Gomez amusing.

I don't move a muscle, surprised to learn how well informed he is about my life.

"Baby doll." Her rude husband comes closer, not looking amused. "We need to leave. One of the altar boys informed me our car has a ticket because we parked in one of the handicap spots."

Samuels's previous words come to mind regarding the subject.

"What the fuck?" Mrs. Tribecca shrieks.

"Language, Mrs. Tribecca. You may not be inside the house of our Lord, but proper behavior never hurt anyone," Father Gomez corrects her with amusement.

"But, what about my injury?" She raises her pinky finger to gain everybody's attention, ignoring the Priest's correction.

"Apparently, it doesn't count as a handicap situation since your motor skills aren't affected by it." He urges his wife forward, leaving her silenced.

"Oh! Thank you for bringing this to my attention, Mr. Tribecca." The Priest claps his hands together. "I wanted to discuss the situation with the bench located at the right of the altar. You can understand the importance of leaving it open for people with more specific needs?"

"But, my..." she complains a little more slowly.

"I know, my dear, and your injury can be quite painful. We should praise the Lord it didn't extend to other areas and that you recovered so fast," he continues speaking. "However, I do recommend arriving before the service begins to get a good seat in the house."

I cover my mouth, hiding the grin, in case Mrs. Tribecca fixes her eye on me. It might not be Christian of Father Gomez to put her in her place publicly, but she did ask for it.

"The kids sitting there didn't present any motor issues, either," she tattles, victorious to find something she can argue.

Father Gomez turns to glance at us and rolls his eyes. It seems his patience can only go so far. "I would love to introduce you to Mrs. Solis," he offers, scanning the crowd. "Such a wonderful woman. An excellent mother to such talented sons and a good example of how to tackle the challenges the Lord presents to us. I'll bet you'll find great inspiration in her." He gently pulls Mrs. Tribecca's arm in the opposite direction of where David and I stand.

"Baby doll, we need to leave now! Abraham texted me. The police threatened to call a truck to tow away our car if we don't move quickly," Mr. Tribecca exclaims, going after his wife and the priest.

Well, what a beautiful example of how karma works.

Thank You, Big Guy!

I can't hold it anymore. Laughter escapes from my lips. I bite the nail of my thumb, trying to stop the giggles. I glance at David. This time he focuses his gaze on a tree that stands a few feet away, but a millimeter grin touches his lips.

"Sorry it took so long," Samuel says, sneaking up behind me. "I had to deal with some handicap parking situation." He studies the two of us. "What's so funny?"

We both shrug at the same time, making me giggle even more. I realize David might be living in his own little world, but he keeps his ears open to whatever happens in reality.

"When did the two of you become friends?" Samuel asks David.

Friends? I mean, we basically just met. It's not as if he's talking to me or anything.

"When her assessment regarding the Tribecca clan equaled my own," David explains, avoiding his brother's eyes.

"The Tribecca's?" Samuel sighs. It seems he's also had a run-in with the terrible family.

"She called them idiots to their faces during Mass," David tells him with his monotone voice, but I finally catch one of his quick glances toward me.

My hands fly to my mouth once his words sink in. David just ratted me out.

Big Guy, come on, who's side are You on?

Samuel's head snaps in my direction, his face in utter

shock. "You did?"

I freeze in place, my face getting warm.

"Yes, she did. Right after she showed me her gluteus, and Mrs. Tribecca insulted her garments."

Now my face boils with heat.

"You flashed my brother?" Samuel asks, full of surprise as he raises one eyebrow.

Now, I'm speechless.

"I assume she didn't do it intentionally since the stitches on her sky-blue skirt broke, leaving two inches of her light-pink, Fruit of the Loom, cotton undergarments exposed," David explains.

Samuel's eyes go straight to the sweater tied around my waist.

Please, Big Guy, make the earth swallow me right this instant!

Obviously, the Big Guy doesn't agree with my reasoning, as I remain standing in front of them. Somehow, I find the tree David studied earlier quite interesting. And the sky, the church, or anything else to avoid meeting Samuel's eyes.

"David, we should keep this between the three of us," he informs his brother with a chuckle. "How about we don't tell Mom."

"Are you referring to the skirt incident or our assessment of the Tribecca's?" David asks.

"Both," Samuel immediately responds.

"Another of our secrets?" David asks.

"Yes, you lucky son—" Samuel stops at the last moment. "How about I take you home? Mom seems to be done speaking with Father Gomez." He thankfully changes the subject. "I'll bring the car around."

I glance around. The area's now empty, and David approaches his mother who sits on one of the outside benches next to Father Gomez. I follow him, internally thanking Samuel for at least warning David not to tell his mom about the skirt incident.

Father Gomez notices me, stands, and approaches with his hand extended.

I take it.

"Always a pleasure to meet one of Angela's grandkids." He smiles widely. "I've heard a lot about you."

"You have?" This surprises me. He's probably the only one who has.

"Obviously," he beams. "She was proud of all of you. When you visited, she really looked forward to introducing us, but never got a chance because other commitments always came up. But she would regularly talk about you and couldn't stop praising your achievements." He pulls me to the side, away from Miranda and David. "Thank you for helping with David. I don't know how you managed it, wrestling the Tribecca's and keeping David calm. It takes great strength."

Oh, you know the usual. Distracting a teenage boy with my bum and insulting the rich people. All in a day's work. I think sarcastically.

"The Big Guy helped," I offer instead. While I do thank him, I also personally blame him for the whole skirt situation.

Why do you like to work in mysterious ways, Big Guy? How about next time we keep my buttocks out of the situation?

"He always has an eye out for us," the priest holds his hand upwards as if high-fiving the Big Guy and then drops his hand. "My door is always open, Little Dove, in case you need to talk."

"Thank you." I smile to hear Grams's nickname on his lips, finding her fingerprint on the priest. She really did talk about me from time to time.

He glances from side-to-side and whispers. "And if you happen to find a lot of baked goods in your pantry, I'll be more than happy to take them off your hands." He rubs his expanding waistline.

After what he did for us with the Tribeccas, I believe next Sunday I might save some of my baking— Wait, I'll bake him a personal stash and hide it from the rest of the family.

"Are you ready, Samantha?" Samuel calls from a few feet away.

I turn and find a black sedan parked at the curb. David sits inside the car next to his mother in the backseat. I give Samuel a disapproving stare. After all, his mom should take the front since she's older and holds a higher rank than me.

"She insisted," he explains as if he can read my mind. He walks to the passenger side door to open it.

Saying a last farewell to the priest, I get in, and I stop from complaining when David speaks up. "The lower right corner is not symmetrical. I've insisted on them replacing it."

"David, honey, they already explained it would be hard and costly to change it," Miranda explains.

"But my design clearly stated the measurement for the blue part. The ignorant person who put it together clearly doesn't know how to follow instructions," he persists. "Point two inches! He practically ruined the mural."

"Honey, he did his best to follow it," she replies tiredly, covering her eyes with one of her hands.

"David, not this again," Samuel intercedes. "Mom needs to rest, and we already discussed this over a dozen times."

"But..." he continues, determined to get his point across.

"David, I loved the mural. It shows great inspiration, and it's a beautiful piece of work," I comment in an effort to ease the tension.

"Don't get him started," Samuel warns me.

"It's not symmetrical. It's not perfect," David whispers.

"Have you considered the beauty in asymmetrical things?" I turn in my seat to meet his eyes. Even if he's staring at the car floor, I get the impression he somehow perceives me. "Most things in the world are asymmetrical, and God created them. Either you say God did a poor job in creation, or your work can be as beautiful as the trees, the mountains, and the people that God created."

The car becomes completely silent.

Oops. I probably went a little too far with my speech.

"She sounds like Fluttershy. Samantha is Fluttershy!" David's voice becomes more alive than during any of our conversations so far and the smallest grin spreads across his face.

Flutter who?

Miranda removes her hand from her eyes, her gaze utterly astonished as she glances at David and then at me.

I expect some translation from Samuel. His eyes stare straight at the road in front of us, but his lips press tightly together to restrain laughter.

"Samantha, would you like to join us this week for our family dinner?" Miranda asks happily. "David and I would love it if you could."

"I would like to," I accept, flattered by her invitation. "Can I bring something?"

Samuel's amusement vanishes.

"Mamá, ella es solo una amiga. No empieces con tus locas ideas y haciéndote falsas ilusiones," he says, assuming I don't know Spanish.

While my lessons didn't go far, I recognize the words *friend* and *crazy ideas*.

Yeah, they're probably talking about me.

Miranda shoots back, "Logro traerte de regreso a Misa. Cuido y defendió a David. Y ahora tu hermano la ha comparado con Fluttershy de Mi Pequeño Pony, tus advertencias llegaron demasiado tarde. La quiero de nuera."

I don't understand a single word of this, but no matter the language, the Mom tone needs no translation.

Samuel's in trouble.

"How about I bring dessert?" I propose to stop the argument. "Samuel and I can prepare it. Last night, he helped me when we made pasta."

"No!" Samuel's snaps at me. By his expression, one would think I revealed the government's greatest secret. Miranda laughs her heart out in the back seat.

"What?" I ask innocently.

"You've done it," he says. "She will never let it go."

I widen my eyes at him. "No dessert, then?"

Samuel only rolls his eyes and chuckles, amused by my comment. He pulls into a driveway and parks the car. "Oh, look, we arrived home."

He quickly gets out of the car, ending the discussion.

"It was wonderful to meet you, Samantha. Please make sure Samuel brings you to dinner, and don't believe any excuse he gives you. You're more than welcome," Miranda tells me merrily, her tired mood vanishes. I nod. "David, say bye to Samantha."

"Bye, Samantha," David complies as he climbs out of the car.

"Bye, Miranda and David." I wave.

Samuel helps his mother to the door, followed by David.

"I'll be back soon, try to rest." Samuel bends to kiss his mother goodbye. "Take care of her, David. Make sure she takes her pills and carries them in her purse."

David gives a small nod.

Samuel returns to the car, and before he turns on the

ignition, we catch David's voice. "Mom, I forgot to mention on my previous assessment her face is more symmetrical than Abigail's."

Samuel closes his mouth, his lips tight, but with an amuse spark in his eyes.

"What does that mean?" I ask as we pull away from their house, because I can't make sense of David's words.

"David practically called you prettier than Abigail," Samuel translates.

"Oh!" My face warms up, and I cover it with my hands, hoping Samuel doesn't notice.

"And, so it begins. The girls guessed right about my mother's future expectations," he acknowledges with a chuckle. When I glance at him, his dashing stare meets mine. "But, you surprised me with David, Samantha."

I shrug and slide my eyes to the car floor, intimidated by the way he looks at me.

I didn't do anything major. I only treated David the way I would like people to treat me.

"What time will you return your mom's car?" I ask to change the subject.

"I don't know. Probably in a couple of hours. Why?" Samuel asks.

"If she needs to rest, I'll be happy to prepare some lunch for her and David. That way she can—"

"Thank you for offering, Samantha," he interrupts. "But you need to review Darcy's notes for tomorrow's test."

Oh, nuts. I completely forgot about that.

233

"Plus, the last thing I want is for my mother to spontaneously combust with excitement," he adds under his breath.

As if it could happen. Why would she get excited about me cooking her lunch?

And they say we girls exaggerate, Big Guy.

CHAPTER SEVENTEEN
Testing, Testing, One, Two, Three

Dreamland is hard to find, and when I almost reach it, it slips from my grasp. Thoughts of the test keep waking me up.

At five thirty in the morning, I give up and decide to get ready for the day. Sticking with my uniform in the hope it can provide me with the confidence and knowledge I need during the exam.

I stole Zach's bed for the night, and as I step out of the basement, the household remains quiet. Simply removing some of the furniture and adding a bed to the attic would solve my room issues, but according to Oliver and Zach, they still need to work on it.

In the kitchen, I inspect the fridge. The team didn't allow me to cook yesterday. Everybody insisted I needed to study. They're worse than Mrs. Johnson at St. Magdalene. Instead, they opted to order pizza for dinner.

Next time, I'll just make the pizza.

I cook a quick breakfast and work on their lunches, putting in different items to entice their appetite. I make a quick note to figure out what they like for future occasions. Meanwhile, I eat breakfast as well, knowing I need the energy to ace the tests.

Joy joins me first. She wears a white, button-down shirt with a red tie, a red cardigan, and a black, skater skirt. Her hair is tied in a high ponytail, and her face shows a light touch of makeup. She looks simple, yet sophisticated.

Over the last few days, I've noticed she may be small, but she can easily out eat any of the guys, including Kellan. As one of the greatest fans of my cooking, along with Archie, she's earned a special place in my heart.

Her face lights up the moment she notices the quesadillas, juice, coffee, and fruit available for everybody. When she notices the bags of food packed, each identified with the name of the final recipient, she chuckles.

"Thanks." She smiles and quickly puts the bag inside her backpack.

The rest come down, surprised when they find food already prepared.

Did they expect milk and cereal?

"Honey, you're too kind to us." Barb fills her bowl with fruit and hands one already overflowing to Kellan.

Her outfit matches Joy's, her loose hair styled to perfection.

On the other hand, Kellan wears black pants, a white, button-down shirt, and the same red tie. He carefully hangs his gray coat on one of the dining room chairs.

"Coffee! Me needs some!" Archie's zombie-like voice comes from the basement door.

When he opens it, he wears the same outfit as Kellan. He stretches, his wrinkled shirt raising to reveal his bellybutton, then runs his hand through his already messy hair.

Why does he remind me of an Archangel? Ha, easy. Because he's so darn cute.

"Archie, we need to discuss..." Lyra trails off as she steps into the kitchen, wearing what I assume is the Calvary uniform.

Her hair is styled in a French braid, while she hardly wears any makeup, except for some blush and lip gloss. But with her perfect complexion, it would be a crime to cover it up.

"Coffee first, arrangements later." Archie approaches the coffee pot, his blue eyes filled with sleep. "Or start planning on walking to school." He points a finger at all the people in the kitchen, stopping when he reaches me. His sleepy grin appears. "Except Samantha."

"Ugh! You're terrible." Lyra brings her hands up and quickly drops them. "Oh, quesadillas! Yum!" Her mood brightens. "I kill at cooking quesadillas."

"You mean you could kill us by cooking quesadillas,"

Archie corrects her under his breath, chuckling at his joke.

Kellan laughs while Barb mysteriously suffers from a coughing fit, drowning Archie's comment.

"Samantha also prepared a lunch bag for each of us." Joy points to the rest of the bags with her finger.

The kitchen goes silent. Awkward stares go from one person to another. Lyra picks up the bag with her name and checks its contents.

"Thanks, Samantha." Archie puts two quesadillas on his plate, and when he passes, he gives my hair a playful tug.

I leave them to their discussion, go downstairs to brush my teeth, and grab my backpack, making sure I packed all of Darcy's notes. With one final check of my simple ponytail and wardrobe, I head back upstairs.

Near the kitchen door, I stop to adjust one of my backpack straps and sigh when I identify the Saint Magdalene logo on it. A lot of changes in such a few days, and all of it this little sucker's fault.

What do you plan for me in the future, Big Guy?

"Don't take it the wrong way, but lunch bags? What are we, in kindergarten?" I pick up a female whisper coming from the other side, but I can't identify the speaker. "We'll look like dorks."

Ouch! Lesson learned. I won't make...

"I don't mind it. I'll be happy to take yours," Joy offers excitedly.

It seems I can trust Joy's appetite to be on my side.

"No! I want it. You already ate half of the quesadillas,"

Archie's grumpy voice flows through. "Ouch!"

"Too slow!" Joy chuckles.

"Either you hand it over, or you'll walk to school today!" Archie retaliates, his voice now fully alert, a sign of the caffeine kicking in or his hunger waking him up.

"Instead of fighting, you could share it!" Frustration fills Oliver's voice.

The kitchen falls silent.

"The two of you are asking for it!" Oliver orders. "See, sharing is caring," he adds after a few seconds, sounding relieved as he averted a crisis.

"Her half of the sandwich is bigger!" Archie complains.

"Are you a two-year-old, Archie?" Abigail's voice comes through. "Here, take my half of the sandwich if it makes you happy."

"Oh, I really appreciate... Ugh! Totally uncalled for, Abigail. Now, your cooties are all over it," Archie exclaims, disgusted. The rest laugh at Archie's words. "I don't want it anymore, and you'll definitely be walking."

"You could avoid it if you stopped behaving like a baby," she responds, laughing.

Oh, my, Big Guy! Abigail knows how to laugh and joke! Hallelujah!

When I enter the kitchen, everybody's spooning, drinking, or eating goes suspiciously quiet. After dropping my bag at the counter near the entrance, I return, make another sandwich, bag it, and hand it to Archie.

When he sees my offer, he crinkles his eyes, which

appear to shine. He happily takes it, and with a big grin, deposits it inside his backpack.

"You're spoiling him," Zach comments from the dining table. His lips twitch as he controls the urge to smile after watching our transaction.

"Technically, she's spoiling all of us," Kellan corrects Zach. "Especially our two toddlers." He points at Archie and Joy.

Joy doesn't seem amused and takes advantage of Kellan's distraction with a quick, smooth move as she steals the quesadilla from his plate. By the time he realizes his food disappeared, Joy already licked the whole thing.

Kellan shakes his head. "See? Completely immature."

I chuckle while I return the food to the fridge.

"Okay, team, we need to leave soon. We don't want to be late," Oliver says.

When I study him, I notice his clothes are different from the others. Instead, he wears gray pants, a white shirt, and a dark blue tie. To complete his sophisticated image, he added a pair of glasses. He comes across as polished.

Nothing like the guy who trained us yesterday.

"This is the plan. Samantha, I'll take you to the administration and admissions office, where there will be an interview with the principal. Afterward, you'll perform a series of tests. When you finish, you'll go to the library, where you'll spend the rest of the day," he instructs, gaze on me. I nod in acknowledgement. "I'd like to give you a cell phone to be able to reach you, or for you to contact us."

He retrieves a small box from the table and hands it over. My mouth falls open when I find a brand-new, state of the art cellphone inside with a charger and additional accessories.

When I imagined getting a cell phone, I knew it would be a basic one since I spend most of my allowance on dancing shoes or necessities. Handling such an extravagant piece of equipment scares me as I imagine the screen cracking by itself.

To my relief, a protective cover secures it. When I turn it over, I bite my lower lip from excitement as I study the picture of light-pink roses, and on top of them, a pair of pointed ballet shoes.

My mouth opens and closes like a fish while I struggle to find the proper words to thank them.

"We broke her again!" Samuel's voice comes from the entrance. "Whose fault is it this time?"

Until now, I hadn't realized he wasn't in the kitchen. I guess he slept at his mother's house, since he didn't come from the basement.

My breath catches at his manly face. His dark eyes, full of worry, stare at me. Like the rest, he wears the school uniform, but his beard makes him appear slightly older than Archie and Zach.

"Thank you," I whisper, returning my gaze to the phone. Not daring to continue touching it, I return it to the box, tempted to keep it there.

"All of our numbers are in there." Zach steps closer, takes it out, and unlocks it. He expertly moves through the icons, showing me where I can locate the information. "If you get in trouble or lost, just call one of us. We all carry our cell phones. But, during class, I would rather you text us, and only use it in emergency situations to avoid getting us in trouble, okay?"

I nod, not trusting my voice with my emotions all over the place, overwhelmed with technology.

"We also added text features. We downloaded a couple of games and music in case you got bored at the library." Archie joins us and points to the different icons.

"Okay." I nod.

"Now, moving to the next topic." Oliver changes the subject and turns to stare at Archie "Car arrangements?".

"Well, you need to drive to school alone. The rest of us will need to split into two cars." Archie sighs and glances at the table, stopping for a quick breath before he continues. "There shouldn't be any trouble getting there. The problem will be returning home with all of our hectic schedules."

"I want to take my car!" Lyra quickly raises her hand, interrupting Archie. "I don't want to stay longer waiting for the rest to finish their training."

"You only want an escape car to avoid our torture session," Archie corrects her.

She sticks her tongue at him, acknowledging he caught her alternate plan.

"I need my car in case of an emergency," Samuel mentions, earning more complaints from the rest.

Annoyed, Archie scratches the back of his head and

waits until everybody quiets down. "This is the deal. Zach will take his car and Samuel, Abigail, Samantha, and Joy will ride with him. We'll also take Barb's car because of the issue—"

"Assignment!" Barb corrects him, overflowing with excitement as she jumps up and down in her seat.

He rolls his eyes and frowns, before he continues with zero enthusiasm. "Because of the *assignment* Barb, Lyra, and I need to complete after school. Kellan can switch places with Samantha on the return trip."

Wow! I didn't know they included me in the assignment.

They continue eating their breakfast while Samuel steps into the kitchen, retrieves a travel mug from one of the cupboards, and pours the rest of the coffee into it. Quickly glancing at the empty plates, his face falls.

"Okay, time to go to school. Samuel, don't forget your goodie bag," Zach reminds him while bringing in the dirty dishes and placing them in the sink.

"Goodie bag? When did we get a goodie bag for school?" Samuel locates the bag with his name on it. He chuckles and immediately turns toward me. "Thanks, Samantha. You're a life saver."

He takes out one of the cookies and sinks his teeth into it.

I wish I were the cookie... What? Treacherous teenage hormones! I leave the kitchen before he catches my blush, which I desperately cover with my hands.

During the drive to school, Joy instructs me on how to

243

use the phone after she catches me attempting to turn it on without success.

When we arrive, I hand Darcy's notes to Zach, trusting he'll return them to her before classes begins. I quietly follow Abigail to the main office, sensing the stare of the other students on my back after we pass. Whispers fill the hall behind us.

"Who is she?"

"Ugh! Another one of their group!"

"Why is she wearing a different uniform?"

"She seems younger."

"She's cute."

"Why does she walk like a duck?"

"Ignore them," Abigail advises me, her head held high with confidence. "Don't look frightened, Samantha. They don't bite."

Ignore them? Easy for you to say.

To her, they might be kids. To me, they're my peers. Some are even older than me. Plus, she's used to meeting new people and talking to boys.

I feel like I entered the twilight zone.

Straightening my back, I walk next to Abigail, trying to convey confidence and hoping I manage to transmit at least half what she does.

The moment we arrive at the office, I thank the Big Guy for secluding me in an area away from the other students' eyes.

"Wait here." Abigail points to a seat outside while she walks to the secretary, joining Oliver's side, who was already waiting for us.

I drop my backpack at my feet and take one of the school brochures located on the table next to where I sit. Reviewing it, I'm surprised at how big the school is. Calvary, unlike Saint Magdalene, is an expensive, private school. White marble covers the floors and the walls are wood paneled. A pricey, state of the art board displays the school announcements. I restrain myself from going to the hall to check if the lockers function with a retina scanner and fingerprint pad as a security measure.

The map shows the office as a small dot compared to the rest of the building. I memorize the layout, identifying the library, cafeteria, bathrooms, classrooms, auditorium, and computer lab. I give particular attention on the big dance studio located at the far end of the north building. Unfortunately, I notice a humongous, inside pool near the studio.

Note to self, avoid it at all cost.

"Samantha Melbourne?" the receptionist calls.

I glance up to find her focus on me and put the map inside my backpack before I stand. "Yes?"

"They're waiting for you." She nods to the open office door.

Dread makes my stomach drop. "Thank you."

I walk into the office to find Zach, Oliver, and Abigail inside, in seats near the entrance. A middle-aged man with thinning, salt and pepper hair sits behind a desk, an empty chair in front of it. The man's mustache softens his severe nose. His light-blue eyes analyze me from head to toe, and as expected, he then studies Abigail.

Yeah, yeah, I know.

Luckily, he doesn't say anything as he stands and walks over to me, offering his hand. "Good morning, Samantha. My name is Peter Stinson."

I move my backpack farther up my shoulders, take his hand, and shake it. His grip is strong and firm without being hurtful.

"Nice to meet you, Mr. Stinson," I reply, dropping my hand in the first instant I sense he opens his.

"You make me sound like my Grandfather. Please, call me Peter," he corrects me with a chuckle.

O-o-okay?

"Now, please, everyone take a seat. We need to discuss your current situation." Once he sits, he pulls a file closer to him. I take the open chair, dropping my backpack on the floor. "I understand you didn't participate in the Phoenix program?"

I nod.

He opens the file and quickly scans it, going through each page, laughing at some of the notes while nodding at others.

"You little rebel! Drunk driving at the age of eight?" He fixes his eyes on me with an amused, yet stern, expression, and shakes his head.

Oliver chuckles behind me.

It seems the eggnog incident will follow me to my grave. But come on! It only happened once, and I blame Sister Josie for letting me taste it. How was I supposed to know there was alcohol in it?

At eight and learning how to cook, I wanted to guess the ingredients and stole more than one sip, disregarding the lightheaded sensation. Besides, who could blame me if I decided to go on a bicycle ride afterward with my judgment and coordination impaired by my intoxicated state? At the moment, the main church aisle seemed to be the perfect bike track, and although I agree my timing wasn't the best. I interrupted the nuns during prayer time with my fabulously out of tune performance of *Ode to Joy* while riding. My presentation was cut short by the wall at the other end of the church.

Again, sorry, Big Guy! But I'll bet You laughed Your heart out at my ungraceful dismount. I know Sister Josie still does.

Mr. Stinson continues his review. Stopping at the last page, his eyebrows rise and he flips back and forth between other documents.

I'll bet Brittany would hate to know how many people review my handiwork of her face.

"What I need to understand, Samantha, is the incident from last Friday." He closes my file, placing his hand under his chin and focusing his attention on me.

Not brave enough to meet his eyes, I divert my gaze to my feet where the guilty perpetrator innocently lays.

I sigh.

My backpack.

"I did not cheat," I respond, not wanting to elaborate on the whole ordeal.

"It says here the name of the unanswered test was

yours and vice versa. How can you explain it?"

"She switched our names." I shrug, replaying in my mind the dreadful minute when she did it.

"You can understand why I might feel a little skeptical?" he asks, not convinced by my explanation.

"You can perform a test on the subject and confirm if she tells the truth," Zach proposes.

"She already had all weekend to prepare for it," Mr. Stinson counters.

Oliver steps closer and glances over Mr. Stinson's shoulder. "Samantha, can you please write your name on a piece of paper?" Oliver asks, studying the file.

Everybody becomes quiet. Mr. Stinson hands me a piece of paper and a pen. Confused, but wanting to obey, I follow Oliver's request.

Without a lot of effort, I write Samantha C. Melbourne and hand it over to Oliver.

He takes the paper and places it next to the file. His eyes widen in excitement. "She's not lying. The handwriting might be similar, but if you focus on the test with her name, the 'a' seems more oval, and the line that crosses the *T* is longer. Plus, the capital *S* has this strange swirl at the end. She didn't use that right now."

Zach and Abigail come closer to compare the copy of the test with the piece of paper I used, confirming Oliver's analysis.

"Oh, that's correct. And did you notice how the 'C' tilts a little more toward the left?" Mr. Stinson adds, earning an approving nod from Oliver.

"Samantha's telling the truth." Zach raises one eyebrow smugly.

Told ya!

"Then, I believe I can put the pieces together of what happened after." Mr. Stinson focuses on me. "You punched the girl because she stole your test. Although, I don't fully approve of the method, I like the fact you stood up for yourself."

Well, technically, I stumbled on my backpack, but whatever rocks your boat, Mr. Stinson. His version of the story is much better than the pathetic reality.

"Then, I believe we can proceed with the next part of the admission process. Oliver, if you could please direct Samantha to Admissions, she can take the tests. Zach and Abigail, I'll give you a permission slip to avoid any problems with your teachers when you return to class."

He pulls a note from a block and writes on it.

"If you run into any trouble, Samantha, please contact me." Mr. Stinson stands and stretches his hand out once more.

"Nice to meet you, Mr. Stinson," I say, stopping when he pulls his eyebrow together and shakes his head. "Sorry...Peter."

He grins after I make the correction, letting go of my hand.

"Let's go, Samantha." Oliver opens the door for us. He extends his hand through it, indicating I should go first.

I grab my backpack, wave goodbye to Abigail and

Zach, and leave the office.

CHAPTER EIGHTEEN
Making Bets

After a series of aptitude tests, I hope my torture is over.

No such luck, though, as the tests keep coming. Math, Physics, Science, Chemistry, History, English – a never-ending parade of knowledge displayed on different pieces of papers, challenging my long-term memory.

By the time I finish, I'm completely drained.

In the final one, English, I get the impression they designed it to verify whether or not I cheated. It's harder than the one at Saint Magdalene, but getting a good grade on it will seal the deal and validate my reputation... At least as far as tests go. There's still the whole drunken incident… And the violence…

When I hand over the last test, a sense of relief washes over me. I put in my best effort.

"We will review the scores and work on a schedule based on your results." The counselor points to the chair in front of her desk. "We need to include one language and two extra classes."

As she waits expectantly for my answer, my heart plummets.

Saint Magdalene never encouraged languages. They only offered one on special occasions at a basic level.

"Spanish," I reply, hoping there's still room in the class. "I've taken a rudimentary course, but don't know it very well."

I hope she doesn't want to test my current knowledge. My fried brain is ready to rebel if I torture it with more information.

Especially in Spanish!

"All right." She grins, writing down the information on my file. "Now, we need an elective. We offer debate, robotics, chess, astronomy, sewing—"

"Somebody told me you offer cooking classes," I interrupt, happier.

"Are you sure?" She narrows her eyes and tilts her head to one side, taken aback by my suggestion. "Most kids enroll, believing they'll get an easy A, but soon discover their mistake."

I nod, confident.

"It will be up to Mrs. O'Flannagan to accept you," she

warns.

Oh! I firmly think Mrs. O'Flannagan will. I chuckle when she writes the information in my file, her eyebrow lifting as if to say, *'You dug your own grave, girl.'*

"Now, about the extracurricular activities. For sport, we offer track, soccer, baseball, tae kwon do, swimming—" I shake my head wildly at the last option. "I believe most of the coaches will be happy for you to join their team based on your siblings' record."

"Thank you, but I like arts better," I respond, guessing ballet classifies as a sport and art.

"Oh!" She straightens in surprised disbelief. I guess Zach and Abigail aren't artistic at all. The counselor reads a list from a piece of paper she removed from her binder. "Well, we offer drawing, poetry, creative writing, band, and theater."

The one class I expect to hear, she skips. I keep quiet, hoping she continues or realizes her mistake. When she stays silent, I stare at her in confusion.

"In the school brochure, it mentioned dancing?" I raise my eyebrows, tempted to pull the piece of paper out of my backpack to show her the proof.

She sighs and shakes her head.

"I could probably put you in introductory level of ballet." She searches through one of her piles of paper, pulling out the information.

Introductory level?

"My brother told me about the excellent ballet program," I encourage her to tell me more about it. "I've been dancing ballet for some time."

She stops her search and faces me with a long, slow sigh.

"Sorry, but the class is full," the counselor explains. "Plus, to be accepted, you need to audition."

Full? And perform an audition? My heart drops to my stomach.

"Auditions closed three weeks ago," she adds, further sinking my hopes.

Oh, nuts! *Big Guy, how about a little help?*

"You can always ask Monsieur Pietro for an opportunity, considering your situation." She kindly offers. "But, I wouldn't get my hopes up."

She continues her search through the pile of papers as if her explanation settled the discussion.

"But, I can ask?" I repeat.

She stops, turns to face me, and her face pulls into a hard smile. "Samantha, positions were already limited, even at the beginning of the school year, and the audition process is difficult. You'll need a miracle to get in."

Are You onboard, Big Guy? I bet You won't let me down.

I straighten my spine, determined. "I'll give it a try."

~

After my meeting with the counselor, she takes me to the library, where I need to wait for Barb to come and get me. The whole ordeal took longer than I expected, but now, alone in the quiet library, I find myself utterly bored.

Of course, I can go through the books and occupy my mind by reading, but I don't want to get hooked on a story only to be pulled away in the middle without the possibility of taking it home with me.

The answer to my dilemma lies within reach. The phone!

Well, they did say I could entertain myself.

I dial the number I know by heart, but hardly ever call.

"Saint Magdalene, how may I help you?" the new receptionist answers.

She started working this year, and as Sister Agatha refers to her, she's a scatter brain. I doubt she'll recognize my voice.

"Hello, may I speak with Sister Josie?" I ask, longing to speak to my old friend. Even though it's only been a couple of days, I miss her demanding nature.

"One moment, please," the receptionist responds and puts me on hold.

Several minutes pass with an obnoxious song playing in the background. When the line finally picks up, I hear movement and questions from the other end.

"Are you aware it's almost lunch time?" Sister Josie's strident voice comes from the other end.

"Yes, Sister, but..." the receptionist answers, her voice nervous.

"Who's calling me?" Sister Josie demands.

"Huh?" the receptionist responds.

"Ugh. Never mind, you don't know squat."

"This is Sister Josie," she answers more calmly, which

means she's not happy.

My eyes immediately fill with tears, picturing her stern face. "Hi, Sister. Sorry for calling at such a terrible time."

"Samantha, what took you so long to call me, you ungrateful child?" she replies, laughing on the other end, her bad mood disappearing. "Are you aware how terrible things are in the kitchen without you around? I thought I died and went to hell."

I grin at the peculiar way she expresses her concern. "Sister, I am sorry—"

"Oh, no! You don't apologize. I know the whole story," the nun interrupts, determined.

"What?" I ask. "How do you know it? I never told anybody about it."

"I've known you since you were a little girl, and I know Miss Murphy. Not a great mystery there," she responds. "It took long enough for someone to stand up to her."

"I hit her. I don't consider the way things..." I hold back a chuckle.

"Excellent, my little darling! Can I get a swing when she returns?" Amusement fills her voice.

I muffle my laughter with my hand, picturing the oldest nun in the convent punching Brittany. "But, you're a nun! You're here to do the Lord's work, and to avoid viol—"

"Exactly! I wish Mother Superior agreed," she responds, cutting me off. "We need to kick the little devil out of this school. She continues corrupting the rest of the girls. All our good work is for nothing with such a terrible influence around." She laughs and immediately whispers, "I plan to gang up the whole convent, but don't whisper a thing to Mother Superior until all the nuns agree with me."

Brittany never gave Sister Josie credit, calling her Sister Senile. If anyone can manage a revolution, it's her, the little rebel nun.

I laugh, earning some ugly glares from the librarian.

"You listen to me, child. When she returns, she will find out why nobody messes with the cook," she chuckles maniacally. "Her taste buds will learn what hell tastes like."

Big Guy, hold the reins on this one. She could get away with murder since no jury in their right mind would find her guilty. I should count my blessings to be far away from Saint Magdalene when this happens.

We only talk for a couple more minutes since she needed to leave to attend lunch time, and I ask her to send my regards to the rest of the nuns. I return my phone to my backpack, and notice the library filled up while I was distracted.

It seems it's also lunch time here.

Trying to avoid unwanted attention, I move to the farthest table. Taking out a notebook, I work on this week's menus, making notes of the ingredients I'll need to order. I get distracted when a guy and girl come near my remote table. They don't seem to notice me; the girl glances at the boy in what I assume is a flirtatious manner, smiling at him and encouraging him to follow her. She walks to the last bookshelf and disappears into the farthest row. The guy turns to where the librarian sits, takes advantage of her distraction, and follows the girl.

I may be inexperienced in anything involving romance, but I can identify kissing sounds. I turn my attention back to my list, but find it hard to concentrate, the noises and giggles constantly interrupting me. I abandon the table for one closer to the librarian, hoping with more distance I won't overhear them.

Wrong!

The giggles become louder, gaining the librarian's attention. She runs in the direction of where the couple disappeared.

Busted!

She returns with the pair trailing a couple of steps behind her. When she quietly chastises them, they don't seem to mind. Instead, they intertwine their hands and keep glancing at each other, holding back laughter.

When I return my attention to my list, I find Barb standing at the other side of the table, a phone with a purple case in her hand.

"Why did we give you a phone if you don't intend to pick it up?" she whispers with a grin on her lips.

I immediately jump and find it in the backpack, noticing the three missed phone calls.

"Sorry!" I pick up my notes and stuff them, together with my phone, into the backpack. "How did you find me?"

"Oliver mentioned you would be here after the test," she informs me while I get to my feet. She wiggles her eyebrows playfully. "Plus, the GPS app on it helps."

What is a GPS app?

"Are you ready?" she asks excitedly once we leave the library.

"For what exactly?" So far, nobody explained what we'll be doing.

"We're going on a field trip, darling." She walks faster through the empty halls.

Yes, that still doesn't answer any of my questions.

"Field trip?" I ask as we approach the school entrance.

"You'll see." She tugs my hand when we reach the door.

When we open it, the sun momentarily blinds me. My hand flies to my forehead to protect my eyes. Once they adjust, I see a sparkling, brand new red Audi car waiting at the curb with Archie in the driver's seat and Lyra in the back with another, unknown figure inside.

The guy who climbs out appears to be around Oliver's age, around half a head taller than me. He wears a flashy purple dress shirt and gray pants. The only way he could style his hair the way he wears it is by using a blow dryer. His piercing green eyes stand out as he critically analyzes me from head to toe.

"Archie, I understand what you mean by a fucking fashion emergency!" His foul language comes as a surprise, since it doesn't match with his polished appearance or the way he carries himself. "Definitely one of the shittiest outfits created by man."

He scrunches his nose as if my garments stink.

Two Hail Mary's in one phrase.

"Excuse me!" My eyes widen with hurt. I wore this uniform for the past twelve years, for five out of seven days of the week. "I believe it's a practical design!"

His face lights up at pulling such a vivid reaction from me.

"Practical if you plan to visit fucking Ireland and hunt for some damn Leprechauns in the sky." He walks over and circles around me, furrowing his brow while his finger touches his lip.

Four Hail Mary's!

"A complete eyesore. First thing on the agenda, removing this thing from your persona. Trust me, I'll be doing you a favor. I swear this rash appeared because I dared to set my eyes upon such shitty fabric." As if on cue, he scratches one of his arms and steps closer to Barb to show her his so-called allergic reaction.

Seven Hail Mary's!

My cussing sensor overloads. I bite my lower lip to hold my tongue against arguing back.

"We need to get started, Edward. We'll need to purchase a whole new wardrobe, darling." Barb urges him toward the car, pulling his arm. "And fast. She needs to be somewhere later in the afternoon."

Shopping trip? Was this the mission they kept discussing at breakfast?

"You need a fucking wardrobe and a kick ass haircut." Edward removes his arm from Barb and steps closer to me, his eyes traveling the length of my ponytail.

"No!" I grab ahold of my hair and sidestep him to climb into the car.

He holds the door for Barb, and once she's inside, he closes it and joins me in the backseat. Archie immediately steps on the accelerator.

"A few, simple cuts here and there and voila! Once I finish, all the fucking girls will want to be you." He changes his approach, reaching for my ponytail, his finger twitching with anticipation.

I slap his hand when it nears me.

Amused, he pulls back.

"I like my hair the way it is," I tell him with determination. "And please stop swearing." I don't want to spend all night praying ten rosaries because of his language.

"No. Fucking. Way!" He laughs and claps a couple times. "Archie, I believe we'll spend a fucking long time cracking this nut out of her shell. Who wants to bet I can get her to say a bad word before our shopping trip comes to an end?"

"I'm not fucking betting against you." Archie chortles.

Not you, too, Archie! Twelve Hail Mary's. I swear my ears will bleed at any moment now.

"Barb? Lyra?" Edward asks, tugging Barb's hair. She shakes her head, and he focuses on Lyra.

"I'm not betting against you," she answers, the same as Archie.

"Come on. I need something to fucking entertain

myself, after all those longs hours I dedicated designing the costumes for diva Pierre." Edward crosses his arms and pouts his lips like a small child as he slumps down in his seat.

Oh, Lord. Thirteen!

"I'll take the bet." I bravely accept the challenge, and his green eyes come alive.

The car becomes quiet, the engine accelerating the only sound to disrupt the silence.

"If I win, I get to give you a fucking haircut," Edward threatens, with a Cheshire smile. "By the time I finish with you, you'll be thanking me and begging for me to return. Once styled by Quinn, you will never return to whatever crappy hairstylist you had before. Right, Barb?"

Sister Theresa would hate to know they refer to her in such a manner. Plus, I don't want a haircut. The length of my hair is a quick way to tell me apart from Abigail. Besides, it's taken me forever to get it like this.

"Hell, yeah!" she says with her southern accent, turning her head from her front seat to glance at us.

Oh, Barb, not you, too.

"If I win—" I stop to ponder my options. Since we just met, I don't know what he could offer. "You get to help me with something in the future."

Sounds safe enough.

The car becomes utterly quiet. His gaze goes straight to Lyra, who shrugs, then diverts back to me. His eyes fix on my hair, and he bites his lower lip, frowning as if it taunts him.

"Jesus Fucking Christ, fine. You got yourself a goddamn deal," he responds, excited by the new challenge. He stretches his hand out to me, which I gladly accept.

What number of Hail Mary was I on? Oh, nuts! *Is this one of Your tests, Big Guy?* Never mind. Simply give me the strength to hold my tongue, keep my hair the length I want, and survive this shopping trip.

CHAPTER NINETEEN
I Am Sixteen Going On...Twelve?

After a couple of hours spent with Edward, I gave up on counting the quantity of Hail Mary's, since the short drive to the mall earned me five rosaries.

However, I understand the use of his foul language is part of his personality and a way to express himself, like a dancer using prompts to embellish a dance. His words weren't meant to insult or wish an ill fate on anyone. Which means that while I don't necessarily condone it, and I haven't gotten used to it, in Edward's case I will ignore it.

At first, he makes me feel like a laboratory mouse with the way he critically studies my body. I never explain to him I dance ballet. He guesses it on his own. After that discovery, he started referring to me as Twinkle Toes.

"Barb, damn it! How many times do I need to tell you, she's not Abigail!" Edward shouts from the other side of the dressing room door.

We began our shopping trip in the undergarments section, where Barb barged into the dressing room to confirm the fit of the underwear. Something I did not find amusing. Well, I should count my blessings. At least it was her and Edward trusted her judgment, stopping him from performing the inspection personally.

After, we toured different department areas before they stuffed me into a stall to try things on, and I've now been playing dress up for the last two hours.

"Well, the color works darn perfect on her. It should be the same for Samantha as well," Barb responds.

"Oh, well then, fuck it! Don't ask for my shitty opinion. You already have fucking Thing One, so let's dress Thing Two up the same and have them fucking parading around as little crappy clones," he argues back furiously.

In my mind, I picture him throwing his arms up, one step closer to pulling his styled hair out of his head.

"I don't look like her!" I shout as I try on what seems like the hundredth outfit of the day.

"I know, Twinkle Toes. She doesn't have those killer legs and helpful attitude. Her style doesn't compliment you." He puts another new batch of clothes to try at the top of the dressing room door. "She likes to be more sporty and tomboyish. Unlike you, who likes more delicate and fucking girly things."

"Then I should dress her more like me?" Barb asks.

"What the fuck!? Don't twist my words, Barbara," Edward answers, annoyed. "Your coloring and hers are opposite, and your style wouldn't compliment her."

"I don't get it! You said girly!" she complains. "I'm girly! All of us are."

"Yes. But there are different kinds of girly. You like modern and sophisticated, Lyra loves preppy, Abigail adores edgy, Joy, well... I can't find a definition for her fashion," he explains. "Samantha needs something more approachable and classy."

"Oh! I think I know what you mean. Be right back then." Barb's tone changes to an awed one, as if the great mystery of life just revealed itself to her, with the quick order to go and get yet another big pile of clothes.

"Can we take a break? I'm starving!" Lyra whines from the chair where she sits.

It's obvious Barb and Edward enjoy dolling me up, but for Archie, Lyra, and I, this is equivalent to a form of torture.

"Next time, keep your goodie bag," Archie mentions merrily.

Oh! Then it was Lyra who didn't want to take the lunch bag this morning, afraid to look like a dork.

A bag crinkles, and I picture Archie taking out the sandwich I made and biting into in front of Lyra, taunting her.

"Ugh! Are we done yet?" Lyra complains for the ninth

time.

"No, we still need footwear, coats, and gym clothes." Barb's voice sounds muffled and soon enough another pile of clothes appears at the top of my dressing room door.

"Jesus! Smite me now!" Archie says, making me chuckle.

Big Guy, if You smite him, can we avoid trying on the rest of the clothes in respect of his memory?

Probably not. Edward and Barb will make me try on clothes for his funeral. There's no winning in either situation.

Okay, then, let's keep Archie the archangel then.

I step out of the small cubicle wearing the seventh pair of tapered jeans, a nice, light-pink shirt with a white scarf wrapped around my neck, and a tan blazer on top.

The argument dies, and all attention focuses on me, their eyes scanning the items, reviewing the fit. Archie's jaw drops, Lyra's eyebrow raises, Barb gives a small ecstatic clap, and Edward finally gives me an approving nod.

"Well, about fucking time, there it is," he says triumphantly. "Can you see it, Barb?"

She nods with an excited, wide grin on her face. "Classic casual with a tinge of street chic it is, using the lighter colors of the season's tones."

Big Guy, I know they're speaking English, but whatever they said, my mind only translated to nice outfit.

Lucky for me, the pile of clothes gets reduced significantly after that. The pieces I try suit me better, each new outfit encouraging me to try on the next one after I receive more compliments. However, as I pass back the last outfit and change into my own clothes, my main concern shifts to how I'll pay for all these items, since I don't have a dime on me, much less a credit card.

I step outside of my cubicle and find a lack of clothes and people. About to search for everyone, I stop from exiting the dressing room when I hear Barb's voice from nearby. Should I stay in here? She might bring me another set of outfits to try on.

I stay put.

"How are things at home, Barb?" Edward asks in a lower tone, probably not intending for me to overhear.

"Mommy's still being her old, snobby self, my sister's still dating a gold digging asshole, and Daddy, well, he still calls me from time to time." Fake joy suffuses her voice. "But, you know, I'd do anything for Kellan."

"Glad to know you two are still strong," Edward says with a softer tone.

"He's the love of my life, plus the rest of the guys and girls help," she replies, a little happier. "But I still miss them."

"I know you don't like it when others criticize your family, but you need to realize how fucked up they are. Get on with the times, people! Welcome to the twenty-first century for crying out loud," Edward exclaims. "Kellan's a fucking gentleman and practically saved you from that shitty situation with your ex. He's smart, caring, and loves the heck out of you. If they can't get past the color of his skin and still prefer the fucker who got you in trouble in the first place, who's gray matter inside his head equals zero and who planned to piggyback ride his way to your family's money, then I say good fucking riddance. You're better off without them."

Never in a million years did I imagine the situation Barb faces. She always seems polished and perfect, with an open manner and a hopeful heart. Even if Kellan seems more reserved, he also welcomed me to the group with open arms.

She chuckles. "Angela told me those exact same words when the shit hit the fan."

My heart strings tug listening to someone's memory of my Grams. Yeah, I can picture Grams giving the same advice to Barb and Kellan, minus the bad wording.

"Always rooting for us and helping us get through when my family turned their backs on me. She liked to refer to our situation as a modern version of Romeo and Juliet and cheered us to re-write the terrible ending Shakespeare gave to the story," Barb continues.

"I completely agree with her, and you'll see, things will work out in the end. So, keep up the good work," Edward says. "Now, speaking of Abigail's family, where the fuck is Twinkle Toes?"

Nuts! I don't want them to catch me eavesdropping.

I run toward the nearest mirror, pretending to study my reflection, totally unaware of the conversation that passed between them. After a moment, my attention actually catches on my clothes and I tug at my skirt. No matter how many times I see it, I don't understand why Edward insists my uniform is an eyesore.

"Damn it, Twinkle Toes! What the fuck? We went through this whole shitty ordeal to get you some kickass clothes, and you still return to your goddamn rags?" Edward scolds me when he comes back into the dressing room.

"Old habits die hard," I try to explain myself.

"Don't give me shit. Now, put on something decent and hand them over." He points toward the dressing room, his nose once again scrunching in disgust. "I will make the fucking earth a better place by disposing of these eyesores."

"What will I wear?" I cross my arms, determined to get a clear answer since I don't plan on walking out of here naked, no matter how nice my new undergarments are.

Nu-uh. Not going to happen.

He rolls his eyes, steps out, and immediately returns with a new ensemble, minus the price tags. "Now, no fucking excuses. Go back and change."

Hoping this will be the last time, I stomp my way back to the dressing room. When I come out, Edward forces me to hand over my uniform. He takes it and drops it in the first trashcan he finds.

We then locate Barb who waits for us with a mountain of shopping bags at her side. She bounces with excitement. "Now, time to try some footwear!"

"Wait, Barb, who will pay for these clothes?" I stop myself from popping the knuckles in my hand while my stomach knots itself with guilt.

"Don't you worry your pretty head. Our sponsor won't notice the small dent in his bank account with our shopping trip," she tells me happily.

What sponsor? And what does she mean with a dent in his account?

"No, Barb, honestly, I can't afford all these items," I object, the stress hitting me harder when I catch my reflection in a mirror with the new outfit I have on.

"And I say don't worry about it. Daddy won't mind. He'll be happy to know I can still count on him every now and then." She gives a small smile that doesn't reach her eyes.

I bite my lip to stop myself from asking her to expand on her explanation. I need to let her be the one to open up to me, not force the answers out of her.

The moment her eyes fall upon the shoe area, her expression changes to complete happiness.

"Welcome to my little piece of shopping heaven," she comments with a chirp, overflowing with emotions.

I don't understand her fuss. They're only shoes. How can someone get excited by them?

"We need to get the basics. Sneakers, flats, boots, and a couple of..." Barb speaks quickly, her eyes traveling from one table to the next, locating the displays we need. "Oh! Look at these beauties!" Stopping, she grabs a pair of ankle boots, her hand slowly moving the pair from one side to the other.

Her hand runs through the small heel, appreciating the

quality of it. She then turns them over, checks the size, and hands them to me. She continues moving through the aisles, grabbing and giving me more and more shoes until I put my foot down. I drop the boxes, and sit to try them on, choosing a pair of flats first.

"Nope, try this one. I want to check your posture and stride with heels," Edward explains, swapping the shoes out of my grasp. "I want to confirm if the duck stride still exists with them on."

Reluctantly, I put on a pair with a small heel, which he calls kitten heels. When I stand, I find it hard to walk in them, not used to the extra height and the change in equilibrium. My ankles threaten to twist.

"Fuck! Twinkle Toes, next time give me a warning about your high heel virginity." He laughs, and my face heats up at his words and attitude. "First rule, which also applies to regular walking, heel to toe and not on your toes. It will give you more balance."

Following his advice, I immediately notice the difference. However, in order for it to come naturally, I need to force myself to walk the way he instructed. It will take time to adjust, but I know I can do it.

"Now, your strides will be shorter. Put one foot in front of the other," he shows me.

I follow his instructions.

"See, now, the movement of your hips looks more natural than your previous duck walk. But try not to exaggerate your hip movement. It attracts the wrong fucking crowd." He tilts his head to one side, telling me to discreetly turn in that direction.

When I do, I notice a group of guys, probably around their mid-twenties, staring at us.

"Then, I shouldn't do it?" I ask.

"Not unless you want to attract unwanted attention," he turns his head in another direction and chuckles.

One of the guys in front of us smirks at me and gives me a thumbs up.

How sweet of him. He encouraged me to continue practicing.

Trying to get used to this new stride without breaking my ankles, I continue walking, ignoring the guy in front.

"Those shoes look beautiful on you," he praises, approaching me.

"Thank you," I respond timidly, not daring to meet his eye for fear of activating the mute system. I might feel more in control with the guys at home, but strangers still represent a problem.

"Are you lost?" I hear one of the guys step closer to me.

"Uhm," I manage to say, searching for Edward so he can rescue me. But he abandoned me to my fate, and now sits with Archie. Both keep an eye on me, their eyebrows raised while they enjoy this new development.

"Because heaven is a long way from here," he replies.

What?

"Okay," I whisper, moving farther away from him, and continue walking in the opposite direction, practicing walking on heels and ignoring the crazy guy in the hope he doesn't follow me.

After all, practice makes perfect.

"Hi!" Another fellow, this one easier on the eye, approaches me. "Excuse me, are you religious?"

His question takes me by surprise.

"Yes," I respond, "I'm Catholic..."

"Cause you're the answer to all my prayers," he comments, stepping closer.

Archie and Edward laugh their hearts out, one of them stomping his feet, while the other grabs the sides of his stomach, bent over in laughter. Meanwhile, I don't know how to react, practically stunned into silence.

"I certainly doubt I am." I sidestep him and walk away.

Returning to my seat, I continue to try on the shoes Barb picked for me. I dare to put on another pair of high heels and try to walk. With all of my attention on not falling, I don't notice as another guy from the group comes to stand in front of me.

"Didn't we take a class together?" he asks.

Twelve years in an all-girl Catholic school. Definitely not. But since Abigail and I look alike...

I respond seriously. "You might be confusing me with my s—"

"I could've sworn we had chemistry together," he answers with a wide grin.

Archie and Edward howl with laughter, attracting the attention of other shoppers.

"No, we didn't," I say and return to where Archie and

Edward sit, my cheeks heating up. I sit to remove the pair of shoes. "What 's so funny?"

"You are," Archie manages to say between laughs. He wipes away a tear.

"Am I making a fool out of myself?" I ask, mortified.

Did my stride evolve to a chicken now, instead of a human?

"Nope, they fucking are," Edward nods to where the group of guys stand. He hands me over a pair of skyscraper, light tan high heels. "Try these ones, Twinkle Toes."

"You want me to break my neck," I comment.

"No, you won't. Just take it slow," Edward instructs.

When I put on the shoes, I immediately notice the difference in my feet. I stand and continue practicing on my small catwalk.

"Did it hurt?" another one of the guys asks, stepping closer.

Confused, I glance at him. I know this isn't my usual stride, and the shoes feel different, but I'm not in obvious pain.

"Did what hurt?" I ask, annoyed.

"When you fell from heaven," he replies, almost closing the gap between us.

Wow. Apparently, nobody explained to this guy what personal space means. And, did he just imply I'm Satan?

"Samantha! We need to take these boots, one in tan and the other in..." Barb stops talking when she notices the guy in front of me. "Hello? How may I help you?"

The guy glances at Barb, and his lips widen.

"I wanted to ask your friend if she would like to join me for coffee," he explains. "Or dinner, perhaps?"

Barb turns her head, raising her eyebrows. Once again, I remain speechless, since the guy never mentioned his offer to me. Barb immediately nods and returns her attention to the guy.

"How sweet of you, sir, but my friend's not interested," she kindly explains with a forced smile, but her tone gives finality to her answer. She gently pulls my arm, putting some distance between the guy and us. "Hun, we need to get these two boots in different colors. They will work fantastic with skirts, leggings, and jeans."

Grateful for the rescue, I follow her.

As soon as we're out of earshot, she stops and faces Archie and Edward. "Care to explain the situation?"

"We only wanted to check out how cheesy their pickup lines were," Archie explains, trying to look serious.

Pickup lines?

"They only asked me about my religion, classes, and my well-being," I explain. "I never got the impression they…"

Barb's hand flies to her forehead.

"Hun, I don't know about the previous ones, but the last one asked you out less than a minute ago," she patiently explains. The chuckles from Edward and Archie bring her attention to them. "And you two are supposed to watch her."

"I'm here as a fucking consultant," Edward corrects

her, amused.

"I was here watching her," Archie comments, unable to restrain his laughter. "So, technically, I comply with my job."

She rolls her eyes and shakes her head. "Where's Lyra? She should be here babysitting the two of you."

"Abigail asked us to pick something up from home," he responds.

"And you didn't offer?" she asks, full of surprise.

"Obviously, I did! But, she won at rock, paper, scissors," he answers, deflated.

"Well, we're almost done. I can purchase the rest of the items later on," Barb tells me with a little disappointment. "We'll take those black flats and those tan ones. The gorgeous boots for obvious reasons! These boots, too, and let's not forget those sneakers." She points at the shoes.

Archie and Edward stand and pick them up, placing them in their boxes. They put them on the counter, and Edward returns with the tan flats.

"Here, Twinkle Toes, wear this pair," he hands them over. "And let us fucking burn the other ones."

After putting them on, I eye the group of guys who keep watching me.

How was I supposed to know they were pickup lines? They sounded innocent and good-natured.

"Ignore those fuckers. They had a bet on who could get your number first," Edward explains as if reading my mind.

"It was all a game?" I ask.

"Oh, they did seem interested, Twinkle Toes!" Edward slips his arm around mine and pulls me closer, away from the group. "You did fucking encourage them with the lovely smile and the whole walking up and down the aisle with the hip moving action. If I didn't know you, I would believe you were flirting with them."

My hand flies to my mouth. "I never intended to."

"Well, you sure as hell fooled them. Innocence mixed with beauty can be a lousy combination," he says with a sigh. "Trouble finds you."

I sense the change of mood. "Is that another pickup line?"

He gives me a chop on the head.

Ouch!

"My heart already found its rightful owner," he confesses. "Lesson number one, a compliment doesn't always equal a fucking romantic interest. I'll repeat myself for the idea to get through your head. Beauty and innocence don't mix well together, got it kiddo?"

Kiddo? What gives him the right to chastise me? He barely crossed the twenty-year mark. Not a whole lot of age difference, unlike Sister Josie.

"I'm sixteen!" I defend myself.

"Age is only a fucking number, Twinkle Toes. I'm twenty-four, probably going on thirty," he chuckles. "You're sixteen going on twelve."

Sixteen going on twelve!

"Hey!" I reply, my ego complaining at his hurtful

words.

"Who's twelve?" Archie returns with the bags of shoes.

"Twinkle Toes," Edward responds.

"Oh, no! She sure as hell is sixteen." He smirks and winks at me.

"And, he's twenty going on ten," Edward states as if making his point.

Archie sticks out his tongue and then pulls a face at Edward, making me giggle and proving Edward's point.

"Lyra texted me. She already arrived," Barb informs us after paying for the shoes, interrupting the conversation. "We should take the bags to the car and continue. We still need to make another couple of stops before dropping Samantha elsewhere." She motions for us to follow her, pointing to the nearest exit from the store.

Elsewhere?

"Can we get lunch first?" My tummy rumbles as I catch up with her inside the mall. After all, the goodie bag can only go so far, and with all the walking, dressing, and undressing, my energy levels are low.

"Sure." She nods. "Right after we search for a coat and sports clothing."

"Oh, darn!" The word escapes my mouth, barely a whisper, and my hands immediately fly to my mouth.

Archie's arm stretches to block my way, forcing me to halt abruptly. His head turns toward me, and his eyes shine in amusement.

Oh, Big Guy! What did I do?

"I've won the fucking bet!" Edward exclaims triumphantly and raises his arms, jumping up and down. His antics earn some ugly glances from the people walking nearby. "I cracked the goddamn nut!"

"No, you didn't. Darn is not a curse word," Barb defends me.

"Yes, it fucking is." He high fives Archie, then turns and singles me out, mimicking scissors with his fingers. "Snip, snip, snip!"

No, not my hair. Protectively, I grab ahold of my ponytail and step backward.

"Lyra, would you consider darn a curse word?" Barb asks the moment the other girl joins us. Her arrival takes me by surprise, since I'm kind of busy hiding my hair from Edward's clutches.

"Technically, the curse word would be damn, but darn?" Lyra taps her chin in thought. "Hmmm, it could be up for discussion."

"The hell it is," Archie drops his bags, takes out his cell phone, and Google's it.

I turn around, waiting impatiently to know the fate of the length of my hair, but my attention shifts when I notice the Dancewear store in front of me.

Stepping closer to the apparel, I study the beautiful leotards with the straps that cross at the backs in a gamut of colors and designs. My mouth practically watering at the sight, remembering all the times I dreamed of changing the plain, short sleeve shirts or camisoles that I could afford for these kinds of beautiful dancing clothes.

My eyes stop on the beautiful chiffon wrap skirt and the tights, together with the beautiful leg warmers and the wrap sweaters.

In my mind, I picture the different combinations I can get by mixing the pieces, achieving entirely different outfits, using only the garments from the display. Inside must exist a world of endless possibilities waiting for me to come and sort them out.

If this is how Barb felt when we arrived at the shoe department, I finally get it. I now understand what Edward meant with finding the right style. He searches for the one that boosts your confidence when you wear it, bringing out the beauty within.

"I believe our Twinkle Toes found her little piece of shopping heaven," Barb says.

"Focus, Edward! Is darn a bad word or not?" Archie demands in the background, oblivious. "Internet sites debate this point. Some say it is, others say it isn't."

"It doesn't fucking matter anymore." Edward walks over to stand beside me. "I'll let this one slide. Her fucking expression is utterly priceless."

"For leotards and tights?" Lyra sounds bewildered. "I don't know what the big deal is."

"Remind me to take a picture of you the next time we go to the gun range, Lyra," Barb replies, laughing. "Time to suit up our little dancer. She needs to be in the studio in one hour, and we still need to feed her."

At the studio? And only one hour? Why did we spend all that time in the other clothing departments? *We should have started with this one, Big Guy.*

CHAPTER TWENTY
Something Beautiful

Unwillingly, I drag my feet out of the dancewear store, mumbling about them leaving all the fun until the end. Barb and Edward chuckle at my childish display while Archie happily declares our shopping trip terminated. Lyra cheers once she hears the news.

Over lunch, the discussion of my bet with Edward comes up. To Archie's dismay, his friend and I agree the bet ended in a tie. Our agreement doesn't stop Edward from offering his grooming services once more. It might be a long time before I meet with Edward again, because I plan to keep my hair long.

Before we leave the restaurant, I quickly changed into

the new dancewear Barb had purchased. The black leotard, with its crisscrossing straps on my back, paired with pink tights and a pink wrap skirt, makes me feel confident and happy. I carry my ballet and pointe shoes in my backpack.

It turned out Lyra's errand during our shopping trip entailed retrieving my dance bag from the house so she can take me straight to the ballet studio after lunch to meet Samuel.

She drops me off at the entrance and drives away without waiting to make sure I get inside. When I enter the building, I notice the reception area first. Different portraits decorate the walls of dancers performing bold ballet moves and wearing amazing costumes. On my right, the phone rings from its resting place on top of an empty desk. I expect the receptionist to run over to answer it. However, the call ends before she arrives. I turn around, searching expectantly for some life form that can help me locate Samuel, but nothing.

On my left, I find a hallway leading to two doors, one of them marked as the bathroom.

My curiosity gets the better of me, and I walk toward the first room, hoping to find someone who can help me. As expected, I discover a standard dance studio with mirrors covering two of the four walls of the room, and a barre installed in the center of each one, extending from one side of the wall all the way to the other. Instead of a fourth wall, a big sliding door allows natural light to come in. It opens to a small, rectangular garden that acts as the central area for at least four other classrooms, similar to the one I stand in.

In the studio on the other side of the garden, I notice a figure moving. I inch closer to the window for a better view of the male dancer. He wears black cutoff leggings, leaving his muscular calves exposed. His torso, covered by a black, sleeveless tank top, shows off his strong arms.

From my position, I analyze his movements, noticing how his lines are clear and sharp, his technique flawless. I stare at the perfection of his jumps, the great height his strong legs can achieve. His body twists with precision and in complete synchrony with his arms. He takes advantage of the jump's momentum to perform an outstanding landing, the exact definition of what the move requires.

He shifts his position, and after a couple of steps, performs a cavalier turn, his strong, supporting heel lifting and falling in each consecutive turn, while his other leg extends at a ninety degree angle.

My heart stops when he performs a Grand Jeté. I would die of excitement if I could reach his altitude in the horizontal jump.

Whoever said male ballet dancers aren't sexy, I completely and entirely disagree. The way their bodies developed in time into a sensual, exquisite and manly form in order to achieve the difficult steps for the choreography. They're hot.

Yeah, Big Guy, I said it, but in my defense, You created them.

With my attention focused on the male dancer, it takes me by surprise when I realize a female dancer performs with him. A bunch of small girls arrive in the classroom with me, cutting my analysis short. Their giggles break my concentration on the—ahem—excellent dancing.

"You're the new student?" A younger woman with a Russian accent stares at me in confusion while the rest of her students step inside the room.

Her confusion's understandable. Most of them appear to be around six years old, leaving a big, ten-year gap between them and me. Is this really the class Samuel enrolled me in? By the way, where is Samuel?

"Yes?" I hesitantly nod.

She shrugs, accepting my answer as plausible.

"Then suit up." She points at my shoes.

After hanging my backpack on one of the wall hooks, I put on my ballet slippers and join the rest of the class with the warm up exercises, stretching my legs and my arms. I chuckle at the little munchkins when they try to reach their little toes, some losing their balance in the process and landing on the floor, making the rest of the girls giggle.

Big Guy, it's been four days since my last dance, but it feels like a million years. I've missed this.

"Positions at the barre." The teacher claps a couple times, and the little girls go to one side of the barre. I go to the wall with the higher barre, better suited for my height. It leaves me with a clear view of the other room where the two advanced dancers continue to practice.

"First position, now second... Laura, move your heels toward..." the teacher continues correcting the girls while directing us to change positions. My brain automatically makes them without any concentration on my part. I've been doing them for twelve years, my body knows the moves by heart. Familiarity allows me to keep my attention on the girl's solo in the studio across the garden.

She moves with precision, although the results are not entirely perfect. While she focuses on completing a step, she loses concentration on another part of her body. Either her arms don't stretch completely, or the angle of her leg seems wrong. She stops and turns around to address her dance partner. Her face is flushed, and she crosses her arms, while the guy tells her something, finalizing the discussion with her stabbing a finger at him while he turns around and ignores her.

"Now girls, we need to work on the routine for the Christmas festival," our teacher tells my classmates, bringing my attention back to the class.

I don't know when we stopped the warm-up.

The teacher shows the girls the routine for a small piece of the Nutcracker, moving quickly and explaining the steps while she shows them. After she performed it once, I have it memorized. The routine's similar to Miss Johnson's back at my old school.

I can practically dance it in my sleep.

"Okay, girls, form a single line here," she commands, and the girls follow her.

I stop near the outside of the line, unsure where I should stand and afraid I'll knock over one of the little munchkins with my height. Eventually, I settle on one end of the room, which allows me enough space to perform my moves freely.

When the music begins, I follow the choreography the teacher marked, letting myself get lost in the dance. I dance my steps with the precision Miss Johnson taught me, not allowing myself to hesitate as I make sure to put the sentiment behind every move to convey the story the dance should show.

When the music comes to an end, I stop, noticing how the girls stare at me, some with their mouths wide open, while others giggle or pull a girl closer to whisper a secret at her friend. The teacher, her eyes narrowed, tilts her head to one side as she regards me with confusion.

"Did I mess up?" I ask, afraid I made a fool of myself.

Every single girl shakes her heads in unison.

"You did better than Miss Katya," one of the girls replies.

Oh, no! Kids can be such little troublemakers with their jokes.

I don't dare to face Miss Katya. I never intended to show off, much less make her a part of her student's poor sense of humor. I simply performed as I was taught.

"You," a commanding voice calls from the door, breaking the uncomfortable silence.

I turn to find a mature woman at the entrance, her dark hair showing a few gray strands at her temples. Her finger points at me, leaving no room for doubt as to whom she refers to. My arms stick to my sides and my back automatically straightens when all eyes fall on me.

She turns to leave. "Follow me."

I nod and grab my bag on my way out.

The woman speed-walks through the halls, unintentionally giving me a tour of the facility. The main lobby leads to the other studios. The building is shaped like a rectangle, and as I thought, the garden was the center.

"You must be Samantha," she says coldly.

"Y-y-yes," I stammer while I try to keep up with her.

"I am Maria." Her tone turns sharp.

"Nice to meet—"

"Samuel mentioned you might stop by, and that I needed to train you," she cuts me off without glancing at me.

"Oh!"

"You are late, by the way. I will not tolerate this kind of behavior in the future," she warns sternly. "*If you manage to prove yourself.*"

"When I got here, the receptionist w—"

"And no excuses," she retorts, frowning at me.

Well, that's my cue to shut up.

We reach the last studio, but don't stop at the door. Instead, we walk a little farther and enter an adjoining door, which turns out to be an office. The only window inside the office opens to the dance studio where the couple I spied earlier continue to dance, oblivious to our presence. His back is toward me, while the girl follows him, trying to keep up.

Maria presses a switch on the wall, and the music they practice to comes through.

The guy reaches for the girl's waist and lifts her. At first, the movement seems precise, but she hesitates in the last second, and what started as a beautiful lift ends with her face almost in his shoulder.

"Are you trying to kill me?" the girl yells angrily, while the guy sets her down. "You messed up!"

"Stupid girl," Maria comments below her breath, barely shaking her head while her eyes single out the female dancer.

The guy turns around. When I register his face, my mouth drops. It's Samuel. His features contorted into an angry expression.

"I messed up, Anya?" He storms toward her. "You need to worry about keeping your legs straight, your arm extended, a beautiful smile on your face, and most importantly, you need to trust that I will not drop you."

"You use too much force. It took me by surprise." Her hands come up, and she takes one step away from him.

"Because you didn't hold your position when I lifted you, and we were about to tip over. Plus, you didn't keep your legs straight," Samuel adds.

The girl glares at him, her hands balling up for being called out in a lie.

Maria releases a sigh. "This is not going to work."

"I'm tired, Solis. We've already danced for over two hours." Anya's tone gentles as she changes tactics from accusatory to innocent.

"Two hours in professional ballet equals warm up,

Anya. You're tired because you only eat rabbit food," he calls her bluff. "You need a balanced diet for your body to produce the energy we require for this type of dance or for any activity."

Anya's expression changes from innocence to a full-on glare.

"I give up! You can't treat me like this. You're impossible!" The girl's face turns red as she stabs a finger at Samuel. She turns, snatches a bag hanging from one of the ballet beams, slams open the door, and storms from the studio, banging the door shut on her way out.

Maria sighs. "Another one bites the dust."

I don't look at her. My mind's still trying to wrap around the idea of Samuel as a dancer. Never in a million years did I imagine his great body came from him being an excellent ballet dancer.

He shakes his head and rolls his eyes. Walking to the music console, he changes the song, and takes position in the center of the room.

"He hasn't been good with partners, after Ella," Maria explains, pulling my attention to her. Her face is expressionless as she stares at the scene in front of her.

"How many..." I stop when a new song begins.

My head snaps back to the window, surprised at the pop song playing. I recognize it as *Something Beautiful* from a group in South Carolina called NeedtoBreathe. Some of my dorm neighbors at my old school were fans of the band and kept playing it over and over. I never complained since I liked it, too.

"Pay attention," Maria tells me.

I nod, acknowledging her request.

Being a dancer, I recognize the complex choreography, but he makes it seem effortless, moving freely, and as I observed earlier, with precise perfection. However, now, I get to appreciate the whole ensemble, music and dancing. The singer tells the story of a man finding the love of his life, expecting her to notice him and accepting him, waiting for his *Something Beautiful*. But while the story is beautiful, and Samuel delivers a perfect performance, the choreography feels wrong.

Maria pushes a button and speaks through some interphone, her voice echoing on the other side. "One more time, Samuel."

I expected the loudspeaker to take him by surprise, but instead, he nods, puts the song back at the beginning, and performs the routine once again.

"Watch and learn Samantha," Maria tells me.

I focus, this time working to memorize his steps, noticing how they repeat during the chorus of the song, making my job a lot easier.

The song comes to an end. Samuel pants heavily, out of breath. He walks over to a backpack on the floor and removes a water bottle, taking a swig from it.

"Now, go inside and show me what you can do," Maria orders.

For a moment, I think my mind played a trick on me. I turn, making sure it wasn't a figment of my imagination. She tilts her head toward the window, silently indicating I join Samuel.

"What?" my voice comes out an octave higher.

A small grin plays on her lips. "You saw the dance. If you need to improvise, do it. Samuel will follow you."

I try to remain calm. The ballet boot-camp I was going to attend in Spain would have required something like Maria's request, although it wouldn't have included a half naked guy.

"Are you slowly going to torture me before you give me hell for Anya?" Samuel asks, facing us.

I inch back, worried he can see me, but when his eyes never focus, it confirms my suspicions about it being a two-way mirror.

"Nope." Maria signals me to go out and join him. "I have her replacement right here."

Her replacement?

Following her instruction, I leave the room, closing the door behind me, and quietly enter the other room, dropping my bag at the entrance.

When he turns around, Samuel stares at me. His examination begins at my feet, moving slowly up, stopping at my hips, and a small smile spreads across his face. I hold my breath, my cheeks warming at his scrutiny. His eyes finally stop at my face, his expression changing. The smile on his lips disappears, and his warm, brown eyes widen. He quickly turns to the mirror in front of him, his reflection angry.

"Maria, no!" he tells her in Spanish, but I don't need any translation. His words are obvious. "Not her."

"You're confident in her skills," her voice calls out through the speakers. "Samantha, put on your pointe shoes."

I'm not going to question her. Quickly, I follow her order.

"She needs to warm up, or she'll get injured," Samuels argues while I wrap tape around my toes to avoid any blisters and put the shoes on.

"She already did in Katya's classroom. No more excuses. You said she was good, so let's see what she can do," Maria proclaims. "Start your dance from the top."

"I said I heard she was good," Samuel corrects her. "There's a difference."

After one final stretch, where I touch my toes with my hand and rest my forehead on my knees, I straighten and offer him a small, encouraging smile.

"And still you want me to train her," Maria replies. "Stop stalling, Samuel."

"You start." I nervously cut off the argument between them. "I'll join in."

He narrows his eyes, taking me in. "If we're going to do this together, you'll follow my lead, okay?"

I nod.

"First part, let me do my thing. I'll cue you in." He walks to the console, pushes play on the iPod, and goes to the center of the room.

Beating drums, quickly joined by a guitar, fills the studio. My heart rate speeds up, and my feet twitch, preparing for the action.

He begins his choreography from the floor, reaching out, explaining to the audience he wants something that's out of his grasp. At the same time, a force pulls him, calling him to move and get that special something, lifting him to his feet. Accepting his fate, he turns toward his prized possession…me.

"Now, Samantha, it's your turn. Dance."

He stops, steps to one side, and with a motion of his hand, he indicates I have the dance floor. I follow the next set of steps the choreography requires, putting all my attention in perfecting my movements, circling him, proving with this solo that I can hold my ground. With an awed expression on his face, his eyes follow me around the room.

I don't know how much he knew about my dancing skills. Judging by his expression, he didn't expect this.

In my mind, I pictured this part as being the introduction of the girl, while the guy watches her from afar, extending his hand to reach her. However, it doesn't mean the girl knows about his existence.

When the chorus starts, I continue with the choreography. Samuel joins me on the dance floor, performing the same steps only a few seconds behind. For a moment, I think my timing's off, but my steps match with the cords of the song.

"Keep it up," Samuel mumbles under his breath. "The guy is pursuing you."

Chuckling, I continue, understanding his vision, feeling him near me.

I let the rhythm mark my pace and make sure my movements are precise, with no hesitation as I try to match his expertise.

After the first chorus, the tempo of the song slows.

"Okay, now how about you flirt with me," he proposes. "And don't let me catch you," he warns with a smirk.

Flirt? I've never done that. At least, not intentionally.

I try to remember the way Abigail flirted with Sherlock, or how the girl at the library kept glancing at the boy, inviting him with a smile to come and join her.

I stop and face him as if noticing him for the first time. I give him a small, encouraging grin, as I observed Abigail do a couple of days ago. He extends one of his arms, almost touching my shoulder, but I move backward and give him a playful, coy smile like the library girl. He follows me. I continue with the next combination of steps, toying with him. He smiles, ready to rise to the challenge, and with a wiggle of his eyebrows, he begins.

Let's play.

He sometimes mimics my movements. At other times, Samuel's movement become fantastic, gaining my complete attention—and not only for the show we're putting on. He wows me, making me laugh when he lands at my feet, inviting me to join him. He's clear with the direction, I'm to flirt with him, but I can't relent to his attentions.

I move along, beaming at him, dancing the choreography, keeping my eyes on him. He does the same, but to the opposite side of where I stand. We join in the center when the chorus comes again.

"Together this time," he directs.

We dance his choreography side by side. Constantly sharing glances, I invite him to come and get me since the guy in the story is no longer off the girl's radar. His existence has been noticed.

When the tempo slows down again, I face him, my eyes asking, *What now?*

"Am I going to get the girl? Or are you going to fade away?" he whispers, allowing me to decide what will be the outcome of the dance.

I am such a sucker for happy endings.

This time, I reach out for him, stepping closer and touching his shoulder. With one hand, I tilt his head toward me and smile, encouraging him. I slide the hand at his shoulder down his arm, get ahold of his hand, and redirect it to my waist.

"You've got me," I breathe out. "Now, let's do it together."

He looks momentarily confused, studying my face before finally settling on my eyes. "Do you trust me?"

I trusted you with the rock climbing wall. Compared to that, this is child's play.

I give him a quick nod. The smile on his lips extends. It's the only invitation Samuel needs. He pulls me closer to himself and dips me.

Then he lifts me, taking me by surprise. I keep my legs and arms extended, maintaining the pose.

He continues the dance, whispering instructions for partnering, improvising while instructing me at the same time.

Back at Saint Magdalene, I studied the steps from ballet videos, but had never done them before. No girls wanted to play the part of the boy, or even had the body strength to lift me.

Now, here I am, with Samuel carrying me and lifting me as if I was a feather.

I stiffen the first time he touches me in an area that has never been touched, but I know from the videos I studied it's a necessity to achieve the movement. I try to relax and focus on the dance rather than the location of his hands.

Not an easy task.

I do the moves as best as I can, trusting he won't drop me. Finding my center of gravity and equilibrium, I put strength in my position to alleviate him from my weight.

When the song comes to an end, he turns me around to face him and dips me one more time. His nose touches mine, his warm breath in my face, his breathing ragged from the effort, like mine.

"You've been hiding your talents, Samantha. You walk like an ugly duckling but dance like a beautiful swan," he whispers happily.

I roll my eyes but chuckle, my cheeks warming at the compliment.

You heard that, Big Guy. Samuel said I dance like a beautiful swan.

He helps me up, my hand in his. His moodiness from earlier gone.

The door to the studio opens, and Maria comes in with a serious expression on her face. Samuel's hand goes around my waist, bringing me closer to his body as if to protect me from the instructor's criticism.

Her eyes glance at the location of his hands, and she gives a short nod.

"How long have you been dancing, Samantha?" she asks with a sweeter tone, not as stern as before.

"Twelve years," I answer.

"You've never danced with a male partner before, have you?"

I shake my head.

"But she did beautifully for her first time," Samuel defends.

Maria raises one eyebrow and gives a small smile. "Your technique needs some minor tweaking, and you need to work on partnering, but I agree with Samuel. For your first time, it was impressive, and I believe it will improve significantly under our tutoring."

She focuses on Samuel who nods in agreement.

"I expect to see you here the days you don't train at school. And I expect you *on time*," she warns, emphasizing the last word.

Oh, nuts! I started on the wrong foot.

"We will work for four hours during the week and three hours on Saturday," she continues, explaining the schedule arrangement.

I nod.

"You both have something to gain out of this." Her eyes dart between us. "Samantha, we will work with your technique and on pax de deux. In return, you'll help Samuel prepare for an out of school commitment. There are still a couple of hours of training. Samuel, work with her on the basics of partnering."

He nods, and she leaves the studio, closing the door behind her.

Samuel breathes out, and his hand abandons my waist.

When I face him, he towers over me.

His dark, intense gaze examines my face. "Let's get the show on the road then. Are you ready to dance something, beautiful?".

Lost in his dark-brown eyes, and impressed with his skills, I'm not certain if I catch the phrase right. Is he referring to the song we just danced? Or making something beautiful with the dancing? Or did he just call me beautiful?

My heart melts a little.

Hold on! Edward mentioned not all compliments mean a person is romantically interested in someone. But this eats me alive. I replay it over and over in my head without reaching anything conclusive.

Okay, Big Guy, I know You're busy with running the world but...did he say: Ready to dance something beautiful? Or did he say: Ready to dance something, beautiful? Commas are important You know.

CHAPTER TWENTY-ONE
Night Closing In

"Hey Samantha, wake up. We're home." From a distance, a voice interrupts the peaceful silence, but I can't for the life of me open my eyes.

I mumble something along the lines of, "Not praying time," and turn around, trying to find a more comfortable position than the one I'm currently in.

Whoever's trying to wake me up chuckles at my reaction. "Come on, sleepy head." A warm hand shakes me.

"Nooooo." I shift farther away from the intrusive person.

"Then, I'll carry you inside," he chuckles.

"Go away!" I wiggle away from the annoying voice, and my surroundings become utterly quiet.

Ah, finally, more sleeping time for...

"Today's dinner menu consists of grilled cheese sandwiches, then," the annoying voice threatens.

"What?" I ask more alertly while regaining consciousness. "At least put some ham on it."

The person laughs.

When I open my eyes, they focus on Grams's house. For a moment there, I expected to find my old dorm room. The events of the last four days come pouring back, stopping at today's. A new school with a welcoming party of tests, followed by the shopping trip, and afterward, dancing ballet with a hot, Latin guy.

No wonder I confuse reality with dreamland. In one single day, nightmares and dreams came together.

I turn my head to find Samuel grinning, staring at me, one side of his face settled on the headrest of the car seat.

I might still be dreaming. I pinch myself to eliminate any potential doubt. Ouch, nope this is reality.

"Sorry," I apologize. "It's been a long day."

"I mean it. We could probably get away with grilled cheese sandwiches," Samuel jokes, his eyes twinkle softening his sharp features.

My heart pumps faster, and I stretch my arms. "Joy and Archie deserve a better dinner."

"Only Joy and Archie?" Surprised, he raises his eyebrows, the smile disappearing from his lips.

"Okay, Lyra and Barb deserve it as well. They did take

me shopping." I joke and cover my mouth when he pouts.

Aw, how can I say *no* to that face? He also deserves it after putting up with me all afternoon.

He was a good and strict instructor. Class with him was entertaining with jokes and a relaxed atmosphere, but he made sure I learned a move expertly, always testing me. Which only made me push myself harder to close the gap between his expertise and my average level.

Before today, pairing seemed like an impossible task. However, Samuel made it possible by teaching me and being my partner. The mere idea of a man touching me in such a manner would have had me stiff as a board, but somehow, over the past three days, I learned to trust him.

At the end of two hours, Maria stopped by to verify the progress we made. She did some minor corrections; the ones Samuel couldn't notice because his attention was on holding me. At the end, I believe she liked the final result of day one.

Mentally and physically drained by the time we reached the car, when my head touched the headrest, I lost consciousness.

"Okay, perhaps, you also earned a better dinner," I agree, my mood lifting when his face lights up.

Once inside the house, we decide to cook something quick, chicken Parmesan on a bed of steamed vegetables, since the small catnap I took only gave me a slight boost of energy and not a full charge.

Samuel helps me wash and cut the vegetables while I work with the chicken. After all, our team is in charge of cooking and grocery shopping after swapping activities with Barb and Kellan.

The moment the aroma of the chicken Parmesan fills the house, I detect movement upstairs, the thumping informing me the upstairs crowd is aware dinner will be ready soon.

While I prepare the lemonade, Samuel sets the table. I grab the jar to take it to the dinner table, but stop when a pair of hands goes around my waist, preventing me from moving any farther.

The action takes me by surprise, and I almost drop the jar in the process.

"I'll go and get the downstairs crew," Samuel whispers in my ear, his warm breath sending shivers down my spine. "Make sure Joy and Archie don't eat everything before we return."

"Okay." Nervous, I get a better hold on the jar.

His hands fall away, and he leaves. However, it takes me a couple of seconds to regain my composure and for the beating of my heart to slow.

This kind of interaction between boys and girls is normal, with no romantic interest whatsoever. *Right, Big Guy?*

After placing the jar on the table, I run back to the kitchen and catch a set of footsteps approaching. I position myself between the stove and whoever dares to come close, arming myself with a wooden spoon to slap away any potential thieves.

"Hello, Samantha," Joy steps in the kitchen, her eyes

scanning the counters in search of food.

"Hi, Joy, did you have a nice day today?" I cautiously ask while watching her movements. She can be fast.

"Meh!" She shrugs. "What's cooking?" She steps closer. "Smells delicious."

She focuses on the stove, then her eyes move to the oven. Putting two plus two together, she knows she located the bounty.

I back closer to the food to make it harder for her to reach the treasure.

"Chicken Parmesan with vegetables," I answer. "Currently in the final stages of cooking inside the oven," I add to buy some time before everyone else joins us.

She raises her eyebrows. "I see."

The whole scene reminds me of an old western movie, two gunmen ready for their duel, eyeing each other, trying to guess when their opponent will draw.

The door to the basement opens. I dare to take my eyes from Joy, my stomach falling when I see the newcomers and realize I'm now outnumbered. Archie arrived with reinforcement, Rasputin.

"It will be done in a couple of minutes." I try to sound calm and composed, while my hand gets a better hold of my weapon. "You should go and wash your hands while we wait for the others."

"Done," they both respond in unison, joined by Rasputin's bark.

"Then go sit down and wait for the others to come," I order, moving my head toward the dining room, my gaze darting from Joy to Archie.

"I'll go when she goes." A glint enters his eyes, and he takes a step in my direction.

"And leave you alone in the kitchen?" Joy counterattacks when I turn to reply.

I stop, realizing she's closer than the last time I had my eyes on her.

They exchange a glance, as if sharing an idea. Joy lifts an eyebrow.

I lift my spoon in front of myself. "Well, either you both go and sit down, or I'll let the chicken burn inside the oven, and then we'll be eating grilled cheese sandwiches for dinner."

I'm lying. The chicken isn't in any immediate danger since I already turned the oven off. However, I don't want it to dry out from the remaining heat inside. The vegetables, on the other hand, might overcook if I don't turn the stove off.

Sorry for lying, Big Guy, but I want to prevent a fight.

Both their head snaps toward me.

"No!" Joy exclaims, her face twisting into a terrified expression. She inches closer, earning a growl from Rasputin.

"You wouldn't." Archie also gets closer, but Joy stops him, placing her hand on his arm.

See? Boy and girl contact is normal. The two of them are practically frenemies, and they touch, which means I need to keep my emotions in place around Samuel.

"Don't tempt me," I warn them, giving the most

aggressive expression I can muster.

Archie turns, glances at Joy, and they continue with their silent communication. She gives a small nod. I sigh with relief. They fell for my threat and agreed to stand down. I lower my spoon.

Big mistake!

They attack me from both fronts. Joy quickly goes for the spoon and pulls it from my fingers. Meanwhile, Archie dives in from the other side, making me protectively back up toward the stove. I may no longer possess a weapon, but at least I still stand, defending my prized position and making it impossible for either of them to open the oven door. Rasputin bounds forward, barking madly.

"We can do this the easy way or the hard way." Archie threatens, moving into my personal space. "Either you hand over the food, or we take it by any means necessary."

His beautiful blue eyes look menacing. The archangel means business.

Oh. No. He. Didn't!

"Either you step away from my kitchen, or help me God, you will never again eat anything prepared by my hand," I threaten him back.

His eyes soften, and he chuckles, stepping away with his hands in front of himself, indicating his withdrawal from the battle. When I focus on Joy, she laughs and pops a piece of broccoli into her mouth, challenging me.

I cross my arms. "No goodie bag for you tomorrow, Joy."

Joy immediately spits the broccoli out of her mouth, as

if this action will buy her back her lunch.

I need to keep my punishment, otherwise they will always overstep me.

"Nope, too late, you licked it, it's yours," I reply, angered. "And if you throw it in the garbage, it's two days without a goodie bag."

"Oh, man!" She puts the food back in her mouth, chews, and swallows it.

After confirming my attackers ceased their approach, I turn the heat off on the vegetables and dare to shift to one side to fetch an oven mitten to take the chicken Parmesan out. I stop when I notice from my peripheral vision that the rest of the family stares at us. Some of their shoulders shake from silently laughing while others cover their mouth, holding back their chuckles.

"Anybody else want to challenge the cook?" I cross my arms and eye them, making sure they understand the warning also applies to them.

Everybody shakes their head, amused at my attitude.

"Excellent. Now, Oliver and Zach, help me get the food on the table. The rest go and sit down," I order confidently. "Nobody eats anything until after we say grace," I add for good measure.

"Yes, Mom," Oliver says while the rest chuckle.

Everybody follows the orders, even pint-sized Rasputin.

Dinner goes without a hitch, everybody happily discussing today's school events while enjoying their food. After I finish eating, I bring my hand close to Rasputin testing how he behaves towards me, and when he comes closer without a growl or bark, I scratch the top of his head, earning some licks on my hand.

"Who's a good boy?" I whisper while the others continue their discussion and pick up the little guy, placing him on my lap. "How was your day?"

As if the little guy can answer, he yaps.

"Oh! Really? Inside the house all day? You want to go out for a walk?" I ask him, earning a loud, happy bark from his side.

The table falls quiet at the sound.

Oh, shoot!

"Archie, can't you leave him downstairs while we eat and discuss today's events and findings?" Barb asks.

"But, the little dude needs more space to run after spending all day down in the basement," he answers with puppy dog eyes.

As if on cue, Rasputin whimpers.

Aw! I get you, and I only did a couple of hours in the library.

"I can walk him," I offer. It's not like I can add anything to the conversation.

"Perhaps later, Samantha. We need to discuss your test results." Oliver's comment kills the discussion, quieting the table and managing to tie my stomach into a knot.

"Okay." I set Rasputin back on the floor.

Please, Big Guy, let it be good news.

"The admissions office seemed quite impressed with some of your scores." He crosses his arms and smiles.

"Your English test showed outstanding results, quieting whatever doubts they had regarding the cheating incident. Math, History, and Physics show good scores and place you at a senior level."

I'm smart! Yay!

"Science and Chemistry, however, were your weakest subjects, which places you at your current level."

Way to kill the happy mood, Oliver. At least I stayed within my class and not lower.

"Abigail, Zach, and I worked together with admissions to create a schedule. We tried to place you with one member of our team during the senior classes, but we couldn't do the same for the classes at the junior level," he explains. "But, Zach mentioned you might be comfortable if we could pair you up with one of the O'Flannagan kids. Therefore, you will share Chemistry and Cooking with Darcy and Biology with the twins."

This is excellent news since I didn't expect to share any of the classes with anyone I knew. I'll bet Darcy will be over the moon when she hears we'll share cooking class.

"The only problem we faced was language and the other extracurricular activity," he tells me. "You requested Spanish at a basic level, but since most of the students pick a language and continue with their option throughout the rest of high school, the only available choice was for you to share the class with the freshman. Peter Stinson spoke with the Spanish teacher and agreed to let you join in the class with Potter O'Flannagan."

Classes with the Freshmen? Oh well, not exactly what I expected. At least I got to stay with Potter.

"Now, our biggest issue is dancing," he continues slowly. "Monsieur Pietro is adamant on not allowing any other exception in. He didn't allow us to talk to him." He turns and eyes Samuel, raising his eyebrows.

"He should be thanking me, not the other way around," Samuel replies. "I hate it when he behaves like a diva."

"Plus, if he agreed, he would make you go through the audition process, which we heard can be quite hard," Oliver explains, making eye contact with me and ignoring Samuel's comment. "There are no guarantees you would make it."

Samuel chuckles, gaining the attention of the rest of the table.

"The audition shouldn't be a problem," Samuel comments. "She needs to work on improving some areas, but she's a natural. You should worry on coming up with a plan for Monsieur Pietro to test her."

Me? A natural? Ha, ha, ha! I've trained for twelve years. It's called practice.

"Admissions asked us to talk to you and sway you to Introductory Ballet," Oliver says.

"It would be a waste of talent. Samantha can easily out dance any of the girls in the Advanced Ballet class," Samuel defends me.

"I know you would love to take the class at Calvary, but Samantha, we tried several times to talk with Monsieur

Pietro and came up empty handed. He wouldn't even listen to Peter," Abigail explains. "You can always train with Maria."

Samuel scoffs and shakes his head.

"Samuel, you know better than us how Monsieur Pietro is. Don't get upset with us for him not listening to reason," Oliver scolds him. "Or do you care to explain what the problem is?"

Samuel breathes in and then out, restraining his annoyance. "I know you did your best, and I'm angry at Pietro. He's burying her talent on a technicality. Do you know how many opportunities Samantha can lose on future job offerings or even scholarships because of a wimp? Calvary's reputation is outstanding. Dance scouts usually attend the recitals."

Wow, I never imagined this situation or considered how it could affect my future. Honestly, I only love to dance.

"Perhaps I can ask him directly and get a better result, since it's harder to say no in person," I propose.

Samuel shakes his head and crosses his arms. "That's never been a problem for Monsieur Pietro, Samantha."

Well, I don't plan on accepting no for an answer. One way or another, I'll get the audition.

"When do I need to submit my final schedule?" I ask Oliver.

"Friday, Monday at the latest," he replies, looking unconvinced. "We can always stall, telling them you want to check out the other classes, but you'll need to attend at least some of your probable options."

"Okay, then Monday it is," I confirm, determined. My mind racing with ideas on how to get the audition Pietro denies me.

After they move on to discuss items regarding their investigation, I decide to get out of the way and take Rasputin for a small walk. I ask Archie for his leash, which he fetches for me. The little dog jumps up and down, overexcited when his tiny eyes land on it, which makes it hard for me to put it on him.

"Hold on, Rasputin," I tell him, chuckling while I struggle to keep him steady enough to clip it to his collar. "Stop moving or we're not going anywhere."

The moment it clicks, he pulls me toward the door. I thank the Big Guy that he's so small. Otherwise, he would be dragging me.

After shutting the main door, the cold wind hits my bare arms and I realize I forgot my sweater. Shivering, I consider going back for it, but Rasputin's already making his way to the end of the driveway, pulling as hard as he can and coming to an abrupt stop when he reaches the end of the line.

"Calm down, Ras. You're going to hurt yourself." I kneel at his side, making sure he didn't cause any damage.

Once I verify he's okay, we leave the yard.

Since my scatterbrain also forgot my cell phone, I keep our walk near the house, only going around a couple of blocks and returning home quickly. The little guy decides it's not time to go back and accelerates his pace the moment we approach the house.

"Okay, okay, we can take another turn around the block across the street," I propose, earning another happy bark from Rasputin.

At the corner, we cross the street and make the same walk on the opposite side. I try to slow down to make it last longer. By the time we get back home, Samuel's car is no longer in the driveway. My heart drops and my smile disappears from my lips, replaced by a pout.

I try to shake off the disappointment, confused why the feeling came over me in the first place. *Oh, well!*

Rasputin tries to make a run for it when we reach the house. I pick him up so he doesn't figure out the hard way how long the leash is.

"Sorry, Ras, but we made a deal. Besides, I need a shower and to go to bed." I explain, patting his head. "Tomorrow, I need to rise early to prepare breakfast and goodie bags."

He whimpers.

"How about I take you out tomorrow? Sound all right?" I propose.

He licks my hand as if sealing the deal.

Once inside, I go straight to the basement, guessing I'll be stealing Zach's room once again. When I get to the lower level, I stop, realizing I don't know which room is Archie's. There's a fifty-fifty chance of getting it right with the two available choices.

Eeny meeny miny moe?

I knock on the first door and cross my fingers. Oliver

answers, wearing only boxers.

Oh, nuts! *Wait, no, no, no, Big Guy! Not those nuts! I was simply cursing. Oh! You know what, shoot me, okay?*

Something about knowing it's his underwear makes me uncomfortable. Although, I can't tell a lot about what's underneath. After all, they're...shorts.

Yeah! Let's go with that!

I divert my gaze from the lower part of his body, focusing on his face.

"Uhm...sorry, Oliver," I manage to say, my face warming to an almost boiling point. "I didn't know which room belongs to Archie. I guess the next one. I apologize for disturbing you and wish you a good night." Listening to myself, I feel even more embarrassed since I manage to say the whole sentence without pause. The worst part is, the longer I spoke, the higher my squeaking got.

Smooth, Samantha! Smooth!

By the way his shoulders shake and how he bites his lower lip, he's holding back laughter.

"Good guess, Samantha," he replies. "And have a good night."

Immediately, I turn and beeline for the next door. I stop in front of it, giving myself extra seconds to allow my color to return to normal.

What if he decides to sleep without anything on? The basement's the boy's area, and I'm the intruder.

I peek at Rasputin, who cocks his little head to one side and gives me the puppy eye treatment.

Sorry, little dude, you're on your own. I kneel down to put him on the floor and prepare to run for Zach's room when the door of Archie's room swings open. Darn! Caught red handed.

I stop moving. The little traitor runs inside the moment the gap's big enough to squeeze through.

"Twinkle Toes, what a surprise," comes Archie's excited voice.

Slowly, I lift my head, stare at his bare feet, and relief floods through me when I see the bottom of his pants.

Thank you, Big Guy! At least he still wears something besides his...um, shorts.

"Hi, Archie, I came to drop Rasputin off." I stand, noticing he wears a T-shirt now instead of his school shirt.

"Oh! I see." A broad grin stretches across his face, and he raises an eyebrow. He leans casually against the doorframe. "Did you two enjoy your date tonight?"

Rasputin answers with a bark.

"Yeah, we had tons of fun." I playfully swing my arms back and forth. "We planned a second one for tomorrow night."

He turns and focuses on the little devil. "Rasputin, you lucky bastard! How did you manage to get a second one? You've got to teach me your moves, dawg." Archie's relaxed posture changes, and he bends down to Rasputin's eye level, continuing with the joke and making the little guy more excited.

Rasputin barks louder.

"Archie!" Oliver's scream comes from the room next door. "First warning!"

Archie laughs and puts his finger to his mouth, quieting the little dog. He closes the door of his room, leaving the two of us standing in the hall.

"I consider it my duty as a gentleman and your friend to warn you about his reputation as a player and advise you to not take any of his flirting seriously," he warns, deadpan. "I could tell you horror stories about the awkward situations I've caught him in." He shakes his head in a disapproving manner. "To preserve your dignity, and keep his little paws off you, I bestow upon myself the duty to become your official chaperone on your future dates."

He gives a small curtsy.

"You'll be my knight in shining armor?" I giggle, the whole act making it hard to keep a straight face.

"If you insist with this crazy obsession of yours, I must," he responds, still in character.

"All right, my brave knight, 'til we meet tomorrow, then." Holding in my laughter, I make a curtsy of my own.

"Good night, my fair lady, Twinkle Toes," he replies with a deeper curtsy this time.

"Good evening, Sir Archibald." I turn and walk into Zach's room, closing the door behind me.

I search for my brother, but stopping when my eyes focus on the girl's uniform folded on top of his bed. The white shirt, red tie, black skirt, and a pair of black flats excites me. I walk over to it and grab the skirt, noticing the rich fabric of the clothes are different from the ones in Saint Magdalene. For a moment, I remember Edward's comment about my old uniform giving him a rash.

I recognize the higher quality of the fabric, I still believe he over-reacted.

I move them in the desk, take my pajamas, and shower quickly in case Zach returns.

When I leave the room, I still find no sign of my brother. Remembering the cell phone inside my backpack, I go to open it and instantly notice a change in the bag's weight. Inside, I discover it's filled with books and notebooks of different subjects.

I find myself speechless. Clearly, getting me inside the school, dressing me, and making sure I get what I want hasn't been as easy of a task as I thought it would be.

If they keep this pace up, they'll spoil me. Perhaps I could return the favor by preparing meals they like.

I retrieve my phone and unlock it, surprised to find three messages there from an unknown number.

Unknown Number: OMG!! OMG!! OMG!! I just heard we get to share two classes together!!!!

Okay, I know the sender's identity.

Unknown Number: By the way, this is Darcy.

Unknown Number: Mom already agreed for us to be partners in cooking class, after I promised to name my first-born child after her and offered my services as her personal minion for the whole month. We're going to have SOOOOOOO much fun!!!!! Talk to you tomorrow.

I laugh after reading her messages and prepare to reply when a new one comes in. My breath catches when I read the sender's name.

Samuel: Hi Samantha, sorry for disturbing you this late. Mom wanted me to inform you she scheduled family dinner this Wednesday at 7:00 pm, and she and David are excited about you joining us.

I chuckle, picturing his mom staring over his shoulder to make sure he sent the message.

Samantha: Hi, Samuel and Miranda! Thank you for the invitation and count me in. I'll bring dessert. Would chocolate cake be all right? Or cookies? Or both?

I send the message and wait for him to reply.

Samuel: LOL! Mom says your company is more than enough. My stomach says chocolate cake sounds fantastic.

I laugh when I read his comment.

Samantha: And what does David's stomach say?

I send it and jump when barely three seconds pass and my phone pings with a new message.

Samuel: Both.

Warmth fills my chest.

Samantha: Then both it is!

Before I lose my courage, I type the next message.

Samantha: By the way, I never got a chance to thank you for standing up for me during dinner. I appreciate it.

I nervously wait for a reply, believing for a moment I made him uncomfortable. The ping of a new message allows me to breath comfortably once again.

Samuel: I did nothing but speak my opinion, and frankly, you deserve it. You have the passion, the motivation, and the right set of skills to make it inside the group, and with the proper tutoring, you'll easily surpass any of the girls there.

I read the message twice to make sure my creative mind isn't editing it. I answer with the only words I can come up with.

Samantha: Thank you, Samuel, for believing in me.

I send it out, then notice how late it is.

Samuel: You're welcome, Samantha. Now go to bed. You have a big day tomorrow.

I type my answer quickly.

Samantha: Sure thing. Good night, Samuel.

I finally connect the charger to the phone when a new message comes in.

Samuel: Goodnight, beautiful.

What? My pulse starts racing as I stare at the message.

Okay, Big Guy, I know I asked You to clarify before, but please explain how You expect me to sleep after this kind of answer? Huh?

CHAPTER TWENTY-TWO
My Favorite Things

After steadying my heart and trying not to over read the whole "Beautiful" nickname, I manage to sleep all night long. Better to let the Big Guy provide the answers later on.

Yeah, right, who am I kidding? I want to know.

But it was kind of late, and it's not like I can call Samuel and ask him to elaborate on the whole thing.

My only available option is to hit the sack and sleep. Otherwise, the bags under my eyes will change my nickname to Beautiful Raccoon.

Not funny!

I get up early the next morning and change. Finding it

impossible to knot the tie, I decide to ask one of the girls for their help once they wake up.

In the kitchen, I prepare breakfast and the goodie bags, saddened not to make Joy one, but after yesterday, she's grounded.

I quickly make the pot of coffee and bring out the orange juice, knowing the smell will smoke everybody out of bed. And, if they know any better, they need to beat Joy and Archie if they want to eat more than leftovers.

I return to Zach's room and pull my hair into a ponytail. Afterward, I go upstairs with my backpack and the tie.

Everybody sits in the dining room, talking. I try to be inconspicuous. With my stomach tied in a knot, I'm not really in the mood to eat. It's been so long since my last first day at a new school that frankly I don't remember how it went.

Instead of eating, I throw a couple granola bars into my bag, knowing once I get past this, my hunger will return with a vengeance.

"Good morning, Samantha." I turn to find Oliver greeting me.

Somehow, I can't find the courage to look him in the eye. Flashes of him in his...shorts still haunt me.

"Thank you for the excellent breakfast," he says.

Samantha, stop it! Everybody will notice how much your face resembles a tomato.

"No problem." I turn around and open the fridge. Hopefully, the cold air will drive the blush away.

"Did you already eat breakfast?" Samuel asks, but I don't dare to turn since my face still feels warm.

"Almost. I wanted a glass of milk." I shift my head up and down as if searching for the milk carton, a perfect excuse to keep my head up in front.

"It's over here," Zach informs me from the table. "Come and join us."

Great! So darn great!

"Oh!" I innocently respond. "Sure."

I need to stall.

Glass! I need a glass for the milk.

After closing the fridge, I go to the cupboard for my newest target. Unfortunately, the whole ordeal doesn't take long. I grab a glass and drag myself to the open chair.

The team talks about the dynamics of today. I reach for the milk and pour myself half a glass.

"May I have some, please?" Samuel asks from beside to me.

My head snaps toward him, his handsome face turned to me as he extends the empty glass in his hand. His steady gaze causes the nervous butterflies in my stomach to create havoc inside.

"Sure." I take the glass, hoping he doesn't notice the slight shake of my hand, and pour the milk.

When I return it, I accidentally touch his warm hand, the action catching me off guard. Good thing he already has ahold of the glass. Otherwise, we would need a cleaning crew after I spilled its contents on top of the table.

Quickly, I pull my hand back and redirect my attention to sipping my milk.

"Then it's settled," Oliver finalizes whatever they discussed. "I'll take Samantha to the admissions office and get her schedule."

Really, Big Guy? Today of all days You decide to change my face color to beet-red?

"Sure," I whisper.

Oliver claps his hands. "Everybody finish up, we leave in five."

After finishing the rest of my milk, I run downstairs to brush my teeth, and at the last minute, I remember my phone on the nightstand. I take it and run upstairs where the rest wait for me to join them.

"Samantha, you ride with..." Zach says in the background.

Please don't say Oliver.

"Kellan and Barb," he finishes.

Thank you, Big Guy.

Samuel, heading toward the door, stops when he reaches the staircase. "Archie, can I swap cars with you?"

"Nope, I need to discuss some items with Kellan and Barb," Archie answers in a heartbeat.

Samuel frowns and his lips take a dip before he continues toward the exit.

"Samuel, I also need to discuss with you another item on our ride over to the school." Lyra follows him out of the house, putting an end to the discussion.

I follow after them. Samuel rolls his eyes when he

reaches Zach's car while Lyra continues asking him something.

I follow Barb and Kellan to the red Audi and realize Joy joins the other car, along with Abigail, which means Barb, Kellan, Archie, and I will be riding in this car.

Kellan opens Barb's passenger door while Archie opens mine.

"Thanks," I tell him, enjoying his attractive smile.

"Here, give me your backpack, and we can put them in the trunk." He stretches his hand out to take it from me.

The bag and I share a long history together after four years. When I hand it over to Archie, I do it with some apprehension. But then I remember its tainted record after the whole situation regarding the nose breaking incident and release it guilt free.

"Wow. What are you carrying in here? Bricks?" Archie lifts the bag like he would a dumbbell.

"My school books," I respond.

"You brought all of them home?" He walks to the back of the car and puts both of our backpacks in the trunk.

"Yes, because I don't know today's schedule." I shrug. "Once I get a locker assigned, I'll drop the ones I don't need there."

I get inside the car, closing the door behind me.

Kellan joins Archie in the back after dropping Barb's and his backpack in the trunk.

Through the back window, I see Kellan take my bag and test the weight. He returns it to the trunk. "Wuss, it's not terribly heavy."

"Says the football defensive lineman," Archie replies dryly, closing the back and going to the other side of the car. Once he gets inside, he glances at me. "I'll help you carry them when we get to school."

"Okay," I answer. I wouldn't call the backpack light as a feather, but I can still carry it myself. But, whatever.

Barb turns to study me from the front seat, while Kellan gets in and turns on the car. "Are you ready for your first day, darling?"

Beginning a new school, one month later than the rest of the students, sharing classes with seniors, juniors, and freshman, should be a piece of cake. Nobody will notice the new girl, right?

Ha, ha, ha! By nobody I only mean the sophomore class, the equivalent twenty-five percent of the school's alumni.

The magic powers in my stomach that creates butterflies out of thin air decide to organize a wild party inside of me.

"Yes?" I respond.

Barb and Archie chuckle at my answer. My face must reflect the same confidence as my answer...which is none.

Barb gets ahold of my hand and gives it an encouraging squeeze. "Honey, everything will turn out all right. You'll be with us or the O'Flannagans."

"Don't be nervous, Samantha." Kellan grins from the driver's seat. "If you get overwhelmed, imagine them naked. That should help."

With those words, my simple mind brings up last night's image of Oliver, sans shorts. My face lights up beet-red once again.

Not helping, Kellan!

I put my hands on either side of my face to hide the evidence of my traitorous mind, but Barb's laughter makes things worse. I'm busted!

Big Guy! Honestly! Why?

"It would probably help if you focus on something else," Archie proposes, but I don't dare to glance at him.

What if... Argh! No! No! No!

My mind's not trustworthy at the moment.

"I believe that would be a better idea," I manage to say.

"How about you imagine your favorite things," Barb offers, leaning in and glancing at me with kindness in her eyes. "For example, what do you like?"

Samuel!

Argh, Big Guy! I need to be stopped right this instant.

To preserve whatever remains of my dignity, I keep quiet.

"Cooking!" Archie answers when the silence becomes longer than expected.

"Ballet!" Barb adds to the list, putting two fingers up as if keeping count of the items.

"The Sound of Music?" Kellan offers.

Archie laughs after listening to the last item and immediately hums the tune of My Favorite Things from the movie, impressing me with his musical voice.

Big Guy, he already looks like an archangel, does he need to sing like one?

Kellan chuckles, identifies the song, and joins in.

I can't help it and peek between my fingers at the whole silly scene.

"Wait, what was the chorus?" Barb touches Kellan's shoulder, interrupting them when they reach that part. "Do you remember the lyrics?"

"I know the German version, but not the English one," Kellan says.

Archie sings it, and Barb joins him, both of them pulling silly faces and making me laugh.

"I believe we can come up with a better version for it." Kellan momentarily deviates his gaze from the road to glance at Barb.

Her lips stretch, and she quickly winks at him before he returns his attention to driving. "I got an idea." Barb attentions goes to Archie. "When Rasputin bites."

Big Guy, how did Barb know? Will Archie now be mad at me?

Extraordinarily enough, the warmth rushes from my face as I feel myself pale. From red to white in an instant. My hand flying to the small bite mark that's almost completely disappeared.

Big Guy, don't let anything bad happen to the little guy.

Barb turns around and notices my sudden change of mood. Her eyes focus on the healing area.

"Honey, I noticed it yesterday when we visited the first shop," she answers my silent question, raising her eyebrows and tilting her head.

"I was a stranger and he protected his family from me," I defend him.

She shrugs and returns to the previous topic. "Has a bee stung you recently?"

She keeps eye contact while waiting for my answer.

I shake my head.

"I know how to replace it." Eyes crinkling, Archie raises his arm as if he's in class, earning Barb's and my attention. "When Abigail is mean?"

His suggestion earns a genuine laugh from Kellan.

I cover my treacherous smile with my hand, not wanting to give away my opinion about my sister.

"Aww, don't be mean, Archie. She's a doll," Barbs defends her.

"I will agree with your statement..." he pauses dramatically. "If you mean Bride of Chucky doll."

Kellan's shoulders go up and down, and all of a sudden he develops a mysterious cough.

I don't know who Chucky is, much less his bride, but the glare Barb gives Archie makes me believe she's not a sweet doll.

"Don't mix up toughness with meanness, Archie. She's loyal and has a big heart," Barb chastises him. "She's a great leader and friend. She keeps her feelings guarded from most people, but believe me when I tell you how lucky we are to be part of her team."

Her feelings guarded? As in locked in the safety box inside the Titanic, meanwhile the key is stored next to the Holy Grail.

"I'm certain she's a wonderful person," Archie deadpans. "But we still need to peel a lot of layers on the Abi-onion to get to this big, mysterious heart of hers. Until then, we can vote for these new lyrics to stay until further notice. Unless you can come up with something better before we get to school."

Barb stays quiet, pursing her lips, but when she offers nothing Archie moves on.

"When I am breaking down," Kellan continues.

"Not the best choice, but it will be easier to rhyme," Archie says, the corner of his mouth stretching upwards.

I find myself sighing at the view.

One of my favorite things.

Wow! Hold on.

Ugh! I'm messed up. The first boy who calls me beautiful and I fall head over heels for him. And now the archangel messes up my feelings with his smile.

Keep them on hold.

"I know, I know! I simply remember how lovely I dance and nothing will bring... me down!" Barb finalizes the song, keeping the rest of the choir lyrics and making me laugh when she purposely extends the last part completely out of tune.

Archie leans forward, nodding. "There, when you are nervous, either go with the O'Flannagans or us and remember your favorite things all right?"

All I can offer him is a small smile in return.

They finish recomposing the song as we reach the school and the guys quickly get out of the car. My hand goes to the door handle, but Barb stops me.

"Allow them to be gentlemen, Samantha. Southern boys like to do that," she explains before Kellan reaches for her door.

Isn't Kellan German?

He quickly moves and opens my door as well, helping me out.

"Now, darling, we need to take you to Oliver." Barb intertwines her arm with mine, guiding me through the parking lot toward the main building.

Argh! Why? I momentarily forgot this little detail.

"My backpack?" I turn around to find Kellan and Archie carrying all our bags.

"I told you, allow them to be gentlemen and set an example to the rest of the guys here," she reminds me as we enter the school.

I can sense the eyes of the students following us when we walk through the halls, some of them whispering.

When Rasputin bites, when Abigail is mean...

Before I know it, I find myself chanting the song, which calms my racing nerves. We enter the main hall of the school.

"Miss Miller, what a pleasant surprise," a teacher says merrily to Barb, stepping forward and stopping our trajectory. "I was wondering if you could help us with a small favor regarding the Talent show."

She turns back to Kellan and Archie, both of them nodding. She quickly faces the teacher with a big grin on her face.

"It would be my pleasure, sir." She lets go of my arm and grabs ahold of Kellan's hand. "Samantha and Archie, I'll talk to you later."

Archie immediately walks to my side once our lovely couple follows the teacher. He takes his cell phone out and makes a face. "My classroom is on the other side of campus. However..."

As if he magically invokes him, Samuel appears right next to me. Archie hands him my backpack.

"See you later, my Fair Lady." Archie bows, making me giggle.

"Just go will you." Samuel laughs at his friend's silly display. "I need to get her to Oliver."

I wave goodbye to Archie before he disappears around the corner.

"Come with me." Samuel indicates with a small movement of his head and slings my backpack on his shoulder.

The backpack alone shouldn't be a problem. However, mixed with the other two bags he already carries, the whole combination probably weighs a ton.

"Let me help you at least with one of them." I stretch out my hand, waiting for him to hand me one of the lighter ones.

"Samantha, if I can carry you around while dancing, I can easily manage these three," he reminds me, chuckling. "Believe it or not, they're quite light."

"Compared to me? Did you just call me fat?" I joke, placing my hand on top of my heart and pulling a hurt face, making him blush.

"I did not say that." He points an accusatory finger at me. "Don't put words in my mouth."

I chuckle at his worried expression.

"Quite frankly, you need to put on some weight. You hardly ate this morning," he adds, raising his eyebrows.

His comment stops me from laughing. He noticed I hardly ate breakfast.

"I was nervous," I defend myself.

"And because of that, I let it slide. But for my sake, please don't be one of those dancers who believes being lighter means getting higher altitude or appearing more graceful. They're completely wrong. We dancers need food in our system to perform correctly," he adds.

Sister Josie already gave me this same speech six years ago.

"I know."

Eyes narrowed slightly, he stops and studies my face as if to figure out if I'm being honest with my answer.

Well, I can honestly say I truly find those dark eyes captivating.

Samantha, breathe! Nobody likes a blue-faced girl.

"Where's your tie?" he asks after a couple more moments, breaking the spell. His eyes drop to my neck.

It's in the...

My hand flies to my forehead. Darn it! It's on the kitchen counter.

"At home," I confess while mentally kicking myself for allowing my nerves to mess with my head. "I don't know how to make a knot in the tie, and I was going to ask one of the girls to help me."

He shakes his head and puts the three backpacks down on the floor.

"School policy dictates we need to wear the whole uniform during class," he explains while his hand lifts to his tie and undoes it. "Admissions will notice it immediately."

Nuts! I don't want to go through this again tomorrow and spend the whole day stuck in the library.

He reaches for my hand and pulls me closer to him. His action takes me by surprise, especially when he pulls the neck of my shirt high and circles my neck with his tie.

Oh my, Big Guy!

"B-b-b-ut," I stammer when his face drops within inches of mine.

What was I going to say? Focus, Samantha!

"You also need a tie," I manage to speak after he almost finishes tying his around my neck.

He grins and puts my collar back in place, his finger brushing the skin of my throat and sending shivers down my spine.

"Don't worry about it." He leans forward, slightly pulling the neck of my shirt closer to him. As if he's revealing a great secret, he whispers, "Zach keeps a spare one in his car, I'll go and get it after I drop you off with Oliver."

"Thank you, Samuel," I answer while he removes his hand from my neck and takes hold of the backpacks once more.

He studies the three pieces, then glances at me. "Did you bring your ballet gear?"

What?

"Did I need to bring it?" My hands move to my lips, while my stomach goes the opposite direction, down to the floor.

"Nobody told you Tuesdays, Thursdays, and Fridays are ballet classes?" he asks.

"Nope," I reply, hating myself for never asking.

And now, I lose the one day to prove myself because of my scatterbrain.

Big Guy, You know I want this, right?

"Okay, we can use this to our advantage. I can talk to Monsieur Pietro today to give you a chance, and we will give it a try on Thursday. Okay?"

I nod.

His hand flies to his chest pocket and retrieves his cell phone, focusing on the screen. "Oliver wants to know where you are." He shrugs the backpacks onto his shoulder, takes my hands, and guides me at a faster pace through the halls.

Ah, Big Guy, a boy took my hand!

We arrive at the main offices where Oliver speaks with the secretary. Samuel lets go of my hand to return my backpack.

"Thanks, Samuel," I say while putting it on my back.

"You're welcome." He steps closer, keeping his voice low. "Break a leg, beautiful. See you in class."

Not that I'm counting or anything, but he already called me beautiful three times, Big Guy.

He turns around before I can react and moves through the quickly emptying hall.

Turning back, I face Oliver and the admissions office ahead. I stop to take a moment to catch my breath and steady my nerves.

"Breathe in." I suck in air.

Oh, Big Guy, when I woke up last Friday, I expected a new adventure and a change from my current life, but You really outdid Yourself.

Never in a million years did I picture this outcome. My Barcelona dreams shattered and Grams gone. Now I live with my siblings back at home, interacting with boys, learning partnering, and attending a new co-ed school.

The safety bubble where I lived burst the moment I tripped on my backpack.

Time for me to stop hiding, become the principal dancer of my life, and hope my siblings have my back.

Grams and Big Guy, prepare yourselves, because the show is about to begin.

I release the breath I held.

"Breathe out," I whisper.

Let's do this!

ABOUT THE AUTHOR

Maya William is a new, upcoming author who loves spending time with her two kids and her loving husband.

She likes to explore alternative realities through a good book, an awesome movie, or by plotting her next installment with the help of Miss Inspiration.

Find Maya William in social media on Facebook at www.facebook.com/maya.william.9461.

Made in United States
Orlando, FL
14 June 2022